To the casual observer Scawdale, in the English Lake District, is a delightful place. There is the tranquil lake, spectacular fells buttressed by steep rock – and a pair of peregrines have nested on Falcon Crag. But the whitewashed cottages of Scawdale conceal sombre activities.

Jack Pharaoh, invalided out of Mountain Rescue, is thinking of settling in the dale and he approaches landowner Randolph Steel with a view to renting one of his properties. Soon Pharaoh is made aware of the bitter conflicts of a divided community fighting for survival, and inevitably he becomes involved.

There are two camps in the dale, one paring its lifestyle to the bone – like Miss Cooper subsisting on stinging nettles and the rabbits her cats bring home – the other surviving by exploitation. Deer are poached, the falcons' nest is robbed, Miss Cooper's cats are threatened. Prostitution and pimping imply abuse and violence while, up in their secret cave on Falcon Crag, two little girls keep a close watch on proceedings in happy ignorance that others are out there watching too.

Disaster strikes with the disappearance of one of the most vulnerable of the dale's inhabitants and Pharaoh's relationship with her makes him a prime suspect. The threat of arrest forces Pharaoh to follow his own line of investigation and in doing so he witnesses the clash between two of the most ruthless and amoral opponents the dale has ever known – and uncovers a hitherto unsuspected crime . . .

The Outside Edge

Gwen Moffat

**MACMILLAN
LONDON**

First published 1993 by Macmillan London Limited

a division of Pan Macmillan Publishers Limited
Cavaye Place London SW10 9PG
and Basingstoke

Associated companies throughout the world

ISBN 0–333–59764–8

9 8 7 6 5 4 3 2 1

A CIP catalogue record for this book is available from the British
Library

Phototypeset by Intype, London
Printed by Mackays of Chatham PLC

Chapter One

'The witch is digging a grave.'

'She's trenching for potatoes, stupid.'

'Not in May. And not in the orchard.'

'Gimme the glasses.'

'Oh, Claire, it's still my turn!'

'Gimme.'

The binoculars changed hands and the little girls huddled together in the mouth of their secret cave, intent on Miss Mabel Cooper, five hundred feet below, digging a hole under a flowering plum.

'There's a sort of bundle in the grass behind her,' Claire said, her eyes tight against the lenses.

'It could be a baby.'

'Be your age!'

Ritual abuse was a recent preoccupation of the media. Miss Cooper picked up the tiny bundle and for a moment held it to her breast, her head bowed. Claire's eyes widened. She lowered the glasses and felt in the pocket of her jeans.

'What's she doing?' Becky was intrigued.

Claire retrieved a flattened cigarette and some book matches. She struck a match and cupped the flame in a fair imitation of a man. 'She's praying,' she said, with contempt. 'Silly old cow.'

Becky glanced at her uncertainly, she was never sure of Claire. At this moment she looked bored and angry at the same time. She was staring at the dale so Becky stared with her, at the shining lake, the woods that were washed here and there with purple among the bright greens of spring, at the fells buttressed by crags. 'No one about,' Becky ventured.

'There are people around. Hidden.' Claire thought about that. 'Hidden in the trees,' she went on, 'deep in the forest, going about their secret lives.'

1

'Claire?'

'What?'

'What *do* they do to babies: those people, Satan folk?'

Claire drew on her cigarette. At eleven she was the younger by a year but way ahead in intelligence. Becky wasn't dim so much as immature but she had the edge in looks. Strangers stared in surprise, fascinated by the hint of the Orient in her colour and the shape of her eyes, in the thick black hair worn in a heavy plait. At twelve she was at least two inches taller than the stocky Claire but wherever they went, whatever they did, Becky trailed behind, accepting the other's dominance with only the occasional flicker of rebellion, and that was quickly squashed by Claire, the articulate Claire who, when facts were unavailable or incomprehensible, filled the gaps with fiction. 'Abusers,' she said now, relishing the word: 'they torture kids before they kill them.'

'How? What do they *do*?'

Claire opened her mouth, then hesitated. She regarded the end of her cigarette. 'With fags and – cattle prods. Sometimes they eat them,' she added as an afterthought. 'They butcher 'em like pigs, and cook 'em properly – on a stove.' Becky gaped. Claire sensed disbelief. 'I told you, last autumn! It was on that late-night programme I watched. I told you next day.'

Becky looked away, embarrassed. Her grandmother had tried to convince her that Claire had been watching a horror video but she knew the Fishers didn't have a video. She shuddered: fiction or fact, it was horrid. It was one thing to cast Miss Cooper in the role of witch, another to be reminded that there really were witches – or even worse, like real people who turned into witches – who dragged you into a car or a lorry and burned you and—'I don't want to think about it,' she said loudly.

'You started it.'

Becky sighed and returned to a survey of the dale, searching for a new focus of excitement. Miss Cooper was filling the hole now, moving with the slow deliberation of the old. Her white-washed cottage glowed in the sunshine and the turned earth in her garden was a rich brown, fringed with the tarnished yellow of daffodils past their prime. Fruit trees formed puffs of blossom in the orchard. There was nothing sinister about Miss Cooper.

'One of her cats died,' Becky said.

Claire grimaced. 'Of course it was a cat. Now what's she going to do?'

The distant figure went back to her house to emerge after a moment, pause, and go to a small barn. She opened its double doors.

'Going to town,' Claire murmured, stubbing out her cigarette. 'Did she lock the front door?'

'You wouldn't—'

'Course not. We leave the thieving to Roy Hartley.'

Becky's eyes came round to the binoculars on the rock between them.

'That were different,' Claire said quickly. 'Laura's rich. Besides, she should lock her car. Leaving cars unlocked is an open invitation. Where's she get all her money from anyway? She's only a cook.'

'Take-aways,' Becky corrected. 'She does take-away food.'

Claire blinked, momentarily silenced.

Becky seized her advantage: 'And she's not rich neither. Her dad's so strapped for cash, he's going to sell the woods.'

'Rubbish! He'd never sell in a million years.'

'He's going to then. My grandad said—'

'What's he know about Randolph's business? He was only the keeper.'

'He was head keeper. Look, Mr Steel – Randolph' – Becky's voice dropped, she hadn't the temerity to refer to their landlord by his Christian name – 'he's got men coming to see the woods tomorrow. He says he's going to make ponds and things. Granpa says that's daft. He's selling. Why would I make that up?'

Claire saw the sense of this. There would be no purpose in a lie and it wasn't the kind of fiction on which they could base one of their fantasies, although now she came to think of it . . . She edged closer to the lip of the cave to get a wider view.

'They're going to develop,' Becky said loftily, proud of the new word. 'That's what Granpa says.'

'You mean, chalets – and camp grounds?' Claire's chunky features were alive with interest. 'I'm surprised at that. I *am* surprised.' It was a prim travesty of an adult. 'That's where he buried his wife, remember?'

Becky gasped. It was ages since they'd developed that story, in fact it had been superseded by the more immediate topic of Satanic abuse, which had been so much more enthralling because it was on television every day, and no one would explain, only condemn, grown-ups varying in their reactions from tight lips and jumpy eyes to explosive outbursts from folk like Becky's grandfather who held that hanging wasn't good enough, they should be nailed to the barn door alive, give them a taste of their own medicine, you wouldn't treat a dog that way. It had made a strong impression on Becky who now found it difficult to remember what had preoccupied them before Satanic abuse. Claire enlightened her.

'We never discovered where he buried her,' she said meaningly.

Becky started to remember the details. 'It had to be near his house because he couldn't carry her far. He's an old man.'

They looked across the woods to Burnbank, the big white house on its knoll at the end of the lake.

'He's strong as a bull,' Claire said. 'He could have thrown the body over a horse and put it anywhere. A wet, dark winter's night, who'd have seen him in his own woods? Everyone would be indoors anyway. We'll need to watch him; if he sells part of the woods we'll know the grave's a long way away.'

'How?'

'Because tractors and back-hoes and that would dig it up, wouldn't they? Sometimes I wonder what you got between the ears, Becky Rudd.' Becky sniffed. Claire continued, 'On the other hand he could dig her up and put the body in the foundations.'

'What foundations?'

Claire sighed. 'Toilets have 'em. They make a car park or a camp ground, they got to have toilets so they dig out the foundations and when they're going to pour the concrete next day, Randolph takes the body—'

'It'd be a skeleton by now.'

'Then he'd put the bones in a bin-bag, right? And he digs a shallow grave in the bottom of the hole they've made for the foundations. It's the way the Mafia do it. I bet half the bridges on the motorway have got bodies inside the concrete.'

Becky was impressed. 'So what do we do now?' They'd been talking for ages and spring was rampaging through the dale; these two needed immediate diversion. 'What are we going to do this afternoon?'

Claire's eyes were on Burnbank. 'I might go along tonight and find out what's happening,' she murmured. 'The window may be open and Trudy knows me. Laura's home and they'll be talking when they eat.' She transferred her gaze to Miss Cooper's secluded cottage. 'Let's go and see if there's anything worth scoffing at Skelgill.'

4

'She's certain to have locked up with the season here and all.'
'She's got skylights, hasn't she?'

Mabel Cooper returned from town with a bottle of sherry and a packet of wildflower seeds. She unlocked her front door, poured herself a drink and left it untouched while she went out to the orchard to sow the seeds above the grave of the young cat which had died of kidney failure.

At seventy Mabel was a little stooped, a trifle stiff but as alert as one of her cats and, to the casual tourist wandering up her private drive, intimidating. Coming upon her stationed at her garden gate, a bush of white hair framing a face as lined as that of a Navajo Indian, the shaken intruder would mumble apologies, turn tail and retreat. She loathed what she referred to as trippers; on the whole she hadn't much time for people, with notable exceptions like Randolph Steel.

Their fathers had been friends, old Cooper having owned land at the foot of the dale. He had made his money from slate but when the market collapsed after the First World War, the money started to dwindle and then the estate. Mabel's mother died young and there were no other children; when she inherited, all that was left was a big Victorian house and debts that absorbed everything she could raise from its sale.

She was homeless and almost destitute when Randolph offered her Skelgill and she had lived there for thirty years, supplying him with vegetables and fruit in season. She didn't consider the arrangement one-sided; had their positions been reversed she would have done the same. She was fond of Randolph and there was mutual respect but the strongest bond between them was their feeling for the dale. They had been born here. Randolph owned the land, she had owned it; they would die here and be buried in the churchyard at Kelton, their market town. Unsentimental but passionate, Mabel would have been puzzled had anyone suggested that she was capable of passion. This afternoon she drove to Kelton for sherry not because she was grieving for her cat but because if she drank she might not notice that one of the animals was missing, and she bought seeds because you planted flowers on a grave. It was the thing to do.

She was not a drinker. One sherry and a glass of wine at Randolph's Christmas dinner was her limit but this evening the routine was disrupted. Normally she would have worked in the garden until sunset but instead she sat on the rustic seat drinking,

5

and time passed unnoticed except for a dim awareness that the shadows slipped like water across the garden, they moved so fast. The cats deserted her to go hunting in the woods but it was the cats that recalled her to the present.

With nightfall she had gone indoors and fallen asleep in her chair. The tortoiseshell woke her, mewing urgently and kneading her thighs. She responded after a while, moving unsteadily to the refrigerator, sobering somewhat as she realized that their meat was cold and had to be warmed. Where was the gravy?

She stared at the interior of the fridge feeling that something was wrong but the cats weaving between her ankles gave her no chance to identify it. Standing at the stove, warming gravy and their rabbit stew, she concentrated on not over-heating, not swaying, not treading on paws. When they had been attended to she went back to the fridge to stare at the shelves, convinced that something was missing, but there was no gap.

At breakfast time she remembered; there had been a trifle: a gift for Randolph and Laura. She had used her own raspberry jam, the last of the sherry from Christmas and bantam eggs. She had made her own sponge fingers. The trifle was gone.

She had made it in the crystal bowl that had belonged to her mother; she always used that for trifle. It was in the cupboard: clean, with small glass bowls stacked inside. Under the stack were paper doilies which should have been inside, lining the crystal to prevent its being scratched by glass.

Panic stirred in her mind, spawned by the image of the cats left unprotected as she was taken away to a *home*. She had dreams – vivid dreams – and so far she'd thought she could distinguish them from reality but it was obvious now that she had *thought* of making the trifle and had dreamed the rest, even to putting the bowl back . . . The thought trailed away as she stared at the crystal on top of the doilies. 'No,' she said aloud, 'I wouldn't have done that.' A cat responded enquiringly. She ignored it.

The bowl had been used; it wasn't a dream, so the trifle wasn't either. She had eaten a whole trifle? Reluctantly she walked into her sitting room, dreading what she might find, visualizing damage. Her typewriter was in place on the mahogany table, covered, with paper neatly stacked, pages of typescript in order. The sherry bottle however was on the piecrust table, a full glass beside it, and bottle and glass had left rings on the polished surface. The table could be cleaned but she was disturbed by the void in her memory. How she had managed to wash the crystal bowl without breaking it was a miracle, and so drunk she had stacked glass inside without lining it first . . . she shook her head: appalling behaviour, but preferable to the suspicion that her dreams were replacing reality. Her brain was still moderately efficient; for instance, she could remember every detail of the afternoon before she started to drink, and there was no doubt about it: after she buried the cat and had gone to town, she hadn't left the cottage unlocked. She could distinctly remember turning the key in the lock on her return. As for the back door – she went to look. It was bolted. No doubt about it, the only person who could have eaten that trifle was herself.

Chapter Two

'Next time you're in need of company,' Randolph Steel said sternly, 'you come over here. Getting drunk on your own can be dangerous at our age.'

They were standing on the lawn in front of his house watching a silver pheasant strut before indifferent golden hens.

'I only had three sherries,' Mabel said coldly.

'That makes it worse. If you have a black-out after a limited amount of alcohol—'

'Randolph! There was no question of a black-out.'

He was chastened. 'Not in that sense. I meant – you forgot' – he became jovial – 'eating a whole trifle! Why weren't you sick? You must have a constitution like a dog.'

'What's been happening? Morning, Mabel.' Laura Steel stepped out of the porch, wearing Levis and trainers. Mabel surveyed her with approval; at twenty-five the girl's blond beauty seemed to deepen with every visit home. She took after her mother, which was fortunate; Randolph resembled a fattened hawk, full-faced yet beaky, impressive even in his threadbare cap and bib-and-brace overalls but a world away from Laura's delicate beauty.

'What happened to you?' the girl pressed. 'You're not sick, Mabel; you look terrific.'

'She lost one of the cats,' Randolph said. 'So she spent the evening on her own with a bottle of sherry instead of coming over here, and she can't remember what happened.'

'What's wrong with that if she was alone?' Laura's eyes sharpened. 'What could have happened?'

'Nothing.' Mabel shook her head. 'Nothing happened. It was too silly. Randolph, you'll have to segregate the gold and silver pheasants; you don't want hybrids.'

'What happened?' Laura asked him, very concerned.

He shrugged. It did seem trivial now that an issue was being made of it. 'She can't remember eating a trifle, that's all.' He threw a glance of apology at Mabel.

'Tell me,' Laura ordered.

'I assure you—' Mabel was flustered.

'I want to know.' She could be a real bully when she felt like it.

So Mabel told the story badly. Pressed for details she confessed that at first she thought it was a dream but that had been contradicted by the evidence of the crystal bowl. They understood, one always lined crystal when it was stacked. Laura regarded her intently. 'Someone was in your house,' she said.

Mabel's lips thinned. 'Impossible. I locked the front door when I went to town, the back was bolted, all the windows were latched. I'm careful about that, particularly now with the season getting under way.'

'How about the skylights?'

'No one could get in by those; the openings are too small, and they'd have to climb the roof.'

'He doesn't mind heights.' Laura turned and they followed the direction of her gaze: across the corner of the lake and the foreshortened woods that sheltered Skelgill to the tall buttress of Falcon Crag over a mile away.

'Getting his own back?' Randolph suggested.

'I wasn't meant to know,' Mabel pointed out.

'I got in through a skylight,' Laura murmured. 'And I was much older than him. You remember, Mabel: you thought you'd lost the key. You must fix those skylights, Dad.'

'You really think—'

'He's capable of anything. Who pinched my binoculars?'

'In one way I prefer that,' Mabel said. 'Three glasses of sherry and my memory a total blank? It's more likely that young Roy saw me leave—' She stared at Laura in consternation.

'Anything missing?' the girl asked. 'Anything else?' she added meaningly.

'I haven't looked. Nothing was disturbed. My typewriter was covered, the paper neatly stacked. Next week's "Fell and Dale" ready for the *Echo* – untouched, but then he wouldn't be interested in a typescript. I never mention rarities.'

Their attention returned to Falcon Crag. 'Little bastard,' Laura observed coldly. 'Have they got chicks yet?'

'Have they, Mabel?'

9

'No. The male's bringing food to the nest but she's only feeding herself. She started laying later this year.'

'He's made no attempt—?'

'Didn't I tell you?' Randolph grinned with delight and Mabel nodded approval. 'We cut down the larches, the ones he roped down from. That is, he used only one, but we cut down all the trees on the edge: five of 'em, cut so close to the ground that the rope'd slip off if he tried to climb down.'

'Great! Have there been any repercussions?'

'How could there be? You can be sure Hartley's reminded him of the consequences—'

'And young Roy will have denied everything again,' Mabel put in drily. 'I wonder what he did with the money, how he hid it from his parents?'

'He won't have got much,' Randolph said. 'The fellows at the sharp end never do; it's like drugs: the peasants who grow the crop get only a pittance, comparatively speaking. I don't expect Roy got much more than fifty for the clutch he stole last year, but the fellows who employed him, and the ones who sell the birds to rich Arabs, now they'll make fortunes.'

'Roy still has to hide fifty pounds,' Mabel persisted. 'Fourteen-year-olds don't come by that kind of money honestly, unless they sell a beast they've reared, and Roy Hartley's not exactly Young Farmer material. His father would thrash him within an inch of his life if he knew Roy was the culprit.'

'Oh, yes.' Randolph was grim. 'I gave Hartley to understand that if I caught any of my tenants stealing peregrine eggs, he'd be out on his ear, and he knows I hold him responsible for his son. If I could have proved Roy stole that clutch last year, the Hartleys would have lost their farm, no doubt about that.'

'They might take you to court.' Laura grinned.

'They wouldn't. In any case, it's history. The peregrines are safe this year and young Roy learned his lesson. His parents will keep a close eye on him. That's a nice little farm, Warthwaite; last thing they want is to lose it. All the same, I'll be over after lunch, Mabel, and put bolts on those skylights; be damned if we can have you living in a place that's wide open to vandals, and worse.' His attention was distracted. 'Hello, we have company.'

A man had appeared at the corner of the house and, seeing the group on the lawn, he started towards them. He wore neat, bleached cords and an RAF jersey and he looked fit and powerful:

a craggy man in his forties perhaps, although deep folds in his cheeks implied age or suffering, or both, but the step was springy enough except for the slightest trace of a limp.

'Mr Steel?' He held out his hand. 'Jack Pharaoh, sir. Your solicitor sent me. I'm looking for a cottage to rent.'

'Ha!' Randolph gave a bark of approval. He liked men who came straight to the point. 'My daughter, Laura, and our neighbour, Miss Cooper. RAF?'

'Retired.' He smiled engagingly. Laura stared. Mabel sparkled and then stiffened, surprised at herself.

'We were about to have coffee,' Randolph said, delighted to have a visitor who promised to be entertaining. 'Come inside.'

'What are those birds?' Pharaoh asked, awestruck.

'That's a silver pheasant and he's making up to golden hens. Where's the golden male got to, I'd like to know? Those are Chinese geese. The little ones are bantams, of course. We have a broody hen, Mabel; any eggs to spare?' They went indoors, talking convivially.

From the outside the house, under its slate roof and flaking whitewash, was square and uncompromising. Inside it looked as if it had been occupied by generations of collectors and slatterns. The room into which he ushered his visitors was lit by large windows curtained with velvet that had once been red, now faded in stripes. The centrepiece was a huge circular table covered with a plushy cloth with a bobbled fringe, its surface cluttered with books and papers and unidentifiable objects. Above the table was a centre light which seemed to be draped with a skirt.

'Sit down, sit down!' Randolph pushed newspapers to one end of a sofa. Mabel took a chair by a window and regarded Pharaoh with interest. Laura disappeared. A leggy springer spaniel trotted in and inspected the newcomer officiously.

'She's taken to you,' Randolph exclaimed. 'She's a wary bitch, aren't you, Trudy? That interests you?' – as Pharaoh peered at a photograph beside the fireplace – 'That's my Sunderland. I was in Coastal Command; we flew North Atlantic patrols during the War. Before your time, of course. What were you?'

'Mountain Rescue.'

'Really. That would be what took you to my solicitor. At one time he was in charge of the team that covered this area. You were one of his men?'

'No, sir, I trained him; he was on a course I ran in the Highlands.'

'Your people must originate from here,' Mabel observed. 'There are Pharaohs in west Cumbria.'

'My grandfather was from Coniston.'

'Ah.' To Randolph this was a character reference. 'And now you're looking for a place to settle, is that it?'

'I'm undecided.' He eased his leg. 'I've not been long out of the Service and it's difficult to know where to settle when you have no commitments and so many places to choose from.'

'Can't do better than Lakeland.'

'There are the Highlands.'

'True, true. I see your point; I might feel the same way if our people hadn't lived in Scawdale for three hundred years. I had some grand shooting when I was stationed at Alness. Magnificent country, the Cairngorms; very bleak, must be a rough old place in winter time. You know the area?'

'Passably. I know the west better: Glen Coe, Nevis, Skye . . .'

They reminisced affably until Laura came in with a tray and Randolph cleared a space on the table by the simple expedient of pushing with both hands. 'Pharaoh was in Mountain Rescue, Laura,' he said happily.

She handed Pharaoh a cup of coffee. 'You climb?'

'Not really.' His eyes went to the window. 'Not routes like the ones on Grey Buttress, not any more. I have a game leg. Old age,' he elaborated in the ensuing silence.

'We all come to it,' Randolph said loudly. 'So – my solicitor told you I had an empty cottage.'

'He said you might have a place available.'

Randolph stroked his chin and stared out of the window. 'You'd have loved Hollins, but that's on a long lease; until September, isn't it, Laura?'

'How would I know? They're your cottages.'

'I can't keep track of everything, and you're always up that way . . .' He threw her a doubtful glance.

'I ride on the Roman road. Tim Armstrong lives at Hollins and he doesn't welcome visitors. Where's the connection?'

'I suppose you don't have much in common. And you don't read his books, but then I've never found anyone who does. Our resident celebrity,' he explained to Pharaoh, 'an author. Lives on top' – he nodded across the water – 'beautiful position beside a tarn, private drive, no tourists; you'd have liked the place but there, so does Armstrong.' He changed tune: 'Tell you what we'll do: you go and look at the Boathouse, see if that'll suit. It was occupied by one of the gardeners but he died last winter and it's empty at the moment. See that spit of land on the shore? The Boathouse is on the far side. I'd show it to you but I'm expecting some people shortly. However, if you were to give Mabel a lift home, she'd do the honours, I'm sure.'

'I'll take him,' Laura said quickly.

'You're going to ride.'

'I've got all day. I'll run Mabel home too. You can follow,' she told Pharaoh.

'Come over for a drink tonight,' Randolph called as they went out to their cars. 'Have a bite to eat as well. You, too, Mabel, but you were coming anyway. We'll open a tin for pudding.' He roared with laughter, then sobered. 'I'll be over this afternoon about those skylights,' he assured her.

The women went ahead, Laura driving a small silver Peugeot with a current registration. Pharaoh followed in his Transit, bemused not only by the unexpected warmth of his reception but by the suggestion of undercurrents between the Steels and Mabel. He wondered about the skylights.

Laura drove up the dale for about a mile then turned left to follow a track through the woods that ended at a traditional cottage: white with black trim.

'I'll see you this evening,' Mabel said, coming to his window, looking casually past his shoulder to the back of the van, not that much could be seen because there were no windows in the side panels. She walked to her gate escorted by a number of cats which had appeared after the vehicles stopped.

Back on the road they continued a short distance up the dale to cross a stone bridge. There were entrances to drives on either side of the bridge and Laura took the second one. At this point the belt of trees between road and lake broadened and Pharaoh realized that they were on the wooded spit. Trees and under-growth were so dense that no houses were visible. A few firs among the hardwoods lent a gloomy air to the surroundings and his heart sank when they came to a house in white clapboard but shadowed and even sinister. Two bicycles lay on the gravel circle, dropped as children drop their toys when out of sight of their parents, or interrupted.

'Neighbours' kids,' Laura observed as he climbed down, but she didn't seem concerned. There was no sign of children.

She ignored the door that faced them and led the way down the side of the house, pushing through nettles: already trampled, he noticed, emerging to sunshine and a breathtaking view across the lake to the fells. Half-left was an islet crowned with gnarled pines, to the right was a miniature inlet with a jetty, and a boat upside-down on the turf. He turned to the house which, although small, seemed to be all windows, with a veranda supported by trellised pillars. The front door, with panels of stained glass, was set to one side of the windows. He had expected a traditional cottage but this was more of a folly, an indulgence rather than a functional dwelling. From those windows you would look across grass – crimson and pink rhododendrons on either side and a magnolia in bloom – to the water and the fells. Sunsets would be out of this world. He tried not to appear enthusiastic; he hadn't a lot of money to spare and Randolph looked as if he could use every pound. Moreover he guessed that Laura, despite the new car, perhaps because of it, would drive a hard bargain if she were to set the rent. He cast about for drawbacks.

'There must be another house near.' He looked across the mouth of the beck. 'We passed another drive.'

'That goes to the keeper's place. He's retired actually.'

'I see. And the bikes belong to his children.'

'Yes. No. That is, they're old people and their granddaughter lives with them. Her mother's in America. The other child's from further up the dale.'

He regarded the house doubtfully. 'Why would they come here to play?'

'They shouldn't; that's why they're keeping quiet. They're scared of me – and my father, of course. The other girl's mother is one of our tenants too.' She regarded him levelly. 'You could call it a feudal set-up.'

There were several comments he might have made but he couldn't be bothered, nor did the thought of Randolph as a feudal landlord disturb him. His attention was held by the house which had an air of expectancy as if waiting for an occupant.

'I suppose you want to see the inside,' she said grudgingly.

Apart from a lobby at the foot of the stairs the ground floor

14

front was monopolized by a sitting room furnished simply with a sofa and matching armchairs, a table in one window, but no ornaments or books, nothing personal.

The kitchen looked out on the drive. The bicycles had disappeared. The two big buttresses of the escarpment showed above the trees. 'Gets the morning sun,' he observed with what should have been her sales pitch. He found her hostility annoying.

'It's a grim place,' she said. 'I never liked it.'

The kitchen was dim but upstairs the main bedroom was decorated in lemon and white and flooded with shimmering reflections from the sunlit water. She stood at one window, her back turned, staring across the lake. Pharaoh's leg gave a twinge and he limped stiffly to the other window and sat on the sill. She glanced at him in surprise and he glowered back, massaging his calf. He wasn't about to tell her his medical history. Instead he said tightly: 'You don't want me to take this place.'

She shrugged. 'Can you afford it?'

'We haven't discussed the rent yet.' He meant he hadn't discussed it with her father but wasn't prepared to say so; it was pain making him churlish not her attitude. He stretched his leg carefully. 'Why the hostility?' he asked. 'Was it something I said?'

'We don't know you.' She was in control now. 'Look, I'm in business and there's no way I would employ anyone without seeing his references *and* calling his referees first. I know you're not looking for work but landlords should ask for references too. How do we know you're not going to—' She looked round, at a loss.

'Fill my van with your furniture,' he suggested, 'and do a moonlight flit, owing a quarter's rent?'

'There are some very odd characters about, particularly during the summer.'

'I have references, but they're from the RAF and I take it you'd like to see something more objective, your father being partial to the Service.'

He thought she would flare up at that but she seemed bewildered. 'Yes, well, I feel protective.' She walked across the room so that he had to follow. 'My father is impulsive,' she went on, leading the way along the landing, pausing in the doorway of a dim room with a single bed. 'And Mabel's just as unsophisticated,' she added, pushing a door, revealing an equally dim bathroom. She switched on a light and white porcelain showed, filmed with dust.

15

'What kind of business do you have?' he asked as they went downstairs.

'Catering. We do executive meals, and weddings, that kind of thing. And what do you intend to do here?' She was trading question for question. 'Walk, garden, write?'

'Potter. What *do* you do after a career in Mountain Rescue?' She regarded him suspiciously but it was rhetorical. 'I might fish—' He thought of evenings on the water, drifting along the shore of the lake, watching herons and kingfishers. 'I write a little but it's technical articles on rescue. I'm not an author.'

'Why don't you climb?' Her eyes went to his leg.

People always wanted to know. He decided to get it over once and for all. 'I had a fall. I shan't climb again.'

It wasn't altogether true but she accepted it. He seemed to have reassured her in some way and she didn't return to the subject of references. She locked up and looked at the key doubtfully as if she might be considering handing it to him but she dropped it in her pocket. 'I'll see you this evening,' she said as they walked to their vehicles. 'Six o'clock.' She looked at his van. 'Keep your doors locked and the windows closed. I had a pair of binoculars pinched last time I was down—' She hesitated as if she would say more but she thought better of it.

'Tourists, of course.'

'Why "of course"?'

'Would a local dare to steal from your family?'

She shrugged. 'Crime's like a virus; it spreads. Dad would say it's socialism, Mabel maintains it's over-population.'

'And you?'

'It's always been there.' She looked at him straight. 'And it is a way of redistributing wealth. See you.'

He watched the Peugeot disappear up the drive, thinking that that was the first time she had appeared natural, without subterfuge, as if she thought thieves might have rights. Hardly a feudal attitude, maybe it was backlash.

At the keeper's cottage they were about to start lunch.

'There's an old man at the Boathouse,' Becky said.

Isaac Garner lowered his newspaper and blinked at her over the top of his reading glasses. 'One of Mr Randolph's friends,' he said weightily. 'What were you doing over there?'

Becky was disappointed with the lack of reaction. She pushed a little harder. 'He was a hippie, living in a van.' She saw her

16

grandmother's face and knew there had been no need to elaborate.

'You didn't speak to him?' Doris was incredulous.

'Doesn't she know she's not to talk to strangers?' Isaac growled.

'You didn't let me finish,' Becky said. 'All I said was there's an old man over there but he never saw me. He went in the house. Laura was with him. They were inside a long time,' she added, toying with her fork.

The old people exchanged glances. 'You shouldn't have been over there,' Isaac said weakly.

'Who were you with?' Doris asked. 'You were with Claire, weren't you? You said you were going to the jumble sale in the village.'

'I met Claire on the way. We were too early for the sale so we came back to the Boathouse to play.'

'You weren't at Claire's house?'

'You told me not to go there.' There was a pause. 'I don't see why I shouldn't, she's my best friend and Mum lets me go to other girls' houses. Why can't I go to Claire's?'

'You know why, Becky.' There was the familiar warning note in her grandmother's voice. She started to serve the potatoes.

'I know you say Hugh Mason's dangerous but—'

'Hush, Becky!'

'You did! And Granpa says he's been in prison, and if Mr Randolph knew I went there—'

'Now you listen to me!' Isaac brought his fist down on the table, startling them. He went on more quietly, but still intensely, 'They're a bad lot and we don't want you mixing with 'em. If a man's been to prison he's done something wrong; I don't know what it was' – that was a lie; everyone knew Hugh Mason had stolen cars – 'but he's a gaolbird and that's enough for me. And we're responsible for you while your mother's in America so you'll do what we tell you. We're trying to bring you up right—' He threw a startled glance at Doris who had jolted his shoulder.

'I don't go to Hugh Mason's house,' Becky said indignantly.

'But he goes to hers!'

'Hugh Mason is friendly with Claire's mother,' Doris said clearly. 'We've been over this time and time again.'

'You mean, because he's a bad lot, so is Mrs Fisher?' Doris gave a heavy sigh. 'And Claire is too,' Becky persisted, 'because her mum's a bad lot?' She looked scandalized.

'Of course not.' Doris was overwhelmed. Had the child been

17

younger there could have been a strict edict; had she been a year or two older they could have explained. Becky, who knew more about the situation than they did, at least so far as Claire chose to tell her, feigned bewilderment.

'Claire's my best friend.' Her lips trembled and Doris was filled with compassion for this waif who had no father, whose mother was on the other side of the world, who had no one to turn to but themselves and another little girl whose mother was a whore. 'There's nothing wrong with Claire,' she said, with a hard look at Isaac. 'She's younger than you, of course, but she's got nice manners' – raising her voice at Isaac who had retreated behind his paper – 'and she's always clean and well turned out, I'll say that for her mother. Anyway' – she was almost shouting now as Isaac refused to react – 'if she's good enough to be Mr Randolph's tenant, who are we to look down on her?'

'Good enough!' Isaac grunted. 'I suppose there's one in every village.'

'What? What was that you said, Isaac Garner?'

'One what?' Becky asked. 'There's one what in every village?'

Isaac slumped lower in his chair. 'Single mother,' Doris snapped.

'Like my mother then.' Becky was smug. 'That's why she's my friend. We're both from single-parent families.' The silence stretched until she couldn't bear it any longer. 'Mr Randolph's in the woods with some men,' she told them. 'They're in ties and wearing wellies. What are they going to develop?'

'Did you speak to them?' Doris was ominous.

'Course not. They were standing by this big car in the quarry. One had a clipboard.'

'What were you doing in the quarry?' Doris asked and Becky sighed ostentatiously.

'We were on our way to the jumble sale. You gotta go through the quarry when you ride along the footpath and you say there's too much traffic for us to ride along the road. We couldn't play at the Boathouse any longer because Laura was there with that man. So we went to the jumble sale.'

'They're letting the Boathouse,' Isaac said. 'That's what they're doing.'

'But Becky said he's a hippie.' Doris turned on the girl. 'What made you say that?'

'He lives in a van, like a little bus but with no windows 'cept in the doors at the back.'

'How do you know he lives in it?'

'There's his sleeping bag and a stove and stuff on the floor.'

'You looked inside!'

They hadn't needed to. Claire, who had been out last night, had come on the van parked in the quarry, at eleven o'clock and without lights.

'We just glanced in,' she said airily, then decided she could improve on that. 'Well, we had a good look actually; you never know what people are up to these days. He might be a thief, or worse.'

Claire handed her mother a napkin and a plate of hot dogs oozing butter and mustard. 'You want beer or wine?' she asked.

'Beer, love. Not a can, I'll have the bitter. It's in a bottle—'

'I know which it is.'

Marlene Fisher leaned back against the wall of the cottage, soaking up the sunshine. She wasn't at all like her daughter but thin, with a long neck and high cheekbones. Her eyes were large with heavy lids, deep lavender eyes which showed above the sunglasses that had slipped down her nose. It was hot in the sun and she knew she shouldn't stay out in it long. She was a redhead and burned like a lobster. Her hair was a gorgeous shade: titian, thick and naturally curling, a copper mane.

It was a blissful day, hardly a cloud in the sky and the warmth drawing a fragrance from the woods that was more sensuous than Chanel. Marlene pulled up her skirt to reveal long pale legs.

'You look like a mushroom,' Claire said, handing her a glass of beer.

'How's that, sweetie?'

'Your legs: they're white, like you'd spent the winter in a cellar. Why don't you use a sunbed?'

'I wouldn't trust artificial tanning, not that you can trust the sun these days, skin cancer and all. Besides, health clubs cost the earth.'

'That's a pity. Because I was thinking: if I was to trade my old Raleigh as part-exchange for a mountain bike, I was wondering if you could make up the difference.'

Marlene pushed up her glasses and stared at her daughter. 'Do you know how much a mountain bike costs?'

'Second-hand? Not exactly.'

'We must have a new fridge, love. The condenser's on the blink

19

in that old thing.' Claire said nothing. 'What do you want a mountain bike for anyway? You don't go on the fells.'

'I would if I had one. But they're better in the woods. You can get off the roads; Becky and me, we always ride along the path between here and her place.'

'Were you with Becky this morning? Has she heard from her mother?'

'She had a letter last week. Her stepfather bought some more oil wells.'

'You're kidding.'

'Fifteen of 'em.' Claire nodded earnestly. 'But they're not working at the moment. He's going to wait for the price to rise, then he'll start them up again.'

Marlene gave a snort of amazement. 'That woman! She lands on her feet every time.'

'Why don't we go to Aberdeen and meet some American oil men?'

'Because I don't have Sally Rudd's looks, that's why. I mean, you've only got to look at Becky – oh, I'm sorry, love' – Marlene spilled her beer as she threw an arm round her daughter and hugged her – 'you look terrific when you smile. You're nice and chunky and English—' She stopped, not wanting to appear racist.

Claire sat up straight. 'Becky had a handsome father,' she said coldly. 'He was a prince.'

'Really. My information was that he was an agricultural student, but I suppose princes can go to college too. Like I said, Sally always gets the pick of the bunch, but she is beautiful, Claire; she has to be or she couldn't be a model, not that she ever has to model again now she's landed a multimillionaire. Me, I'd never dare give up this place and go to Aberdeen, rents would be sky-high there.'

'Hugh could get a job.'

'Can you see Hugh on an oil rig? No, sweetie, if we did go, we'd be independent. We'd be on our own.'

'Except for the oil men.'

'Oil *man*. Watch your mouth.'

'Laura's got a man. They were in the Boathouse.'

'What's he like?'

'Old, big, fierce. He lives in a van.'

Marlene, who had been reaching for her cigarettes, checked and turned in astonishment. 'A hippie? With Laura? You're joking.'

'I'm not. We watched them. He camped in the quarry last night. I saw his van parked there this morning,' she added quickly. Her mother might just possibly find a way of stopping the nocturnal excursions if she knew about them. She watched Marlene light up and inhale, expelling smoke luxuriously.

'What makes you think he's her boyfriend?' Marlene asked.

'I don't, but why else would they go in the Boathouse?'

'Because the Steels are letting it, of course. Randolph doesn't have a bean; he needs all the money he can get.'

'So why doesn't Laura let him have some? She's just bought a new car. She must make a fortune with take-away food.'

'It's not take-aways. My God, don't let her hear you say that! It's posh meals for directors – bosses – and stockbrokers – and weddings; she does big weddings. And she works like a horse – imagine: cooking all day, driving out to the country, carrying heavy pans from trucks to kitchens, having to work with servants – and they'll be foreign and won't understand a word. The Peugeot will be on hire purchase, come to that; I expect she's up to her ears in debt, and paying interest.' She paused. 'You know about interest?'

'I'm not thick. It's buying money.'

'That's great. Who told you that?'

'I don't know. I pick things up.' Without a change of tone she went on: 'Randolph was showing some men over the woods this morning.'

'You've been busy. What were they doing?'

'Becky says they're developers. What really happened to Laura's mother?'

Marlene's jaw dropped. 'She ran away with a jockey, or was it a trainer? What's that got to do with Randolph developing the woods, whatever that means?'

'But didn't she never write home to Laura, like Becky's mother does?'

'Becky's mother is on her honeymoon. She'll come back and fetch Becky soon—' Marlene sighed and her eyes glazed. 'And they'll all live happily ever after on a ranch like the one in *Dallas*. The difference between Becky and Laura is that Becky's *father* disappeared, see? In Laura's case she has a father.'

'All the same, you'd think she'd write letters to Laura.'

'How do you know she doesn't? What is this? Why the sudden interest in Laura's mother? It's years and years since she left. For

21

all we know, Laura sees her in London. Why don't you ask her yourself? No, better not. Remember, we stay on the right side of the landlord.'

Claire's eyes moved. 'There's Hugh at the cattle grid.'

The cottage was several hundred yards from the road, set at the top of pastures that sloped gently and formed the southern extremity of the farm called Warthwaite. The farmland had been carved out of oakwoods that climbed the slopes behind. A cart track curved up the hill from the road mostly out of sight where it was obscured by hawthorns. Hartley's Friesians were grazing in the lower meadow, their colours bright as those of painted animals on the new grass. A small van was coming up the track.

'You going out?' Claire asked without much interest.

'I might go to town. How about you?'

'I haven't decided.'

Hugh Mason reversed until he was level with them on the bench under the gable end. He regarded them critically: Marlene like a movie star in the huge sunglasses and that hair glinting in the light, Claire grave and wary, but with a suspicion of a smile on her lips before she stood up and went indoors.

'I'm ready,' he said pointedly, frowning at Marlene's dark skirt. 'Go and get dressed.'

'Let's leave it a while; I'm enjoying the sunshine.'

'I'm not coming back till late, and I'm going now.'

'I need new shoes.'

'So buy them, but look sharp; I'm meeting a guy at two.'

'You've got heaps of time.'

He said nothing. Marlene sighed, stood up languidly and went indoors. He took her place on the bench as Claire returned with a can of beer. She sat sideways on the driver's seat of the van, the door open, and studied him with the absorption of a small child.

Everything about Mason was a little too good; his eyes were clear and grey with very long lashes; he had a sculpted nose, a wide mouth and perfect teeth. His fair hair had been cut fashionably short and expertly but this was his only concession to vanity, or the only one apparent. Women turned to look at Mason in the street; even Claire was fascinated, occasionally disconcertingly so. This, he felt, was one of those times.

'How much would a second-hand mountain bike cost?' she asked.

'You might get one for a hundred.'

'What would I get for my Raleigh in part-exchange?'

He smiled indulgently. 'Ten if you're lucky.'

'So where can I find a hundred?'

He helped himself to one of Marlene's cigarettes and lit it with a slim lighter. She watched his movements like a dog. He proffered the packet.

'I'm cutting down,' she said primly.

'Not before time. With that voice you must get through twenty a day.'

She picked at the lining of the van's door. 'It's not much: a hundred pounds. Some folk make that in a night.'

'In London. This is Scawdale—' He did a double-take. 'Perhaps you weren't thinking of those sort of people?'

'The locals are destitute' – a lovely new word – 'but tourists have cameras although you got to go a long way to fence 'em. There's things that fall off the backs of lorries. I wish mountain bikes did but they're not valuable enough: only a hundred quid.'

He gaped, then pulled himself together. 'You little bastard,' he said, grinning.

'You would be too if you didn't have a father.' She stood up. 'You want another beer?'

'No, we're leaving. Hey, did you never think you could earn money yourself? Proper money?' His eyes were innocent, he could have been asking if she would wash his van.

'That's daft.' She stuck out her lower lip and glowered. For a moment she looked stupid, and childish, and uncomprehending. 'I'm only eleven.'

'You could have fooled me,' he muttered as she stalked away.

Chapter Three

At two o'clock Stephen and Anne Hartley left Warthwaite farm to do the weekly shopping. At lunch time Roy had said no, he didn't want to go with them, and as soon as he finished eating he went up to his room. After a moment they heard the beat of heavy metal only slightly muffled by distance.

He waited until his parents' car had cleared the cattle grid on the main road then he switched off his cassette player, picked up his binoculars and left the house, heading for the wooded slope behind the farm. On the fringe of the woods there was a broken crag about sixty feet high. He scrambled up its side to a corner lined with crushed ferns. He settled himself comfortably and looked north to where Falcon Crag rose above the timber, full in the sun and less than half a mile away.

Roy wasn't a prepossessing boy. With deep eye sockets and heavy brows he produced an impression of menace. He had a strong nose and his full mouth turned down sullenly. His hair was dark and thick and fell over his forehead. His school nickname was Thal, as in Neanderthal. He wasn't bothered about that; Roy thought of himself as a survivor: a cunning opportunist like the fox. The implication that he had a small brain was part of his cover, like the sullen expression; Roy knew himself to be alert, devious, always one jump ahead, or working towards it, which was exactly what he was about at this moment: making sure that the peregrine still had the eggs, that no one else had robbed the nest.

There was a flash of light from the top of Grey Buttress, way beyond Falcon. Roy raised his binoculars. A man was standing on the skyline looking south through his own glasses. He moved then – sat down stiffly like an old fellow – and transferred his attention to the lake. He could be a bird watcher but he didn't know much about it because he was showing no interest in the

24

male peregrine which had just arrived on the scene. Roy hadn't seen the bird himself but it was around because the female was calling from the nest. So everything was in order. It was time to put his new plan into operation.

On top of Grey Buttress Pharaoh was trying to distinguish bird calls and thinking that the afternoon was surprisingly noisy. Swallows were squealing as they jinked round him after flies, a thrush was proclaiming his territory from a Scots pine, a moment ago something had chattered like castanets. It was a gorgeous afternoon and there were no climbers on Grey Buttress, which was as well, it made him miserable to hear climbers' calls. He stood up and looked around and decided to see how far he could walk.

A green track, known locally as the Roman road, ran parallel with the escarpment and some distance above. He followed a zigzag path that climbed through the trees to emerge on the open fell where the ancient drove road was fringed with yellow and white flowers and the turf was indented by horses' hoofs. He turned south into a faint breeze that was heady with the scent of warm rock and flowers. A cock grouse ran through the heather and got up, skimming like a stone, to land and shout at him to go back. He grinned; in winter he might shiver at the warning, in summer the Roman road was heavenly.

An hour and a slow mile later he saw a white cottage below him on the shore of a blue tarn. He remembered Randolph Steel saying how he would have liked a certain cottage, only it was occupied by an author. It was indeed ideally situated if you didn't mind isolation. He got out the map and saw that it was approached by a narrow road, the one that ran along the top of the escarpment: a dead-end road with no houses on it, and none nearer than Randolph's place over two miles away although no doubt other houses were closer on foot. The farm called Warthwaite was just below, and there was one called Starfoot on the same patch of cleared land. The escarpment wouldn't be an obstacle for an active person although he suspected only children were interested in the easy gullies. This chap had chosen a good place to write his books – but he wasn't that much of a recluse, he had visitors this weekend. There were two vehicles outside the cottage.

He walked on, the track curving left and starting to climb as it deteriorated to a stony path. After a further mile his leg began to protest and he turned back, aware that he might have done too much. He came to a fork which he hadn't noticed going in the other direction and saw that a path diverged, dropping down to the cottage. Horses had gone that way. It wouldn't shorten the distance to his van but it would cut out the steep descent through the woodland. He turned left.

The cottage boasted a front garden which was entered by gates at either end of the façade. The horses' tracks went round the back and he followed them, glancing at windows as he passed. There were only two at ground level, the first draped with net curtains, the second so small it could only serve a larder. On the far side of the cottage was the access road that broadened to a space under the gable-end. Only one car stood there now and a man was about to open the driver's door. At sight of Pharaoh he froze and stared, giving every appearance of shock.

'I'm sorry,' Pharaoh said pleasantly. 'Am I trespassing?'

'Where did you come from? You're with Randolph?'

'Well, earlier on.' Pharaoh was surprised himself at the reaction he'd produced. 'That was Randolph?' He looked along the road.

'You're not Conservancy then? Who are you? You're *with* Randolph?' He was floundering between anger and doubt.

'We're at cross purposes,' Pharaoh said easily, aware that writers could be a bit odd. 'My name's Jack Pharaoh and I was visiting Randolph this morning. You must be the author. He spoke about you.'

The anger was replaced by wariness. The fellow knew he had gone off at half-cock. 'But you weren't with him just now?' he asked carefully, gesturing towards the road.

Pharaoh, respecting that hair trigger, said, 'No, but I was walking on the Roman road and I saw them down here so I came to see if I might cadge a lift—' He hesitated, not wanting to tell a stranger that his leg hurt.

'I see. You missed them. I'm Tim Armstrong.' It was grudging.

They shook hands. 'I'm afraid I haven't read anything of yours,' Pharaoh said.

'I keep my head down. If people know you're an author you get no peace; everyone wants you to speak: Women's Institutes, literary societies, you name it. I'm no good at public speaking.' He glowered, then asked explosively: 'What do you do?'

'I write technical articles occasionally: search and rescue mainly. It was my job. What kind of books do you write?'

Armstrong reddened. He had a high balding skull with a few

26

straw-coloured wisps of hair and the blush was obvious. He wore tinted spectacles and it was difficult to judge his expression but he was fidgety: shifting his feet, wiping his hands on his jeans. 'You wouldn't read them,' he said, not answering the question, and then, in the face of Pharaoh's expectant silence: 'I write for money, you see, and under an assumed name.'

'And you want to preserve your anonymity. No wonder no one can find them' – Pharaoh was being friendly – 'people are looking for books under your own name.'

'How do you know people don't read them?'

Pharaoh blinked, then understood. 'Quite. They may be reading your books but they don't realize they're yours. That explains why Randolph and Laura don't know your work.'

'Laura— Of course, you met her this morning.'

'I saw she'd been here.' It was an innocent remark and it produced an unexpected reaction in Armstrong. His glasses flashed as he glanced up the fell.

'She wasn't. No way would she come here. No one does when I'm working. It's private land. They respect that.' His voice had risen.

'Randolph was here,' Pharaoh pointed out, knowing he was out of order; he was on private land.

'That's different,' Armstrong snapped, adding more carefully: 'Randolph's my landlord but even he respects my privacy. I have to work without interruptions. It was different today because he had the Conservancy people with him—' He stopped short.

'It's none of my business,' Pharaoh said.

Armstrong licked his lips. He must be on the wrong side of thirty but he had as much poise as a schoolboy. 'I get lost,' he confessed, as if justifying his behaviour. 'I lose all sense of time and – and what's going on outside when I'm writing. People walk past, Laura rides by and I know nothing about it—'

'Until you see the horse's tracks.' Pharaoh nodded. 'That's how I knew she was here, by the tracks.'

'She comes by occasionally: exercising the horses. But there's no right of way.'

'I understand that. I won't do it again.'

'I didn't mean – it's just that if hikers start to treat it like a public footpath— There's a Private notice at the end of the drive but none on the fell. I came here because I thought there wouldn't be interruptions—'

Pharaoh said he had to be getting along and took his leave. As he walked up the drive between outcrops of rock he was wondering why the fellow should be so prickly. He dismissed the idea of an affair with Laura; in the nineties there was no such thing as an illicit liaison – quaint phrase! But the anonymity, the reluctance to talk about his books, was significant.

He came to a wall, an open gate and the back of a notice. The front read: Private Land No Trespassing Poison Traps Set. He grinned, recognizing Randolph's hand.

After a few yards he was back in the woods and moss replaced lichen on the rocks. Now the road approached the edge of the escarpment and the far side of the dale could be glimpsed through the tree trunks. He turned aside. There was scarcely any undergrowth, only bedrock and boulders, dead leaves and pine needles – except that these weren't pines but larches, now clothed in the most delicate feathery green. He was puzzled to see that some had been recently felled, and very professionally: cut close to the ground.

There were five stumps and they were at the edge of the escarpment. He glanced sideways and saw Grey Buttress in the distance with someone on the summit. So he was on Falcon Crag. Now if *this* were Grey Buttress, the larches might have been felled because they provided anchor points for climbers on the upper pitches, but there was no climbing on Falcon . . . and then he tumbled to it.

From the top of Grey Buttress Mabel Cooper watched him through her binoculars and wondered how to handle him. He was behaving too openly to have designs on the nest but his very ignorance could be a menace. He moved out of sight and after a moment she left the top of the buttress in order to intercept him as he returned to his van. She had discovered it earlier, not that it was hidden; he'd left it in full view of anyone passing on the road.

When they met they greeted each other without surprise. They both carried binoculars.

'What have you seen?' she asked chummily. It was a routine question among bird watchers.

He shook his head. 'I'm only learning. I know the common species and highly coloured ones, and that's it. What's nesting on Falcon Crag?'

'It's full of birds: very vegetated, you know, and there's a lot

28

of ivy lower down; there are wrens and jackdaws and pigeons; blackbirds of course . . .' She trailed off.

'Something chattered earlier on.'

'Chattered?' Her heart sank.

'Well, shrieked is more like it. Would it be a falcon? It's Falcon Crag; there has to be a reason.'

'The crag got its name centuries ago. There are kestrels. They're falcons.'

'I didn't know that.'

'Think of the silhouette: pointed wings, long tail, that's the falcon shape. Buzzards and sparrow hawks have chunky, rounded wings.'

'Why have the trees been cut down?'

She didn't waste her breath asking him what he was talking about. 'It's to stop boys bird-nesting, one boy in particular.' Her face was set.

'Just one?'

'How many do you need?'

He misunderstood her. 'If one boy abseils, and climbs back up the rope, he's taking a chance on nothing going wrong while he's out of sight on the cliff.'

She was intrigued. 'What could go wrong?'

'The rope could run over a sharp edge and fray. Or some other kids might come along – tourists for instance – and start to play with it.'

'I never thought of that.' She was thinking of it now, and her eyes gleamed. 'Because,' she went on, 'he stole a clutch of eggs last year and got away with it. A pity.' She stiffened. 'And he's still stealing; there were Laura's binoculars . . . why, only yesterday he climbed on my roof and came in through a skylight, can you believe that? Randolph had to come over this afternoon and put bolts on my skylights. What do you do with a boy like that?' Her eyes jumped as she looked beyond him. Pharaoh turned to see empty air above the dale. He heard the chattering.

'Kestrel,' she said, as if it were of no consequence: 'the male coming in with food. Female's on eggs. Corporal punishment,' she said with a return to intensity. 'That's what we need in this country. I'm no liberal, Mr Pharaoh.'

'Who would be: guarding peregrine falcons?'

Her hand flew to her mouth. Her eyes searched his face. 'You knew all along!'

'Not at all. But I do know that kestrels are common, and

29

Randolph cutting down trees, and you getting so incensed, that couldn't be just for kestrels. I know about peregrines however, all the same I wouldn't be able to recognize one.'

Mabel's lips had thinned as she listened and weighed him up. Now she sniffed. 'Come here,' she ordered, her hand on his arm, guiding him to the edge and sitting on a boulder. 'Sit down and watch.'

They were looking along the side of Falcon Crag and into the sun. The face of the cliff was hidden. As they watched a surprisingly large bird shot out from the rock, diving, not into a silent void, but space that was suddenly loud with the clap of pigeons' wings. The falcon zoomed up like a fighter plane, gave a quick beat of its wings, turning up-dale, and vanished round the corner.

'Missed,' Mabel said. 'A pity. He expended a lot of energy there. Funny, they don't usually hunt so close to home.'

'Aren't you afraid of attracting attention to the nest by sitting up here?'

'My clothes are drab but yes, I am exposed. Usually I watch from my garden, although the shore below the Boathouse gives the best view of the nest. There are view points in the woods too. The reason I came up here was because I saw you on Grey Buttress.'

He smiled. 'You keep a close watch. You really thought I was after the eggs? The risk of roping down this cliff in the dark – it would have to be in the dark – isn't worth the returns. How much would the eggs fetch? A hundred quid? I could earn that in one night, writing off the top of my head. If I wanted risks I'd be in civilian rescue.'

'It was stupid of me.'

'Not really. I'm a climber – or was; I know how it's done: roping down, and I'm used to heights. Is this lad a climber? He has to be.'

She looked doubtful. 'He doesn't climb with other people so far as I know but then you don't have to, do you? We'd always assumed he was acting on his own; I didn't realize that it was risky for him not to have anyone on top when he went over the edge. And there are no other boys of his age, well, there are—'

'Who's that on top now?'

'What? Where?' She followed his gaze, raised her glasses and was just in time to see figures on Falcon Crag who turned their backs and faded into the trees. 'No,' she said, lowering the binoculars, 'They're not chums of Roy's; they're two little girls, I know their families. Roy doesn't have any friends in the dale.'

'Do his people know about his activities?'

'Know is the operative word. No one has any tangible proof but I saw him hanging about the top last spring and when the nest was robbed and I confronted him he told me that falcons were vermin and their only value was as "commercial properties" – his own words. When I pointed out that he had admitted he was the thief (he hadn't, but that's immaterial) he said I had no witnesses. But the worst thing was that he told me to take good care of my cats.' Mabel looked at him with cold eyes. 'If he touches one of my cats I'll kill him.'

Pharaoh repressed a shiver. 'Did you tell Randolph that?'

'No. He'd turn the family out of their farm.'

'He'd hold the family responsible?'

'Wouldn't you? Spare the rod and spoil the child' – her face changed, became animated – 'although it doesn't always follow. That child' – she gestured towards Falcon Crag – 'Claire is eleven years old and her mother – well, it's a single-parent family: no father and the child's been brought up without any discipline. You can smell cigarettes on her breath – honestly, I'm not exaggerating. Her mother—' She checked, pursed her lips and went on: 'She has a full social life, which leaves the little girl on her own a lot . . . The two of them, mother and daughter, treat each other like equals; the child is more than spoiled, there's a total absence of moral values. And yet little Claire is the most engaging, well-mannered child in the dale, and bright as a button. So you see, how the child turns out doesn't depend on strict discipline after all. Now Becky Rudd, her friend . . .' She was off again. Like many solitary people, when Mabel found someone new to listen to her, there was no stopping her. 'Becky is different again. Such a beautiful child, just wait till you see her! Illegitimate, like Claire – but there's always a story of a fictitious marriage; one accepts it for form's sake. But who could have been Becky's father: a waiter, a student, a prince? Certainly a fellow with classical features. Her mother was a model: now on her honeymoon with an American. Becky is staying with her grandparents, next door to the Boathouse actually, he was Randolph's keeper . . .' She paused for breath.

'Only one keeper?' Pharaoh put in quickly, standing up.

'Oh yes, Randolph's poor as a church mouse, like all of us, alas

31

– but we manage. My point about Becky was that here's another child brought up without a father and although she's very different from Claire, shy and not very intelligent, she's so polite! Her grandmother sees to that; they're old school, the Garners know their place, but then they're all Randolph's tenants—'

'Randolph!' Pharaoh exclaimed in feigned panic, glancing at his watch. 'He said six o'clock. Can I give you a lift down?'

'No, dear boy. I'll drop down the gully at the side of the buttress, the way I came up. Look, there's Jackson on the parlour window sill, see: that black splodge? He's Mildred's eldest. She's spayed now, of course; kittens are just a memory for us old folk. You must come and visit us. I can let you have eggs, vegetables and fruit in season. I do hope you take the Boathouse; the dale needs new blood.'

Chapter Four

'Have you tried that electric-shock treatment?' Randolph asked. 'They tape electrodes on your skin and send a charge through you. It did wonders for my knee. You should have shouted; we'd have given you a lift.'

'I didn't know it was you,' Pharaoh said. 'I don't know your car—'

'Wasn't using mine. The Nature Conservancy people ran me up there. We're working out a management plan for the estate. It's amazing what you can do to improve habitat; you can even bring species back that haven't been recorded in the area for decades. Eagles are obvious, of course, and then there are the harriers – and so on.' His eyes strayed to the tall crags standing proud and bright in the westering sun.

They were settled on a wooden seat in front of the house, sherry and glasses on a rusty iron table. Below them the lake lay like a pool of pewter and the air was so still Pharaoh thought he could hear the flutter of the bats. Occasionally there were sounds from the kitchen where Mabel and Laura were preparing dinner.

'What happens when the peregrines run out of pigeons?' Pharaoh asked.

Randolph's eyes stayed on the crags but he had stiffened. Pharaoh went on: 'I heard them calling. Mabel tried to sidetrack me but I knew they weren't kestrels. I won't talk, you know.'

'Ah. Good.' But Randolph didn't sound convinced.

'I can keep confidences,' Pharaoh said meaningly. 'I've kept a few in my time.'

'Such as?' The sharp eyes were turned on him.

'Fatal accidents.' Pharaoh held his gaze. 'Sins of omission, carelessness, the kind of mistake we all make climbing, even walking, but this time someone died. Who was it said there were no accidents, only human error?'

'And you kept quiet about it?'

'Naturally. The survivor's got to live with his mistake. You're only going to make it harder for everyone if you bring in the law. You don't cover up; you just go along with the coroner's verdict of accidental death.' Pharaoh nodded, as if confirming his own thought. 'So I can keep quiet about a peregrine's nest.'

'I'm glad to hear that. We were a bit worried.'

'Laura was?'

'Laura was what?' she asked, coming down the steps, looking very fetching in a loose jumper that was slipping off one shoulder.

'I was saying: you were bothered about the peregrines,' Randolph said. 'He knows all about them.'

'Mabel's been telling me. I misjudged you, Pharaoh. Now we know you're not after the eggs we can call off the surveillance.'

'You were watching me too?'

'Oh, yes. When I left the Boathouse this morning I went back to Mabel and we plotted how to keep you under observation. I went riding on top and Mabel watched the cliffs from below.'

'I didn't see you anywhere; I thought I was following you along the Roman road.'

'You don't know the country. I doubled back through the woods. Now come and eat.'

Pharaoh felt a lifting of his spirits as they went into the house; her hostility had been a fly in the ointment and he hadn't been looking forward to her antagonism across a dinner table. Fleetingly he thought that she didn't seem the type of girl to be that concerned about a pair of birds.

They dined in the drawing room, the table having been cleared by transferring everything to a sofa. Under the chenille cloth the table was revealed as fine mahogany that gleamed dully. The dinner service, somewhat chipped, was a mixture; some pieces had an intricate pattern in red and gold, some were in white with a delicate border of blue flowers. The glasses were plain glass and the knives and forks had plastic handles. They drank white burgundy with a prawn gumbo. Both were delicious.

'We eat like fighting cocks,' Randolph said smugly when Pharaoh expressed his appreciation.

'Only when Laura comes,' Mabel put in. 'You're no chef, Randolph, you ruin my young vegetables. Like all men,' she told Pharaoh, 'he's terrified of food being under-cooked.'

There was a muffled sound from beneath the table and the springer padded out of the room.

'Fox,' Laura said.

'More likely a cow,' Randolph countered. 'She'd be yelling her head off if she'd smelled a fox.'

Laura stood up and went to the kitchen. Mabel stacked the plates. The springer trotted along the passage to the back regions.

'What's your management plan?' Pharaoh asked politely.

Below the open window Claire hugged her knees and waited for the reply. She was bored. The excitement of eavesdropping lay more in the frisson it gave her to know that grown-ups were unaware of the outsider than in the content of the conversation, which was usually uninteresting anyway. She wanted to hear about people she knew, starting with herself and working outwards. Tonight they had talked about the Air Force, the War, mountain climbing and even – for God's sake! – wine. The only excitement had been when Trudy caught a whiff of her scent and came out to see what she was doing, but even that had passed almost without comment. Now Randolph was droning on about marshes and draining and danger. *Danger?* But she'd misheard. 'Which species are endangered besides the peregrines?' came the visitor's voice, and now they were off on birds. Claire's eyelids drooped; she'd been out all day, and part of last night – a dead loss, last night: the Steels had kept the window closed, she'd heard nothing. Now she was bushed. Her head dropped on her knees.

'Hartley at Warthwaite.' The names penetrated a dream and she jerked awake.

'But they're safe this year?' This from the newcomer.

'Nothing's ever safe.' Miss Cooper's voice cut like a knife. 'If he's started entering houses and eating food, where's it going to end? It was a warning to me. He was *playing*. Next time he could harm a cat.'

'You said you weren't meant to know he'd eaten the trifle,' Randolph said. 'But don't worry, there won't be a next time. Your place is secure now.'

'The cats roam all through the woods. So does that boy. He's a monster.'

'He's graduated,' Laura said. 'An escalation in crime. First vandalism, now petty theft – not so petty actually, my binoculars cost a bomb. I bet they're in his bedroom right now.'

'It's more likely that he keeps them in some place from where he can keep an eye on the peregrines,' Randolph said.

There was a pause. A chair scraped. 'Is it warm enough for coffee in the garden?' Laura asked.

Claire started to ease her way through the rhododendrons.

When she reached home both the cottage and the caravan were in darkness so Marlene wasn't in yet. She was almost too tired to eat but she opened a tin of baked beans and ate half of them cold before crawling upstairs to her bed. She flicked the light in Marlene's room as she passed but the bed was undisturbed. Her own room was at the back of the house. It was stuffy from the heat and she opened the window and breathed in the dank smell of the woods. Tonight she would sleep like the dead.

She was awakened by a crash. She stared at the ceiling, listening. Sounds approached: breathing . . . breathing hard . . . Her mouth opened but she held her breath. It – he – the breathing passed with an accompanying brushing sound, there was another crash, and silence came flooding back.

She ran through the sequence again. There was no one in the house, the noises had come from outside. She got up and hung out of the window. There was no sound, no owls called, not even in the distance; normally the dale was full of owls. She wondered what time it was. She crept along the passage and stood in the doorway of her mother's room. She could hear steady breathing in the darkness. She went back, dressed and let herself out of the cottage.

There was no moon and the night was so quiet that she could hear the cows cropping in the meadow. She hadn't looked at a clock, indeed she hadn't switched on a light, but she guessed it must be around two or three in the morning; she was fresh and alert so she'd had a good sleep but it was nowhere near dawn. She loved the night, when all the grown-ups were fast asleep and the only things awake (apart from cows and they didn't count) were wild beasts on the prowl. It gave her a feeling of superiority to be out at this time, moving silently through the meadow, past the somnolent cows, hearing the surprised croak of a water bird on the shore – another fox down there? She stopped. Foxes *panting*? She'd never seen a fox chasing a rabbit; she'd seen foxes but she'd never heard one, apart from when they were calling to each other at night. You couldn't imagine hearing a fox breathe, let alone pant.

36

She looked at the slope behind the cottage: so black that trees were indistinguishable, the hill was merely a dark bulk against the stars. There was a light in Warthwaite – no, you couldn't see the farm from this point, but the light was in that direction. It went out. Hartley must be tending a sick beast in the paddock. She blinked, thinking she was imagining it, but there it was again, and another, and now she realized that they were beyond the farm, in the woods.

'It was men after the peregrines' nest,' Becky said.

'I told you: the lights weren't on the cliff; they were low down, in the trees.'

It was Sunday morning. Most people were still in bed, like Marlene, or dawdling over a late breakfast; the girls seemed to be the only people about.

Becky didn't believe that Claire had seen lights in the woods, she thought this was another fantasy; Randolph was moving his wife's body, Claire said, because the Nature Management men were going to make improvements.

'I never heard of them,' Becky said as they pushed their bicycles through the quarry and concealed them behind some brambles.

'It doesn't matter. What we have to do is find out where he put the body.'

'Where in hell you going to start?' Claire usually did the swearing but Becky was wearing her new dinosaur T-shirt which would be torn to shreds if they didn't keep to the paths.

'We're going straight to where I saw the lights.'

'You don't know where—'

'Yes I do! Come on, there'll be people here shortly, walking dogs.'

'No one walks dogs here. Randolph don't allow it.'

'What's that then: dog tracks everywhere.'

Becky glowered at what were unmistakably the marks of a large dog – or dogs – in mud. They were following the main path up the slope and in the damp places there were lots of tracks: of Wellingtons, trainers, the cleated soles of climbing boots. Falcon Crag loomed ahead.

'It musta been Roy,' Becky said sulkily.

'Roy went down from above, and he can't do that now 'cause Randolph cut the trees down. Besides, there were two lights.'

'So if it was Randolph, who's helping him?'

'Laura, you silly git!'

'You're making it up! Laura'd never—'

'Look!' They stopped. Claire pointed up the slope that was a haze of bluebells. 'Something's been dragged. Not long ago either, these broken flowers are still fresh.' She started to scramble up the slope.

'I'm staying here,' Becky said, not wanting to shout. Claire didn't stop. After a moment she followed, casting wary glances about her, cringing as pigeons erupted from a tree. She reached a boulder, clawed her way round it and came up against Claire's legs.

'He buried her again,' Claire said. 'I told you so.'

Becky sprawled against the rock, gasping for breath, looking blankly at the patch of ground behind the rock where there was a mat of dead leaves.

'He dragged her up the hill,' Claire whispered. 'She must have been buried lower down first of all.' She had the strangest expression on her face: wild and excited as if someone had given her a present which she'd been looking forward to for a long time. 'You didn't believe me,' she hissed.

Becky swallowed as the dead leaves swam into focus. They were oak leaves which should be biscuit-coloured but these were mottled with something that was dark brown. Claire picked one up between finger and thumb. 'It's blood,' she said. 'It's still sticky.'

'It's been years,' Becky whispered, but Claire wasn't listening; she was scooping the leaves away in handfuls. She came to soil stamped with a cleated sole.

'No,' Becky breathed.

The footprints overlapped and they were fresh. Claire plunged away and returned with a broken branch. She started to scrape at the earth. Becky felt sick.

It was only a thin layer, merely an inch or so, but the soil had made such a mess of what lay underneath that for a moment they were both mystified. Claire lifted the branch, but she had to use both hands. Something dangled from it: long, cream and grey, slimy under the dirt . . . Becky screamed.

Claire dropped the branch, whirled and hit her. 'Someone'll hear you!'

Becky clapped her hands to her mouth, looking from Claire to the thing in the hole.

'So what is it?' Claire hissed. 'It can't be her.' She looked furious but Becky knew she was frightened. Claire didn't understand but then her grandfather wasn't a keeper.

'It's a deer,' Becky said. 'A deer's insides. Them lights was poachers. Let's get out of here. They'll kill us if they find us.'

'Who's the little coloured girl?' Pharaoh asked.

Mabel smiled. 'You must mean Becky. That was her on top of Falcon Crag yesterday, the keeper's grandchild. Did she come visiting?'

Pharaoh had moved into the Boathouse last night, Randolph insisting that he should sleep in a proper bed. This morning he'd come over to Skelgill for eggs.

'I met her on her bike,' he told Mabel. 'Not really met, we didn't speak; I said hello but she was terrified: strange man emerging from the woods. She rushed down the keeper's drive without speaking.'

'You must have startled her.' Mabel walked into her larder. 'In my opinion Becky isn't wary enough. She enjoys attracting attention.' She emerged with a box of eggs.

'You didn't tell me her father was Asian. She's going to be stunning when she's older. I'm surprised—' He grimaced and hesitated. Mabel switched on the kettle and turned, attentive. 'In these days,' he went on lamely: 'cycling alone, you don't know who she might run into.'

'She's never alone. If her friend Claire wasn't with her, then they'd only just parted.'

'Her reaction was so – intense.' He was puzzled. 'It's disturbing to realize one can inspire such fear in a child.'

'You took her by surprise. Do sit down; let's move this clutter.' She stacked loose typescript on a small typewriter and put them on the dresser. 'I'm working in here today,' she explained. 'It's cooler.'

'You work on Sunday?'

'My dear! This time of year there's so much happening you can't keep up with it. My piece for the local paper has to be in the office by Tuesday—' She checked, and went on shyly: 'And I keep a detailed journal, just for my own interest. One day I might do something with it.'

'A natural history of Scawdale?'

'Bless you, I'm not a Gilbert White. But it occupies the time and they allow me such a small space in the paper. I can spread myself in private. And there's so much I can't publicize: the peregrines, Randolph's plans for the land . . . Everything can go in the journal. If it's ever published, I'll need to do a lot of editing, but that's a long way in the future. The point is I can let it all hang out in the journal. Is that the expression?'

'Why don't you write – professionally, I mean?'

'Oh, I couldn't! Never. I wouldn't have the slightest idea how to go about it. This is just for my own amusement.'

She made coffee and gave him a mug decorated with badgers. Her tanned cheeks had gone a deeper shade. He sought to change the subject.

'What kind of books does Tim Armstrong write?'

She stared at him and licked her lips.

'Forbidden subject?' he asked with forced lightness. 'I thought as much. He was cagey himself, hostile in fact. I thought it had to be pornography?'

'I wondered.' She was tight-lipped. 'Now you come to mention it, pornography could well be the explanation.'

'Under an assumed name.'

'Of course, because no one's heard of Tim Armstrong – neither in book shops nor the libraries. We've all tried to find his books. So you think it's pornography.' She sat down and regarded him calmly. 'Well, where there's a demand, there'll always be someone to supply the product.'

'You don't disapprove?'

'Oh, my dear boy, there are far more important things in life than dirty books. Have some of this shortbread; it's made with sunflower margarine. Do you like cooking?'

The change of subject took his breath away. 'I'm learning,' he said. 'I haven't been alone all that long.' There was a stunned silence. 'I lost my wife and daughter in a road accident,' he muttered, disconcerted. He stared at the badgers on his mug. 'I'm a pretty raw housekeeper, but I find cooking absorbing.' He looked at her in pleased surprise. 'I'm still amazed when I manage to follow a complicated recipe and produce something that actually tastes good.'

'I see.' The tone was deeply apologetic. With her wild courtesy she went on: 'What cookery books do you use?'

He warmed to her. They discussed cookery books and she repeated her offer of fresh vegetables in season. 'Randolph and

I have a barter system,' she said. 'He does odd jobs for me.'
Pharaoh asked about Laura's mother.

She had left twelve years ago, she told him. 'She came from
Yorkshire, a bit of a butterfly, not enough social life for her in
the dale, or not enough of the right kind. She's married to a
racehorse trainer in Lincolnshire now. Randolph wasn't cut out
for marriage – although he made an excellent job of bringing up
Laura.' She shook her head and her eyes widened as she remembered that Pharaoh didn't have a daughter to raise.

He came to her rescue, suggesting that she show him her
garden.

'You're back early.' Doris turned from the sink. 'Isn't Claire
coming out today?'

'I don't know.' Becky sidled into the kitchen and picked up a
tea cloth without being asked. Doris glanced at the lowered head
and returned to the washing-up, scrubbing diligently at a plate.
The silence stretched. Becky was wiping the same cup over and
over again. Doris dried her hands and lifted the child's chin. The
cup fell and smashed on the stone floor. Becky's arms dropped
and she stood limply. She was crying without a sound.

Doris pulled out a chair and pushed her into it. She put the
kettle on the gas, grabbed a box of tissues and waited for the
storm to pass. She was tight-lipped, guessing that Roy Hartley
had made another brutal comment on the colour of Becky's skin.
She was glad Garner was out of the house; he'd be bound to
make some blundering remark that would only make the situation
worse.

She brewed the tea and pulled a chair out for herself, the
familiar words of comfort on her lips: 'Ladies spend fortunes
trying to tan themselves to your colour, and they never make it,
they go all wrinkled and hard; I don't know whether you're going
to be a model like your mother or a film star . . .' – trying to
think of new ways to phrase the old anodyne. But today was
different. Instead of drinking her tea and submitting to comfort,
acknowledging finally that because she was different she was
better, today Becky stood up, her face set. She's angry, Doris
thought; good, she's learning to fight back – but she didn't say it
because the situation was unprecedented and she was uncertain
how to handle it.

'Drink your tea,' she said diffidently.

41

Becky picked up her cup but she didn't sit down. She stared out of the window at the trees on the edge of the garden. They were spruce here, dense and gloomy. She shuddered. Doris's eyes widened.

'What happened?'

The dark eyes returned to her. They looked flat. Doris was concerned. 'Nothing,' Becky said. 'I don't feel well. I'm going upstairs.'

'It's not—' Doris stopped. She was only twelve but they started younger these days, and then there was the Indian blood. Had her mother told her? Becky turned to go. 'Er' – Doris raised her voice – 'let me know—' Becky halted. She's only a child, Doris thought, floundering. 'If there's anything you want, like – if you want to ask me – don't be afraid to ask.'

Becky stared, her expression unreadable in the dim passage. 'I started months ago, Granma, so I suppose that's what it is. I'll sleep it off.'

Doris collapsed and reached for her tea. She'd put a lot of sugar in when she'd meant only to put it in Becky's. Sugar for shock. You're not shocked when you start your period, particularly when it's not the first time, and why had she been crying? Maybe she hadn't been shocked, just upset. Little girls are so touchy, Doris thought, cradling her tea; she'd quarrelled with young Claire, that's what it was, and Claire had said something she shouldn't. Them as lives in glasshouses, Doris thought grimly, I'll give that Marlene a piece of my mind when I see her.

Chapter Five

Scawdale basked in the warmth of yet another glorious day, the shimmering air sweet with the scent of flowers. People went happily about their Sunday activities, even Isaac Garner, a chronic grumbler, taking pleasure in the progress of his broad beans, his satisfaction marred only by the conviction that the blackfly would arrive before the end of June.

Isaac was working at the far end of his garden, the kitchen hidden from him by the raspberry canes, so he had no knowledge of the movements of his family and wouldn't have been interested if he had. Women and children had their own occupations; men looked after game and such, and grew things – and came in for their Sunday dinner at noon, on the dot. Isaac was a stickler for routine. He would smell the meat before he reached the back door, the table would be laid, pans steaming on the stove – on Sunday the Garners had a roast, winter or summer regardless of temperature. He sniffed appreciatively as he clumped up the back step and then he stopped.

The kitchen was empty. There were pans on the stove but they were cold and the table was bare.

'Doris,' he shouted. 'Doris! Where are you, woman?'

He went out in the passage and bawled up the stairs. There was no reply. He swore and returned to the kitchen. He opened the oven door and stared at the sizzling roast as if it might tell him something. All ready to be eaten and not a spud cooked, no gravy, nothing – no *wife*. There wasn't even a note.

He went upstairs. He stood in the doorway and surveyed their empty room, the windows open, the bed neatly made. He glanced in the bathroom, saw that Becky's room was curiously dim so he went in and pulled the curtains back. Her bed was made too but indented where she'd lain on it since it was made. There was a piece of paper on the quilt. "Gone to Claires" it read.

The devil! She'd gone to that tart's house when she knew she wasn't supposed to, Doris had gone after her – and now he had to go and fetch them back. He would *not* go to Starfoot, let them walk back . . . but there was his Sunday dinner: roast beef waiting to be eaten. Doris had to come home; he'd drive to the cattle grid below Starfoot and sit there sounding the horn until they came.

The boss's old Volvo was parked at the bridge below Falcon Crag; he hoped Mr Randolph wouldn't see him traipsing up and down the dale looking for a wife who'd gone off without a word at Sunday dinner time. He found her on the road this side of the quarry so he went on and turned round and waited. In the mirror he'd seen her turn and start to run after him. He was going to give her what for but when he saw her face he changed his mind.

'Is she home?' she gasped.

'Becky?'

'Of course, you old fool!'

'Isn't she with you?'

'You bloody idiot!' He goggled at her. She never swore. She wrenched open the door and got in.

'Where to?' he asked. 'What's happening?'

'Home,' she gulped. 'She'll be home by now, surely? She'll have gone through the woods. We missed her.'

'The note said she's with Claire.'

'She's not – and Marlene hasn't seen her, and I'll tell you something else: Claire's gone missing too. Not that Marlene cares, she says they're always going off together – so I suppose' – she turned to him, pleading for reassurance – 'they're together? And if they're together they're all right.'

Pharaoh was watching a strange duck when Randolph came down the side of the Boathouse. 'What's this duck . . .' He trailed off because Randolph was already speaking.

'How's the leg? Feel like an outing?'

'It's fine. Better for a night in a comfortable bed.' Pharaoh studied his face.

Randolph held out a piece of paper. 'Dropped inside the car,' he said.

Pharaoh took it, still watching him. Randolph was furiously angry.

There was one short sentence on the paper and it was typed: "dead deer up back of quarrey."

44

'Poaching?' Pharaoh asked.

Randolph scowled. 'I don't even know if it's genuine. It could be a hoax: someone making trouble – although it doesn't accuse anyone.'

'A typist didn't do this. He – or she – didn't know how to get a capital letter, nor how to spell quarry.'

'Anyone could get access to a typewriter. We don't always lock our doors.' Randolph stared at the escarpment. 'Good mind to fetch my shotgun,' he muttered, then shook himself. 'You coming?'

'Of course.' It seemed wisest to humour his landlord. 'Are you picking up Garner?'

'I went there; the place is empty, no one around. God knows where they are, lunch is cooking in the oven. I'd rather take you anyway, you're not involved. And Garner's old and arthritic. It's probably a hoax.'

The act of driving seemed to calm him somewhat. 'Are you sure about your leg?' he asked as they went up the drive. 'I've got the bitch, you know.' Trudy was in the back of the Volvo.

Pharaoh snorted with laughter. 'Her legs are certainly in better shape but I can manage. It seems to me the knickers are in a bit of a twist.'

It worked. 'Sorry,' Randolph muttered. 'I've been knocked for six. Damn it, bitch, lie down, will you!' – as Trudy licked his ear. 'You see, that note: it's got to be someone who knows us. Trudy didn't bark. That's how the windows came to be open, I'd left her in the car. Don't normally take her in the woods; not there, anyway. I was taking a look at the peregrines. So the chap who dropped the note knew Trudy; she didn't make a sound. I would have heard, I couldn't have been far away. That's where I was parked.' He indicated a gate above a low bank with enough space for one car on the verge.

They came to the quarry where several cars were parked. Randolph said they belonged to tourists who were probably down on the lake shore. They started up a well-used path where large paw-prints showed where there was mud. Randolph regarded them moodily. Trudy ranged ahead and when she came racing back he sent her out again. A cock pheasant shouted his alarm, wrens scolded, a woodpecker fled towards them, veering at the last moment with a flash of scarlet. Randolph trudged ahead and Pharaoh knew that he was growing angrier by the minute. He guessed that Trudy would always be at heel in the woods, at least in spring and summer – and she would be quiet; now she was barking frantically.

'She's found something,' Randolph said, and plunged up the slope. Pharaoh followed, taking a zigzag line. He came up with Randolph to find him glaring at a pile of intestines that was swarming with blowflies. Trudy sat a few yards away, her tongue lolling; she'd done her job.

'I'd say,' Randolph began shakily, trying to control his voice, 'they scraped a shallow hole and buried the guts more or less, then someone else came along, with a dog, and dug it up. See this branch: guts still hanging on it.'

'He didn't have to bring a dog,' Pharaoh said. 'There's a drag mark down to the path; you missed it. The second party on the scene followed that.'

'Oh, yes? Could be. The poachers had dogs though; they made those tracks below. Have to use dogs to bring down deer. Daren't use rifles. But someone else knew, or suspected. Why come here otherwise?'

'Neighbours?' Pharaoh suggested. 'Some kind of feud: a person getting his own back?'

'That's what I was thinking.'

'A local chap would be afraid of retaliation so he informed you anonymously. D'you think more deer were taken?'

'Sure to be. These are roe: small beasts; they'd need a few to make a profit. The worst thing is' – he was suddenly fierce again – 'using dogs to bring deer down! They take anything, even pregnant does. We've never had it before, thank God, not in my time, but lurchers have been used to take fallow deer in the Eden Valley, and there's a lot of poaching on Forestry Commission land.' He sighed heavily. 'We'd better see if there are any more.'

It was Trudy who found the next site, and when they'd scraped away the trampled top soil ('Vibram soles,' Randolph said. 'Doesn't tell us much. Everyone wears Vibram soles.') – under the spill of intestines they found a mangled fawn.

The mood changed. Randolph didn't swear. He picked up the torn body that was covered with blood and dirt and placed it tenderly on the bluebells, exposing the savage wounds. He wiped the tiny muzzle and looked back at the guts. 'I'll kill the man who did this,' he said quietly, and Pharaoh marvelled at his priorities: blaming the man and not the dogs.

*

46

'No.' Hartley was adamant. 'I didn't hear nothing in the night. Why? Was something stole or—' He glanced at his wife who was pouring the tea. Her hand shook.

'How about you, Anne?' Randolph asked. 'Did you hear anything?'

'I wouldn't,' she said. 'Both of us sleep like logs—' She gasped as she spilled tea in the saucer.

'Perhaps Roy—' Randolph murmured.

'He were safe in his bed! He heard nothing, he'd have said.'

Randolph regarded her grimly and she moved to the stove. He wondered how Pharaoh was getting on with the boy. They hadn't driven to Warthwaite but approached on foot from the quarry which was close to the boundary of the farm. Seeing the lad dodge into a barn as they entered the yard, Randolph had left him to Pharaoh, himself tackling the parents. 'I'm surprised you didn't hear cars in the quarry,' he said.

'We wouldn't notice 'em.' Anne turned quickly. 'Lots of folk park there nights: couples like and campers.' She was stiff and pale but it was difficult to know whether the pallor was from anger or fear. She was a big plain woman, strong as a horse, and proving equally strong in defence of her family.

'Was it poachers?' Hartley asked.

Randolph inhaled sharply. He had tried to stay cool but the question recalled the image of the fawn. 'Have you acquired a lurcher?' he asked harshly.

'No, Mr Steel! You knows I don't have no lurcher.'

'We never kept 'em!' Anne was furious at the implication, lurchers being bred for chasing.

'They used dogs to take the deer, and they took a doe and a fawn.'

She pulled out a chair and lowered herself into it, staring at him. She was breathing hard but after a moment she said shakily, 'No one left this house last night. Ever since them hawks' eggs was taken we locked up when we went to bed. Folk like that about: you can't leave your place unlocked no more. Last night I took key out of lock and I wasn't thinking, slipped it in me pocket. It were there this morning: in me skirt pocket. No one were out.'

It was bluster and they all knew it. The lad could have gone and come back by a window.

*

47

'So you're not police,' Roy said. 'You still got no right to ask questions without me dad being here.'

'Right?' Pharaoh repeated with feigned naïvety. 'This isn't an interview. I'm your new neighbour, getting to know you. Sunday morning's the time for calling.'

'So why're you asking me what I were doing last night? Told you, I were in my bed.' Roy's jaw worked and his brows drew together as if he were about to say more. Pharaoh studied the lad's body, already well formed at fourteen: the arms muscular, the chest straining the black T-shirt. There was no sign of blood or mud on his jeans; his trainers were grubby but you'd expect that on a farm.

'You'll know me next time you see me,' Roy said nastily. 'What you doing here anyway?'

'I'm a climber.'

There was a flicker of interest, a hesitation. 'Allus thought I'd like to climb,' he said.

'It's dangerous.' Pharaoh was casual, even bored, turning to look up the dale.

'I'd like that.' He was eager now. 'It looks great: that jumpin' down – you know – down sheer walls?'

'Abseiling. It's a sport on its own; some people prefer it to climbing.'

'Why don't the rope break? How's it fastened on the top?'

'You put it round a tree.'

'Yeah, but suppose—' His eyes jumped.

'Ah, there you are!' Randolph was crossing the cobbles. 'Is that young Roy behind you? Been asking your dad about last night, Roy. Did you see anything in the woods?'

Roy scowled. 'I wasn't in the woods.'

'When you were coming home?'

'No.'

'What time did you come home?'

'Dunno.' He threw a glance towards the house and shifted his feet. 'Around seven, eight maybe.'

'Who owns lurchers?'

Roy gaped. 'I don't know anyone as does.'

Randolph turned away. 'He's lying,' he growled as they left the yard. 'Did you get anything out of him?'

'Nothing about poaching but he was trying to pump me about abseiling. I told him to use a tree. You arrived before he could ask me what to use if the trees had been cut down.'

Randolph turned and stared at the crag. Pharaoh thought that they were probably being watched from behind the blank windows of the farmhouse. 'Don't worry,' he said. 'He doesn't know how to abseil. He'd probably kill himself if he tried.'

Randolph shot him a glance. 'Two crimes,' he said. 'Within half a mile of each other.'

'Coincidence?'

'Not if the same person was involved.'

Marlene Fisher came round the corner of her cottage in response to Randolph's shout. She was barefooted in a long skirt. The scooped neck of her blouse revealed fine shoulders and the gorgeous hair framed a face without make-up. She looked as if she'd not long been out of bed.

'I've brought your new neighbour,' Randolph said gruffly. 'Meet Jack Pharaoh.'

She didn't apologize for her appearance nor for having nowhere to seat them other than a plank on cinder blocks below the gable-end. She seemed to take it for granted that no one sat indoors on a summer's day. She brought them cans of Budweiser.

'This isn't a courtesy visit,' she announced, smiling, opening a cheap folding chair and sitting down with her back to the light. Pharaoh felt like an insect being inspected by a collector. 'I'm sorry!' she exclaimed. 'You're looking straight at the sun.' She moved her chair as Pharaoh mumbled protests. 'Not really a Sunday visit,' she insisted gaily. 'No one's dressed for it.' She looked pointedly at their trousers which were splashed with dried mud.

'I would have warned you,' Randolph said, 'but you're not on the phone, and we didn't know we were coming ourselves. We were overtaken by events.'

'How fascinating. Like Doris Garner.'

That took them by surprise. 'Doris?' Randolph repeated. 'Why was she here?' He stopped, aware of a gaffe – possibly. He frowned.

Marlene looked wicked. 'I'm sure they can't be related: the reasons behind your visits. Oh no, impossible. Young Becky's sloped off and left a note to say she was coming here. But she didn't.' There was silence. A shadow crossed her face. The atmosphere changed. 'What did you come for?' she asked sharply.

'Oh no, nothing like *that*.' Randolph was shocked. 'Not the children, of course not! They're off somewhere, playing – down

49

by the lake,' he added wildly. Pharaoh fidgeted. Marlene stared. Randolph pulled himself together with an effort. 'Sorry, my dear, I'm shocked – angry, rather. What happened is that poachers were after our deer last night. We found the remains.'

'Oh.' Marlene relaxed with a sigh. 'Poaching!' And then quickly: 'I'm so sorry, Randolph; those lovely little deer.'

'That's not the worst of it.' He was bitter. 'They used dogs, and they killed a fawn. They left that: no good to 'em after the dogs had finished with it.'

She stared as if hypnotized. Her eyes brimmed over and, searching and not finding a handkerchief, she lifted her skirt and wiped away the tears. Pharaoh turned, embarrassed, to see Trudy streaking down the track towards a small figure pushing a bicycle.

'They should be shot,' Marlene exclaimed angrily, following his gaze. 'They used to bring down deer with dogs but *they* were hung. You know what'll happen to these? They'll get fined. You never heard of a woman poacher, did you? At least, not using dogs.'

Randolph stood up. 'What we came about – we've been to Warthwaite – was to ask if you heard or saw anything last night that might help: in the woods under Falcon Crag.'

'I got home around ten,' she said, thinking back. 'I didn't see any lights – I mean, any that shouldn't be there, but then I didn't look. And I sleep at the front so I wouldn't hear anything in the woods, but then, if they were under Falcon— Here's Claire. Ask her, she sleeps at the back. Hi, sweetie—' as her daughter arrived, escorted by the springer. 'This is Jack; he's going to live at the Boathouse.'

'Hello.' Claire stood by her bike and surveyed them calmly: a solemn little thing, Pharaoh thought, but not shy.

'We had poachers in the woods under Falcon last night, Claire,' Randolph told her. 'Did you happen to hear anything – or see anything, come to that?'

Claire looked at the trees behind the cottage, giving the question her full attention. 'I didn't hear any shots,' she said slowly, 'but would they wake you up? Not if they was as far away as Falcon.'

'They used dogs.'

'They chased deer with dogs? That's beastly. So they wouldn't make a noise, would they?'

'Unless you heard men calling,' Marlene put in, a trifle desperately. 'Or, well, anything.'

50

'Like crashing through the undergrowth,' Pharaoh said. 'Deer being chased by dogs must make a lot of noise.'

'Falcon Crag is still a long way off,' Claire said dubiously, studying him.

Randolph nodded. 'I didn't expect you to have heard anything, not here. Warthwaite was more likely,' he told Marlene, 'but we drew a blank there too. Not that you can believe anything that—' He checked, throwing a glance at Claire who was gazing along the front of the cottage. 'Warthwaite's nearer the quarry,' he said flatly. 'And that's where these fellows would have left their cars.'

'How do you know that?' Claire's interest was awakened. 'How did you know anyone was poaching in the first place? Were they caught?'

'A bit early for that, love,' Marlene said.

'A good question,' Randolph was saying, avuncular now, playing it down. 'I had an anonymous letter saying that there were dead deer near the quarry.'

'There's no post today,' Marlene said in surprise.

'Delivered by hand.' Randolph was grim. 'I was parked at the bridge below Falcon and someone put the note in my car. I'd thank you to keep it to yourself for the time being, and that goes for you too, Claire. Understand?' She nodded gravely. 'You see' – again the adult talking to the small child – 'whoever wrote that note has done me a good turn. And no way do I want—' He glanced at Marlene for help.

'What Randolph's saying, ducky, is that if the poachers find out who shopped them, they're going to have it in for him.'

'That's all right,' Claire said. 'I won't say anything.'

'She won't either,' Marlene assured Randolph. 'You can trust her implicitly.' Her tone changed. 'Did Becky go home, love?'

The girl stared at her and frowned. 'Mrs Garner was here,' Marlene explained. 'Becky left a note on her bed saying she was with you.'

Randolph exchanged looks with Pharaoh. Claire was saying: 'When was Mrs Garner here? I haven't seen Becky.'

'Never mind.' Marlene was flustered. 'You're going, Randolph? I'll let you know . . .' She trailed off, uncertain what she should let him know.

'That's a hell of a way to give a visitor tea,' Laura exclaimed, entering Burnbank's kitchen to find Randolph and Pharaoh eating doorstep sandwiches, with pint mugs of tea at their elbows.

'This is our lunch,' Randolph said. It was five o'clock.

'I knew you didn't come home because I had lunch between horses: Sable this morning, Blaze this afternoon. What happened to you?'

'We had poachers last night: below Falcon. They used dogs and they took a fawn and two adults – at least. They left the fawn. We found the guts of the others. They heard nothing at Warthwaite and Starfoot.'

The colour drained from her face and for a moment Pharaoh thought that she was about to faint but her eyes were bright and intent.

Randolph looked a trifle daunted. 'We'll get them,' he assured her.

She licked her lips delicately, unhooked a mug from the dresser, poured herself tea and sat down, her movements slow and deliberate. Randolph watched her uneasily.

'What did Roy have to say?' she asked.

'Ha! What would you expect? But it was Pharaoh here who tackled him, I went for the parents. Anne tried her damnedest to convince me the lad hadn't left the house; naturally my conclusion was that he did.'

'And he said?' She turned to Pharaoh.

'That he was in bed; he heard nothing and saw nothing.'

'What put you on to this?' she asked Randolph.

He found the note in a pocket: creased and dirty. He smoothed it out on the table and she studied the message.

'The chap who typed that's on our side,' Randolph said. 'So don't try and work out who's responsible. I wish he'd told us before the event though. It's time I reported it to the police.'

'They can only patrol the roads,' Pharaoh said. 'And probably just this one: watching the quarry. The poachers could go in from the top next time, if they come back.'

'What they can do is put out feelers: try and find out which hotel bought venison at the back door this weekend.'

'No one's going to put venison on the menu this time of year,' Laura said. 'And it's got to be hung; that means a cellar.'

'Cellar first, then deep-freeze,' Randolph said. 'If deer are taken then there's a market for the meat, stands to reason. The trouble is, they could have removed the carcasses some distance, and the local police have access only to local informants.' He frowned at the note. 'Impossible,' he murmured. 'She'd have come to me direct.'

52

Laura stood up. 'I'm taking Sable out again; she's fat as butter and pulling like mad.'

'Fat horses don't pull. You're going to be late starting back or are you leaving early tomorrow?'

'Dad! I told you Friday: I'm taking time off. You're getting old, not listening to what I say. You're tired too. You and Pharaoh have a quiet drink and I'll give Sable a short work-out and come back and cook something special. There's nothing more you can do this evening—'

'I must call the police . . .'

'That were boss on phone,' Isaac said. 'We had poachers last night and he only just let me know! Took three deer. Set dogs on 'em.'

Doris stared at him. 'And she was out alone this morning—' gesturing towards the parlour where Becky was watching television.

'They was long gone by then,' Isaac growled. 'But don't you let her out this evening.' He raised his voice in warning as Becky appeared in the passage. 'You're not going out, girl!'

'I wasn't going to.' She stood in the doorway, looking from one to the other. 'What's wrong?' And, with the contrariness of the young: 'Why can't I go out?'

'Because there's poachers about, that's why.' Doris was grim.

Becky looked unhappy but she hadn't been herself since the old people came home at lunch time to find her lying on her bed. She hadn't found Claire, she told Doris, and no, she hadn't meant she was going right to Starfoot when she wrote that note, only that she would wait at the cattle grid, hoping that Claire would see her and come down the track, but there was no sign of life at Starfoot so she came home. She must have missed Doris and Isaac when they were on the road and she was cycling through the woods. Now Doris remembered her telling them about cycling along the footpath.

'The poachers were in the woods, Becky!'

'Last night, woman!' Isaac shouted.

She rounded on him, beside herself with worry. 'No matter when! She's not going out of this house alone. Why, they killed a keeper in Wales, what would they do—' Her eyes shifted to Becky as she visualized what they might do to a little girl.

Becky swallowed. 'I'm not going out, Granma; no way.'

Doris tried to retract. 'There, love, I didn't mean to scare

53

you; it's just until they're caught, isn't it, Granpa? And nothing happened this morning, it was just I was so worried because we're responsible for you while your mam's in America – although I'd be just as concerned if you was one of my own, which you are, of course. Still – all's well as ends well; you go and watch the telly, can't have you moping, can we? And I'll bring you some chocolate ice cream.'

Becky said, 'Why don't you keep your gun loaded, Granpa?'

He opened his mouth and closed it again as he caught Doris's eye. He nodded. 'Good idea. I'll do that.' He looked back to Doris for direction.

'He will too,' she said meaningly. 'We'll be ready for 'em if they come, don't you fret, love.'

'I meant – you take it with you.' Becky was terrified. 'You think they'll come *here*!' Her voice rose hysterically.

'Of course they won't,' Doris said in wonder, studying her face. 'Granpa's the keeper. We'll bolt all the doors and windows and – and he'll take the gun when we go to bed. What's *wrong*, Becky? There's no call to go on so. Now you watch telly and I'll bring you a nice bowl of ice cream—'

'There's something wrong with that child,' she whispered to Isaac as Becky drifted back to the parlour. He ignored her. And now she'd have his bad temper to cope with because he was going to spend the whole evening speculating how last night's villainy would affect him, and why he should be the last person to hear about it.

Chapter Six

Randolph reported the poaching incident to the police, and talked to friends on the force but he derived little satisfaction from the exchanges. He was told that men would be sent out but that there was not much that could be done other than to make enquiries at suspect hotels and to ask questions concerning the movements of those locals known to possess lurchers. He was reminded that dogs could be hidden, witness pit bulls. Nor was it illegal to own a lurcher; it was what use the animals were put to. And there he could be sure that everyone would have a cast-iron alibi for Saturday night.

Uniformed men arrived at Burnbank Monday morning and he guided them to the scene. He'd wedged the fawn's body in the crotch of a tree to keep it from the foxes, and after the police had taken photographs (he'd insisted on their bringing a camera) they buried the remains. Back at the quarry the driver of the police car informed his sergeant that they were to proceed to a Miss Cooper at Skelgill. There had been a burglary.

Randolph swore and led the way down the dale, driving too fast. Mabel met them at her garden gate. 'Are you all right?' he shouted, struggling out of the Volvo.

'Of course I am.' He could see, couldn't he? 'I didn't know until I got up' – she nodded a greeting to the sergeant – 'not until I went to my bag, in fact, and I found my wallet was gone – and all the pounds and fifty-pence pieces from my purse.'

There was a significant silence, the police thinking that this was an old lady but one who was also a friend of a man who carried considerable weight in the community. Randolph was thinking merely that she was old.

'Are you sure—' he began.

'I am perfectly sure,' she interrupted coldly. 'Had it been only one item, the wallet or the change, I might wonder, but not both.

There were a hundred pounds in the wallet – I only went to the bank on Friday.'

'Is anything else missing, ma'am?' The sergeant looked vaguely round the kitchen, his glance lingering on the typewriter. People still used typewriters?

'Binoculars?' Randolph suggested.

'No,' she snapped. 'He has Laura's.'

The sergeant looked at her sharply, then at Randolph. 'My daughter's binoculars were taken from her car recently,' he said. 'It was parked in our yard.'

'And this place was broken into last Friday,' Mabel put in. 'In broad daylight. That time he stole food. Last year he took the peregrines' eggs. He was skulking in the woods yesterday morning too.'

'Ah, that one—' The sergeant had caught on but Randolph was speaking.

'How did he get in? Did you leave the skylights open?'

'Of course I didn't.' But she was embarrassed. They stared at her. 'My own fault,' she muttered. 'Although, how could it be? Doors bolted, ground-floor windows latched, all except one, but go and look.' She indicated the larder where sunlit trees showed beyond a small window.

'No one could get in there!' the sergeant exclaimed.

'He got through the skylight.' Mabel was morose. 'And this is the same width.'

'Mabel!' Randolph was shocked. 'Why on earth did you leave it open?'

'For the cats, of course.'

'My God! I'm going straight home for some cement and an iron bar. And until the cement sets you turn those cats out at night and make the place secure. You'll do that, won't you?'

She shrugged. The sergeant was saying: 'What makes you so sure it was young Hartley, ma'am?'

'I know it was him.' She was icy. 'He threatened me after he stole the eggs and I confronted him. In fact, he threatened worse.' Her eyes blazed. 'I suppose we should count ourselves lucky the cats are unharmed this morning. When I think of that – that monster roaming round my house with me sound asleep upstairs I'm – I feel I've been outraged. It's like rape—' No one dared to smile. She turned on Randolph like one of the Furies. 'Turn the cats out overnight! How can you suggest it? If the cement takes

56

a night to set I'm coming over to Burnbank for one of your shot-guns.'

'Oh, now, ma'am—'

Randolph was mouthing at her and she exhaled slowly and swallowed. 'I'm very fond of my animals, sergeant,' she said shakily.

'Of course.' He was known as a tactful man. 'But shooting the culprit's not the way.' He smiled, dismissing the outburst. 'We'll follow this up, don't you worry.' He turned to Randolph. 'I'll get CID along, sir, see if we can find fingerprints. If you wouldn't mind not going in your larder until they've been, ma'am . . .'

'This is a fine time to come in for breakfast,' Marlene scolded. 'What time did you get up?'

'Just this minute.' Claire went to the sink and dashed water on her face.

'What's wrong with the bathroom?' Marlene stubbed out her cigarette and came over to the draining board with her empty mug.

'I slept in the caravan.'

'You what! You never did that before.'

'So it's time I started. It stinks in there; you should keep the windows open all the time in summer.'

'I don't want you using the caravan, sweetie. I've told you that before.'

'It was just last night. It's cooler than my bedroom – once the windows have been open a while.'

Claire threw the coffee grounds outside the door, rinsed the pot and switched the kettle on.

'I'll make it,' Marlene said. 'You make it too strong. And you shouldn't be smoking,' she added as Claire sat down and reached for the cigarettes. 'The earlier you start the harder it is to give up.'

'Look who's talking.'

'I've given up giving up.' Marlene spooned coffee into the pot. 'We're nearly out of Continental so we'll have to live on instant for a time. We're low on cash.'

'Buy half a pound. I can let you have some money.'

The kettle boiled and Marlene filled the pot. 'Where did you get it?' she asked in the tone of one who has asked the question times without number.

'Hugh gave it to me.'

Claire was normally so inventive with her answers that this was remarkable on more than one count. Marlene froze.

'Why?'

'I asked for it.' Claire's eyes were innocent.

'Just like that. You asked for money and he gave it to you?'

'I chose the right moment. He had to have the money on him—' She left it hanging.

'And?'

Claire smiled with pleasure. She had blown a perfect smoke ring. 'Where does he get his money?' she asked, as if the thought had only just occurred to her.

'It's unemployment benefit, of course.'

'Not on Sunday. And I know how he got it. The point is, do you?'

Marlene pulled out a chair and sat down. She lit a cigarette and shook the match out slowly, staring at her daughter.

'Does Hugh know you – what you suspect?'

'Suspect balls. Hugh and me have an understanding. What I wanted to know was how much you knew.'

'Hugh's all right,' Marlene said absently. 'But sweetie' – her eyes were pleading – 'you've got to realize how important this is. Look at this dump' – she gestured wildly at the dim kitchen with its old stove and refrigerator, the rough shelving made of planks – 'it's not much but it's all we've got. It's our *home*. We're poor, ducky, we can only afford the kind of rent Randolph charges, and if we didn't have this place we'd have to go into a Bed and Breakfast like those ghastly holes you see on the telly. Christ, we could be homeless, thrown out on the street—'

'Give over, Mum.' Claire was incisive. 'You're getting worked up about nothing. You know damn well I'll keep my mouth shut.'

Marlene collapsed, pushing her hands through her hair. 'You're growing up so fast, I can't keep pace. Here I'm still thinking of you as my little girl, other people mistake us for sisters, and now I feel' – she laughed helplessly – 'why, I feel as if it's you who's looking after me.'

'Bloody hell, someone's got to. The only person *he* looks after is Hugh Mason.'

It was another scorching day. Pharaoh thought that if it got any hotter they'd be reduced to taking exercise in the early morning and evening. By mid-morning walking was out of the question and he'd taken the dinghy and rowed out to the island, which was really only a rock with a couple of Scots pines and a few larches. It rose abruptly from the water but there was a sloping shelf on the far side where he had pulled the boat up. Now he sat in the shade, binoculars to hand, watching the peregrines. Already the male had come in with something small in its talons, small enough that he anticipated it would return shortly with more substantial prey.

A movement caught his eye; there was someone on top of Grey Buttress. He raised the binoculars to find the second man but there wasn't one, and no rope so it wasn't a climber, just a tourist who was dangerously near the edge. The man raised something like a stick in the classic attitude of firing, but there was no sound. Pharaoh was surprised; the fellow was black as soot.

The male peregrine was back, the female welcoming him. Pharaoh swung sideways to view the nest and at that moment a shot was fired. He gasped and returned to the black man who was now pointing his weapon downwards, but it wasn't a stick. It glittered – it was a gun. And what the hell was he firing at? He was wearing pale gloves, Pharaoh thought irrelevantly; anyone would think he was aiming at Skelgill . . . *long* gloves? There came another report and for a moment the fellow stood there, aiming down, then he lowered the gun and *waved*. Not pale gloves but a white man – with a black head? He looked like a terrorist. Of course, it was a balaclava. He turned and vanished into the trees.

'It was Roy Hartley,' Mabel said grimly. 'Firing at me with an air gun. He waved to make sure I knew it was him. He was taunting me, and we haven't a shred of proof. You saw him, but neither of us can prove it was him, not in that balaclava.'

'That wasn't an air gun,' Pharaoh said. 'I heard the shots.'

'That was me, dear boy. I've borrowed one of Randolph's shot-guns.' She gestured to where it lay on the dresser. 'Roy was here last night.' She told him about the burglary and the visit from Randolph and the police. 'Something has to be done about that lad,' she said, looking thoughtfully at the shotgun. 'Of course, I couldn't hit him where he was standing on top of the buttress; I fired to let him know that now I have a weapon, and a lethal one at close quarters.'

'He waved after you fired,' Pharaoh pointed out. 'He wasn't intimidated.'

She smiled. 'He wouldn't have waved if he'd been on the other side of this kitchen. I phoned Randolph and he's up there now, and he's armed. Don't look so surprised. He has every right to shoot vermin on his own land.'

'You can't be suggesting—'

'Crows, magpies, ravens: anything that would rob a peregrine's nest. Accidents happen.' She gave him that chilling smile again. 'He was in the woods under Falcon Crag yesterday; the police didn't seem interested but when I reminded Randolph I think he got the message.'

'What was Roy doing in the woods? You mean something to do with the poaching?'

'No, that was Saturday night – but he could have gone back: to see if you'd found the remains?'

'What time was this?'

Mabel sat down and the tortoiseshell queen jumped on her lap. She scratched its skull absently and the purr filled the room. 'It was around midmorning; I remember because I was making a snack and this one got the ham. I rushed out and forgot to close the door.'

'How did you know he was there? Was he firing at something?'

'I hope not. It was Becky: she came running in to say she'd seen him under Falcon Crag. Naturally my first thought was the birds so I ran as fast as I could but he must have heard me coming. That boy can run like a deer and I didn't even glimpse him. Nor will Randolph; he'll fade into the woods, whip off that horrible balaclava, hide the air gun – he's probably walking down the road right now, innocent as a bird.' She grinned. 'If he had a charge of shot in his backside he'd have to go to hospital. With a good aim I might get more important parts. That type should be sterilized.'

'What would Freud say to that?'

'Darwin's more to the point. Bad eggs should be broken. Talking of eggs, let's have some lunch. Clear up this mess for me, will you?' She put the cat down and went to the larder. 'Randolph's coming to put a bar across this window,' she called. 'As soon as he comes down from the top.'

'Good.' Pharaoh was trying to place a typescript in sequence. 'You seem to have two manuscripts here,' he told her as she emerged from the larder.

'I've just remembered,' she was saying, 'I'm supposed not to use the larder because of fingerprints. Never mind, they'll take mine for elimination. You were saying?'

'These pages are one to' – he peered at the corners – 'five, but here's one numbered 168.'

Her jaw dropped. 'It can't be!' They stared at each other, Pharaoh amused by her intensity. 'You did tell me,' he reminded her gently.

'How much – I *told* you?'

'You said you thought of publishing your journal one day. I promise you I haven't breathed a word, not even to Randolph, and I won't. It was a confidence and I respect that.'

'That's very thoughtful of you. Most embarrassing.' She put a bowl of eggs on the draining board and, coming to the table, retrieved the rogue page. 'I would hate anyone to see this in the raw.' She gave a self-conscious giggle. 'I consider it as private as – er – the most intimate act.' Her face brightened. 'The short pieces are different. That's the draft of next week's nature notes you have there. Read it, do; tell me if there are any mistakes.'

He bent his head obediently. She'd seen flycatchers and a cuckoo and *Primula farinosa*: exotic but less intriguing than the glimpse he'd had of page 168: ". . . came up the coral beach, gloriously tanned, in a white bikini. He stepped out of the shade of the palm trees. 'I came as soon as I got your message,' he said." It was a far cry from a natural history of Scawdale.

Becky was profoundly bored. She could have slipped out of the garden but there was nowhere to go because no way would she risk another confrontation with Claire. The morning's fright had faded although it might return with darkness but for the moment life was dull. Isaac was away in the woods and her grandmother was gossiping with Mrs Bell from the village – a nosy old bat who'd come just to ferret out information about the poaching.

Becky picked up a magazine and went out to the garden. The magazine was the pits (her mother took *Cosmopolitan* and *Vogue*) and when she heard someone approach the back door and saw, not Isaac, but the man from the Boathouse, she sprang up without thinking, delighted for the diversion.

He was carrying an egg box. 'Can I help?' she asked quickly, before he could knock. She blushed, excited and a little frightened.

Pharaoh, startled afresh by the child's beauty, tried to appear solemn. 'I'm Jack Pharaoh from the Boathouse. Miss Cooper asked me to bring these eggs over for Mrs Garner.'

She put the box on the window sill and turned away. He turned with her, hearing a laugh from indoors, but the girl was grumbling about its being so quiet and there was nothing to do because the school was closed . . . In order to follow what she was saying he was forced to move with her across the lawn. 'It's asbestos,' she told him. 'It's in all the walls so we're off school until they bring in some huts where we can have lessons.'

'Do you all go to the same school?' he asked: 'Roy and your friend – Claire, isn't it?'

She looked sideways at him. 'Who told you Claire was my friend?'

'I've seen you together. You were at the Boathouse when Laura brought me down on Saturday.'

'We don't play there now,' she said quickly. 'I mean, we won't, not when you're living there.'

He could think of several responses: that he didn't mind children playing round his house but their mothers would, that the top of a cliff – where he'd seen them Saturday afternoon – was a sight more dangerous than a bachelor's pad, but such statements carried undercurrents; he sought to be objective and succeeded only in sounding inane: 'It can't be much fun: riding bikes in all that traffic.'

'The fumes are *toxic*! We use the woodland path mostly but it's awful rough. Claire's going to get a mountain bike but my grandmother says I won't be here long enough. I'm going to live in America,' she added carelessly. 'My mother is on her honeymoon with my stepfather and in a week or so I'm going to have to go and live in Texas.'

'You don't sound very happy about it.'

She sat down suddenly and, picking a daisy, started to shred it. 'All my friends are here,' she said. 'What's culture shock?'

He sat down himself, grateful for the rest.

'It's when you go to another country and people do things differently. You can work it out though if you don't panic.'

'But it's the same language, isn't it? They talk different, but you can understand them. Will they laugh at the way I talk?'

'They'll love it. Americans think all English people talk like royals.' He knew she wasn't bothered about accents.

'What about—' She looked away. She touched her cheek. 'Are they racist in Texas?'

'Who cares? Beauty's the same in any country.'

She stared at him. 'Roy Hartley calls me a nigger.' Her eyes filled with tears.

He gazed back, appalled. What could he say? Kick him in the balls? Young Roy should be throttled. 'I think Cleopatra must have looked like you,' he said, meaning every word of it. 'The boy's terrified of you, he's trying to drag you down to his level.'

'Claire says he's stupid.'

He thought about that while she watched his face. 'I wouldn't say stupid, not stupid all round. He's cunning but he's not a good judge of character. He thinks about himself all the time' – he smiled, remembering – 'not like Claire, who thinks about the person who's doing the talking.'

'When did you talk to her?'

'Yesterday.'

'Was it after— What did she say?'

He hesitated, seeing the solemn child holding her bicycle and answering questions politely, interested in the anonymous note . . . 'Mr Steel asked her if she'd heard anything the night before – when the poachers were about?' She nodded quickly. He thought he'd better not mention the note; the last thing he wanted was to make trouble for the writer.

'Did she hear anything?' Becky asked in her careless voice.

'No. Haven't you discussed it between yourselves?' It was odd if they hadn't.

'I haven't seen her for some time.' She was off-hand. 'But I want to see her,' she added emphatically. 'Trouble is, my grandmother won't let me out on my own.'

Pharaoh was intrigued. 'What's she afraid of?'

Becky was suddenly shifty. 'Poachers, of course. Men are bad enough' – she shot him a sly glance – 'they're always telling us not to talk to strange men, but *poachers*! They're criminals. Granpa says they've all been in prison.' She shivered and stared at the trees outside the garden.

'I'm sorry I startled you yesterday,' he said, trying to bring her back to the present, and a harmless man in a country garden.

'Yesterday?' She was puzzled.

'I came out of my drive and you nearly ran me over.'

'Did I? I didn't see you.' Her eyes returned to the wood.

'Becky?' someone said tensely.

Pharaoh got to his feet and turned to face the grandmother. He smiled. 'I'm your neighbour,' he said, extending his hand. 'Jack Pharaoh.'

'Becky should have brought you in.' She was flustered. 'I'd no idea anyone was here.'

'You had company.' Becky was sulky. 'He brought the eggs from Miss Cooper. He's going now.'

Pharaoh managed not to look taken aback but he noted that Doris didn't press him to stay either. As he moved towards the cottage Becky said quickly, 'You're never going all the way round! It's miles; I'll show you the short-cut—'

Doris opened her mouth, then closed it. She looked at Becky meaningly but the girl ignored her. Pharaoh followed her down the garden, past neat rows of young vegetables and raspberry canes to a wicket that opened on the lake. The woodland started immediately to their left hiding the inlet and the Boathouse, and in a moment they were in the trees.

Beyond the spruces the woods were flooded with sunshine. Bluebells were vivid in the foreground, a mauve ground-mist beyond, broken by stitchwort and a mass of carmine rhododendrons. The brilliant colour was broken by a flash of russet.

'Fox,' he whispered, grabbing at Becky.

'No, no!' She pushed him sideways and he lurched on his bad leg. 'Down here,' she urged, pulling at his hand. He forgot the pain in his relief: for a moment there he had the impression she thought she was about to be raped.

'There was a fox,' he said as they scrambled down a bank to stepping stones across the beck. 'Behind that rhododendron.'

'We see that old fox all the time. There, you know the way now. You don't have to go all the way round.'

'Thank you. The same goes for you, if I can do anything.' His eyes wandered. He frowned. 'Like putting young Roy in his place – although you're old enough to do that yourself—'

'Oh, him.' She grimaced. 'All he's good for is bird-nesting: kids' stuff. I'm not bothered about Roy Hartley. See you.'

She turned, so did he, carefully not watching which way she went. It could have been a fox, he thought, it could equally well have been a russet T-shirt; whatever it was, she wasn't worried.

He drove to town for a load of provisions. On his return he was cooking Moghul lamb and studying the recipe when a voice said: 'Something smells good.'

She was back: standing in the doorway, silhouetted against the sunlight.

'Indian spices,' he told her. 'I'm doing lamb; I'd ask you to supper but it won't be ready for an hour.'

'That's all right; Granma wouldn't let me anyway, you know what old people are like.' She sidled into the kitchen, peering at his little jars of spices, picking up the cumin. He turned back to the stove and added coriander to the meat. Becky sniffed and wiped an eye with the back of her hand.

'Something wrong?' he asked, keeping his tone light.

She picked up the bottle of sesame oil and pretended to be reading the label. 'I always wondered why Granpa didn't have a dog,' she said casually. 'Gamekeepers always have dogs. You know what he told me this evening?'

'Something not very pleasant.'

She nodded, her eyes shining in the dim light. 'Have you got some tissues?'

'On the window sill in the living room.'

It was a few minutes before she came back; he could hear her moving about, picking up objects and putting them down, composing herself. He continued with his cooking, waiting for the revelation, praying that there wouldn't be a flood of tears.

She came and stood in the doorway again. 'He had a little Jack Russell,' she flung at him. 'And that Roy Hartley, he stole her and sold her. Her puppies were worth a fortune.'

'If your grandfather knows Roy stole her why can't he get her back?'

'That's what I said but Granpa says he would if only he knew who had her now but Roy isn't going to tell him, is he? I would have loved to have a dog—' Her face crumpled. 'Roy Hartley's a villain. I hate him.'

'I expect you'll be able to have your own puppy in Texas.'

She changed in an instant, as if he'd thrown a switch. 'I never thought of that! I could have anything I liked; I could have an Afghan hound!' Her face fell again, the change so complete it was ludicrous. 'That makes no difference to me now, and *not* having the little Jack Russell. He's cruel, look at what he did to that baby fawn.' She threw him a look. 'Granpa told me. Granma tried to hush him up but he was so angry he told me anyway.'

'Has Roy got a lurcher?' Pharaoh asked.

There was a long silence. He stirred the lamb carefully.

'He'd borrow one – or two,' she muttered.

'He wouldn't have been working alone.'

'Why not? He stole the hawks' eggs on his own; he's old enough to work dogs, he can work his dad's sheepdogs. And you don't have to be clever to send lurchers after deer, you just loose their collars.'

'Who'd drive the car? Someone has to bring the dogs here, and then the deer carcasses have to be taken away.'

'Roe are small.' But she was thinking about it. 'Maybe he was working with someone else,' she said doubtfully. 'Does it matter?'

'This afternoon you were convinced it was grown men doing the poaching. You said all Roy was fit for was stealing eggs.'

'That was before – before I knew about the Jack Russell. And Granpa says it was Roy doing the poaching. He threatened me too.' She paused to see what reaction this would produce but Pharaoh was measuring bouillon. However, he'd heard.

'Roy threatened you? What did he say?'

'He said' – she hesitated – 'said he'd get me one dark night.'

'Did you tell your grandfather that?'

Again the hesitation, then: 'No, I was afraid to.' Pharaoh said nothing. 'Granpa would tell the police and he'd be put in prison. Do you think I should tell Granpa?'

'If it's easier to tell your grandmother, do that.' There was something fishy here. He turned to her. 'Who was hiding behind the rhododendron this afternoon? We both saw him. Was it Roy?'

Her hand went to her mouth and she showed the whites of her eyes. She took a step back and for a moment he thought she'd turn and run, but she said slowly, breathing hard: 'I didn't think anyone was there, I thought it was a fox, but when I went home I heard him laugh. And then I saw him. Yes, it was Roy.'

'Was he wearing a mask?'

'You don't believe me.' She was sullen.

He regarded her thoughtfully. 'But he didn't attack you.'

'I ran too fast. And I screamed – I mean, I would have screamed; I said: "You touch me, Roy Hartley, and I'll scream so loud Jack will hear me" – I pretended you were my friend – "and my Granpa, he's got a gun" – that's what I told him.'

'And it was Roy you saw in the woods Sunday morning?' She stared at him with parted lips. 'You went to Miss Cooper and told her you'd seen him.' She nodded wordlessly.

He drained a pan of turnips. She seemed to be waiting for more questions, her eyes following his movements. 'Well, you've

66

certainly convinced me that young Hartley's a right villain,' he said. 'And now do you want me to escort you home?'

She smiled engagingly, her moods going up and down like mercury. 'I'll be fine,' she assured him. 'He was gone ages since. You be sure to keep all the doors and windows locked. He can get through the tiniest spaces, like skylights. He got into Miss Cooper's place and stole a hundred pounds! And he steals from cars; he took Laura's binoculars. Is your van locked?'

'I'll see to it.'

He followed her out into the garden, half expecting to hear Doris calling but the evening was silent except for the birds. He watched her run down the bank and wade across the beck, the water reaching to her knees, but then she was in shorts. He wondered why she was so concerned to convince him of Roy's criminal activities.

Chapter Seven

'Roy's very young to be a member of a poaching gang,' Laura said dubiously.

The Steels were at breakfast, the door open wide to the passage and the yard in an effort to dissipate the heat from the Aga.

'He could be their informant,' Randolph said. 'Letting the gang know when it was safe to come.'

'But any time's safe here; you haven't got a keeper. Poachers don't need Roy. No one needs Roy,' she added darkly. 'He's victimizing Mabel by threatening her cats; you know that, don't you?'

Randolph reached for the corn bread. 'I wonder if that cement's set,' he mused. 'Nothing happened in the night or she'd have phoned. She was going to sleep in the porch with the gun beside her.'

'You're making that up.'

'She'd have slept with the gun anyway.'

Claws grated on flags, shrieks filled the passage and dust flew as Trudy launched herself at intrusive hens.

'Here, girl.' Laura put the kedgeree bowl on the floor. 'But they do need someone local' – she reverted to the original subject – 'the gang has to know you don't have a keeper, where to park their vehicles, where the deer are.' Her eyes narrowed. 'Do we know who it is?'

'He's got too much money,' Randolph said meaningly.

'We-ell – there's the dole, and what Marlene pulls in, one way and another, but she's got to find her rent and the poll tax, clothes and food; she's supporting two, probably three people—'

'Two or three roe aren't going to bring in much. They'll be operating elsewhere: red deer on the eastern fells, fallow in the parks; they could be rustling sheep, even horses. Incidentally,

68

when you ride today why not go through the woods, show any interested parties that they're being patrolled?'

'And put myself in the way of cross-fire between Mabel and Isaac? Not bloody likely.'

'There you are, sweetie!' Marlene peered over her sunglasses. 'Where've you been?' She shifted along the plank to make room.

'Playing.' Claire nodded at the wood. 'You were late up,' she added disapprovingly.

'Late night.' Marlene yawned. Beside her was an empty mug and the inevitable cigarettes. She'd not yet done her hair, nor washed. Claire regarded her thoughtfully. 'Is Hugh coming today?' she asked.

'Some time. He has to go to town.'

'You can drive. We should have our own car.'

'We will one day.' Marlene leaned back against the wall, her eyes closed, wondering what she might do about that, how she might find men with more money, even snare a rich husband like Sally Rudd. She asked, without much curiosity, 'You're not jealous of Becky, are you?'

Claire was astonished. 'Why should I be?'

'Her stepfather will have a car.'

'He's got a plane.' It was stated without emphasis, merely putting the record straight. All the same Claire was thoughtful.

'I have a better time than Becky,' she said. 'You're not always stopping me from doing things.'

'Nor does Becky's mother, she's never there, always jet-setting somewhere.'

'Her grandma doesn't let her do much, but then Becky's timid anyway.'

'Timid?' Marlene opened her eyes. 'That's a new word.'

'She's terrified then; frightened.'

'What's she frightened of?'

'I don't know. I haven't seen her since Sunday.'

'Have you two quarrelled?'

Claire fingered the cigarette packet. 'Not really. I just got fed up with her. "I'm not allowed to do that" . . . "I have to go home for my dinner" . . . "I'm scared . . ."'

'What's she scared of?'

Claire shrugged. 'Roy Hartley, I s'pose. He talks dirty.'

'I can guess. He wouldn't try that with you.'

69

'He said worse things to her.'

'Worse than what?'

'Than what he said to me.'

Marlene sat up, jolted out of her lethargy. 'What did that bugger say to you?'

'The usual things.' Claire opened wide eyes, saw her mother was serious and elaborated. 'He told me to take my jeans down.' Marlene gasped. 'They all try it on,' Claire assured her solemnly.

'Did he – force you?'

Claire giggled. 'Of course not.'

'What did you do? How did you get away?'

'No sweat. I kicked him where it hurts. You just got to do it the once; after that they leave you alone.'

Marlene exhaled on a long breath.

'Here's Hugh,' Claire said. 'You better go and get ready.'

'What are you going to do today?' Marlene asked weakly.

'I'm coming with you.'

'I thought you'd want to play with Becky.'

'She's not allowed out, and I want to go to town.'

Mason arrived in his van. 'Jesus!' he exclaimed, staring at Marlene. 'You're not ready *again*. You look as if you just got up.'

She walked calmly round the front of the cottage. Claire came and leaned on his door. He eyed her warily. 'What do you want?'

'I'm coming with you to look at mountain bikes.'

'I'm not looking at bikes.'

'OK, we all do our own thing. You can't leave me here, all on my own in an empty house; it's against the law.'

'Your mam and me, we got business in town.'

'That's what I was saying. You can just take me there. Of course,' she added airily, 'I could hitchhike; plenty of cars on the road, someone'd be sure to pick up a little girl.'

His mouth stretched in a thin smile. 'I'll give you five quid to stay here.'

Claire's face didn't change. 'You can give me five quid to go away once we reach town. I'll meet you back at the van tonight' – now she grinned – 'or I can get a cab home.'

'Does Marlene know about this?'

'That's covered; I've got a friend in Kelton and we'll watch telly in her house till it's time to meet you. Now I have to go and change. Don't leave without me.' She knew he wouldn't, he had to wait for Marlene.

*

'There goes Marlene Fisher,' Mrs Bell said resignedly, driving Doris home after their weekly shop. 'That was her in Mason's van: off to start the day's work in the bars.'

'Live and let live,' Doris murmured. 'And be thankful for small mercies; it doesn't seem to rub off on the child. Can't you go faster, Joan? They'll be wondering what happened to me.'

'We're nearly there. You worry too much, Doris. Didn't Isaac never have a puncture? And how often have you had to hang around waiting for him?'

'That's the point; when I say I'll have dinner on the table for one o'clock, he expects me there – and look: it's turned one thirty!'

'It can't be helped, girl! I didn't get a puncture on purpose. Anyway, we're here.' She turned the Cortina down the Garners' track, bumping through the potholes.

'They'll be that hungry,' Doris moaned, still blaming Joan.

'Then they could make themselves a sandwich. I got no time for men as can't look after theirselves. Bell can roast a joint, he can even peel spuds . . .'

Doris saw Isaac's car ahead, anticipated a scene and thought wildly that she might stave it off by inviting Joan in for coffee. Joan, predictably, declined. She stopped the car and got out as Isaac opened the back door and approached.

'We had a puncture,' Doris shouted.

He glanced in the car. 'Where's Becky?'

The women were on their way to the back of the Cortina. Doris turned, her eyes jumping to the cottage.

'She's not here,' he told her. 'Isn't she with you?' He peered into the back of the car as if Becky might somehow materialize.

Joan Bell said comfortably, 'She'll be playing with young Claire. We passed Marlene on the road; Becky will be along at Starfoot.'

Isaac glared at his wife. 'Are we going to have that all over again?'

Doris sagged visibly. 'Shall we get the shopping indoors?' Joan suggested. 'Then you can drive to Starfoot and fetch her home for dinner.' She nodded firmly at Isaac, stressing his subordinate position, demonstrating how menfolk should be treated.

They carried the shopping indoors and Joan drove away. She glanced up at Starfoot as she passed but could see no sign of the little girls. Small wonder, she thought: one of them with a mother gadding around America with a millionaire, the other with the village tart for her mam.

Isaac, following her up the dale, turned in over the cattle grid and drove up the track to Starfoot. 'I don't know why you had to come as well,' he grumbled. 'You should be home, seeing to the dinner.'

Doris said nothing, her eyes on the cottage which could be glimpsed only intermittently through the hawthorns. No one was visible and the front door was closed.

It was, in fact, locked. Isaac stood on the level space in front of the house looking across the dale, angry and embarrassed at his wife's behaviour. Not content with peering through the windows she had run to the tacky old caravan at the far end and actually gone inside.

She came back to him. 'Where can she be?'

'How would I know, woman? I been in the woods all morning.'

'No!' She turned on him in horror. 'I left her with you! I only went to town because you was working in the garden—'

'I had to help Mr Randolph out—'

'Rubbish, you're retired. You just want to show off in front of the tourists: patrolling the woods with a shot-gun! You're just a kid pretending: cowboys and Indians, cops and robbers; you and your damn stupid gun, where would you be without it?'

Isaac couldn't cope with hysteria, moreover if there were poachers around he felt guilty about leaving Becky. He went back to the van and started the engine but he didn't dare leave without Doris. She twisted her hands. 'No note this time,' she murmured. She'd been in Becky's bedroom. She looked round wildly. 'There are no bikes. Did she take her bike from home?'

'I didn't see it.'

'So they're out on their bikes.'

'They always are.'

'You're not bothered, are you? You're not concerned your grandchild is missing – she could be anywhere, she could—' She stared at the lake.

'She'll be back,' he said. 'Just like last time. Soon's she gets hungry she'll be back for food.'

'She's not a dog!'

'All right! Perhaps she'll find food somewhere else, or someone's already given her dinner—' She looked at him and he shrank in his seat. 'She'll be back,' he repeated sullenly.

But she wasn't. Doris spent the afternoon telephoning, insisting that Isaac drive her everywhere that she thought Becky might have gone. The only person other than Marlene who wasn't on the phone was Pharaoh. He was sympathetic when she came across to the Boathouse but he didn't offer to help. Doris was at the stage where she was hoping desperately that Becky was merely being naughty, that she'd gone to town on her own, or with Claire, or was visiting someone they'd not yet thought of – an unknown friend but a real friend, not someone posing as one. To offer help at this juncture implied that Becky couldn't find her way home; it would suggest that something was wrong. It was a good thing that he hadn't seen her, that she had slept in her own bed last night and been her normal self – whatever that was – at breakfast. It would look bad for him if she'd vanished on her way home after visiting him last evening.

He went down to the beck. Small footprints were obvious in the mud and there were more at the stepping stones, along with his own. Behind the huge carmine rhododendron he found a trail where bluebells and campion had been flattened by something heavier than a fox, and in the centre of the bush was a kind of cave. The ground there was a litter of twigs and dead leaves and told him nothing.

He went home to potter about his kitchen, to concentrate on cooking and shut the children out of his mind but they kept intruding, above all Becky, with her riveting beauty and her ambivalent attitude towards Roy. Finally he abandoned the effort at domesticity and went out to the veranda with a bottle of whisky.

He sat and sipped the Scotch without tasting it, consumed by curiosity to know where the child was now, at this very moment.

It was ironical to realize, an hour or two later, that the police thought he did know, that he was the only one who knew; that he was the man responsible for her disappearance.

Chapter Eight

Pharaoh didn't realize how low the level had sunk in the bottle until someone said, 'Good evening, sir,' and he looked up to see two strangers. He responded bemusedly, then glanced at the whisky, thinking that these were neighbours and he must find glasses. It was then he noticed the level. He looked back at the men and realized that they weren't dressed like neighbours – one actually wore a tie – and they were too confident, walking in as if they owned the place.

'Mr Pharaoh,' said the big one, 'Jack Pharaoh?'

He nodded. About to ask them to sit down he waited until they introduced themselves. He sensed hostility. The other fellow – younger, thin, in jeans – stared bleakly at him.

One was Buckle, the other Fleming: chief inspector and sergeant. CID. He blinked. They'd come about Becky. *CID?* As his brain started to replay the last words Buckle repeated them heavily: 'We're looking for Becky Rudd.'

Pharaoh closed his eyes, realizing how much he'd drunk, trying to clear his head. 'Why CID?' he asked.

'A little girl's missing. Perhaps we could sit down?'

'Please do.' He was aware that he was sweating. 'Will you have a whisky?'

They wouldn't, nor would they have coffee. Perhaps they thought that coffee would sober him up and they wanted him to stay drunk, and indiscreet. They didn't seem in any hurry to speak so they were leaving the initiative to him. He craved a coffee but to get up and make it might look suspicious, as if he needed time to compose himself. He was aware that he had waited too long before asking an obvious question. Why did innocent people feel guilty on such occasions? What did they have to fear? He plunged.

'What rules out accident?' he asked. 'It's the first assumption.'

'Accident is possible.' Buckle, the chief inspector – rubicund

74

and heavy with big hands and meaty thighs like a retired farmer – was suddenly expansive; Pharaoh, in speaking first, had turned a key. 'And of course,' Buckle went on, 'all the hospitals have been contacted: that is, Kelton and Carlisle, and the ambulance station, just in case they forgot to tell us they'd picked up a little girl.' He smiled deprecatingly; there was no hint of irony in his tone. Fleming watched Pharaoh as if he were a butcher buying sheep.

'But then,' Buckle went on, 'she could be lying somewhere, badly injured or worse: hidden away where no one's come across her. Yet.'

'Under the floorboards,' Fleming suggested, 'or in a loft.'

'Not a loft,' Buckle chided. 'How could she come to grief in a loft? But she could have fallen through rotten floorboards and be lying in a cellar somewhere. When did you see her last, sir?'

'Last evening,' Pharaoh said. 'At supper time. Around six o'clock.'

'Oh, yes? Her grandmother didn't tell us that.'

'She may not have known.' Pharaoh thought that Fleming stiffened.

'That's right,' Buckle agreed comfortably. 'She may not have known.' His tone changed. 'She knew about the earlier visit of course, when Becky came here before supper.'

'She didn't come here; she came as far as the beck and then turned back.'

'She was gone twenty minutes. She told her grandmother you kept her talking.'

Pharaoh's face set. 'I'm not surprised. Someone was in the wood, watching us from a big rhododendron the other side of the stepping stones. She said it was a fox. She must have joined – them.' He mumbled the last word but Buckle caught it.

'Them? There was more than one person?'

He shrugged. 'I didn't see anyone at all, just a flash of foxy red—' He stopped; it was far too easy to incriminate someone else – Roy? – and much too desirable when he felt that he himself was under suspicion.

'She was over here,' Buckle said, watching him.

'Afterwards. At supper time.'

'Why did she come?'

He hesitated, defeated – but if Roy was innocent he had nothing to be afraid of. The detectives made no move to break the silence.

'She came over to convince me that Roy Hartley was a bad lot,' he said. 'She cited every theft that's occurred recently and blamed him for it.'

'And you believed her?' Buckle asked.

'No, I didn't.' He frowned, recalling that list of delinquencies.

'Why didn't you believe her?'

'Because she's a rotten liar. First she was crying – I was cooking and she was suddenly there: in the doorway, and she was angry and upset because her grandfather had just told her his dog was stolen. That seemed true – I mean, she cried over it. But she said Roy stole the dog and sold it. I doubt that because if Isaac Garner knew who'd stolen it he'd surely have followed it up, it was a valuable bitch. He'd have reported it to the police, confronted Roy's father, got it back somehow.' Fleming was looking bored, Buckle was puzzled. 'On top of that,' Pharaoh ploughed on, 'she listed everything else: robbing the peregrines' nest, Miss Cooper's wallet, Laura Steel's binoculars. And then the poaching, she said Roy was involved in that. It was gilding the lily. I couldn't see a boy of fourteen – who doesn't even own a lurcher – being one of a poaching gang.'

'Why would she tell you all this?' Buckle asked.

'I wondered that. It was obvious she wanted to convince me that the lad was a criminal.'

'And so she tells a string of lies.'

'Not a string of them; it was fact mixed with fiction.'

'What were the facts?'

'Well, facts.' Pharaoh shook his head. 'I only know what I've been told: that it was Roy who robbed the nest last spring, and most people – I mean, adults, reckon it was him who stole the wallet and the binoculars.'

'But you have no theories yourself?' The tone was silky.

He refused to be intimidated. 'Not theories, but yesterday morning I saw Roy on top of Grey Buttress here, firing an air gun at – or rather, towards – Miss Cooper. He was wearing a black balaclava pulled down over his face. Miss Cooper saw him plainly.' Thank God she had, it sounded like something he'd just dreamed up.

'And where were you when you saw him?'

'On the island.' He gestured to where its northernmost point was visible beyond the magnolia. 'I was watching the falcons.'

Fleming stood up and walked across the grass to where he could view the island in its entirety. He regarded it for a moment, turned to look over the Boathouse roof, and came back, expressionless. 'Where do you keep the oars?' he asked.

'At the foot of the stairs, with the rowlocks.'

'So no one could have borrowed your boat,' Buckle said, and Pharaoh realized that although Fleming hadn't so much as glanced that way, they knew he had a boat; but then how long had they been here, studying footprints on the banks of the beck, before they'd approached the veranda?

Fleming found the oars and rowlocks and went down to the beck.

'Where was Claire?' Pharaoh asked. 'I understood they were together.'

'That will be her friend Claire Fisher you mean.' Buckle's eyes were on the island. 'She went to town with her mother. Mrs Garner passed the van and didn't realize the little girl was with them, sitting in the back.'

'And she's no help?' Buckle's attention returned, his eyebrows raised as he waited for more.

'They're close friends,' Pharaoh pointed out, aware that he was being tested, that all the questions were loaded. 'They know each other well, perhaps better than sisters. Was Claire asked what she thought, if she had a theory?'

'You think a little girl's theory would carry weight in this instance?'

There was a clonk of wood on wood, and the boat slid out of the inlet, Fleming pulling without haste towards the island. Pharaoh thought that he should have told the sergeant the landing-place was on the far side but he decided to let the fellow discover that for himself.

'What do you think's happened?' he asked, and then – truthfully: 'I don't like the CID being called in. It implies you think there's been foul play.'

'What do you think?'

'There's always that possibility, with young girls missing. The grandmother – Doris – was over here yesterday, after she came home from Kelton and found Becky gone. Doris was panicking even at that stage.'

'But you didn't offer to help.'

The boat was no longer visible. Pharaoh had the dreadful feeling that Becky could be on the island. The evening was still, the sky drained of colour. He waited for a shout from Fleming.

'You didn't look for Becky yourself,' came Buckle's voice, soft and insidious, like a man selling a pornographic video.

Pharaoh sighed. 'Doris was trying to hang on to the belief that Becky was safe with Claire; she was treading a thin line between anger and panic – thinking she could be lying injured somewhere, as you said, and in need of help. If I'd offered to search, it could have sent her over the edge.'

'She is now; she's had to be sedated. Her husband's searching, so is every other able-bodied man – or will be.'

'Then I must too.'

'You don't sound too eager.'

'I'm not.' He felt anger rising. 'For one thing I don't want to admit that she needs to be searched for and, more to the point, I'm not good on rough ground. I'm lame.'

Buckle ignored this, or appeared to. Fleming was rowing steadily towards the shore. He didn't look over his shoulder.

Pharaoh said coldly, 'Would you like to see my house?'

The large head turned slowly. Grey eyes bored into Pharaoh's, then looked beyond him to a living-room window. 'I would be grateful if I could use your toilet,' Buckle said.

'Straight ahead and up the stairs.'

Pharaoh listened to the retreating footsteps. The bathroom door closed. Fleming approached carrying the oars.

'Where's Mr Buckle?'

'Inside.'

The sergeant replaced the oars in the corner at the foot of the stairs and Pharaoh heard him step to the doorway of the living room then walk to the kitchen. Upstairs the cistern flushed. Silence fell again except for the hiss of water in the pipes. A heron croaked. The bathroom door opened and Buckle made no effort to tread softly as he walked along the landing to the front bedroom, then walked back to pause in the doorway of the spare room. He descended the stairs and Pharaoh pictured the raised eyebrows, the negative shake of heads. They came out to the veranda.

'Can you use my services?' Pharaoh asked.

Buckle blinked. The man looked puzzled. 'I suggest you contact Mr Steel,' he said. 'It's his land; he'll know where you should go: barns, ruins, that kind of thing. Thank you for giving us your time. Good evening.'

No "sir" but then the courtesy had been fulsome to start with. They'd given nothing away, but he had passed on a lot of gossip about Roy Hartley, except the crucial item. He looked at his watch. Ten o'clock. Late, but not too late on this night. He locked up and went out to his van, wondering why they hadn't asked to look in that, but of course they'd have done so before they found him on the veranda.

'Laura came to fetch you,' Randolph said. 'She saw the police car and retreated. This is a nasty business.'

'Nothing's *happened*!' Laura was exasperated, as if they'd been arguing. 'She could have run away. Sit down, Pharaoh; you look bushed.'

He joined Randolph at the kitchen table. 'I'd been punishing the Scotch when they turned up,' he admitted. 'I'd be grateful for some strong black coffee.'

'Were you drunk?' Randolph was interested.

'I was indiscreet. I gave them all the gossip.'

'You what?' Laura turned from the Aga. 'You've only been here four days.'

'True, but with a chap like Roy in the dale conversation always comes back to him. As it happens, I didn't volunteer information; Buckle – you know Buckle? – he wanted to know why Becky visited me last evening.' They were astonished. He went on quickly: 'It does sound bad, put baldly like that, but she did come over and I had to tell them why. To cover myself,' he pointed out, sensing that hostility was replacing amazement. 'She came ostensibly because she was upset about Isaac's Jack Russell. What happened to it.'

Laura turned to her father. 'What did happen to it?'

'It died,' Randolph told her. 'It would upset—'

'Died?' Pharaoh repeated. 'A Jack Russell bitch? It died?'

'What's so odd about that? Died of pneumonia.'

Pharaoh was staring at him. Laura said, frowning, 'What did Becky tell you happened?'

'She said that Isaac had told her that Roy stole the bitch and sold her—'

'But that's not true!' Randolph exclaimed.

'I didn't believe it,' Pharaoh admitted. 'I did believe that the bitch had been stolen but not that Roy took it. I thought Becky was trying to pin the theft on Roy, particularly when this was just

79

one of a string of accusations. She said he took your binoculars, Laura—'

'Which he did; she was correct there.'

'And Mabel's wallet, and the other stuff—'

'The trifle.' Randolph chuckled.

'The trifle?' Pharaoh repeated. 'I meant the change from her purse – and the peregrines' eggs, of course—'

'Oh, no doubt about that.' Randolph was positive.

'And the poaching: she said he was involved in that. Isaac told her so. At least, that's what she *said* – the second time. You see, we talked twice. The first time was when I took some eggs from Mabel to the Garners. Becky was in the garden and she showed me a short-cut across the beck so that I didn't have to go all the way round by the road. She told me then that all Roy was capable of was robbing nests: kids' stuff, she said. But when she came over later she'd done a U-turn. That was when she couldn't find enough crimes to accuse him of. She even said he'd threatened her.' He paused. 'I didn't tell Buckle that.'

'How did he threaten her?' Laura asked.

'He said he'd get her one dark night.'

'Why on earth would he say a thing like that?' Randolph was amazed.

'The implication was that she should keep quiet about his involvement in the poaching.' Pharaoh smiled wryly. 'I knew there was something fishy going on but it could have been innocent, it could have been a game.' He told them about the rhododendron and the supposed fox. 'With hindsight she wasn't bothered so much about the watcher, whoever he was, but that I should see him. Someone was certainly there; I went to look after Doris came over this evening to ask if I'd seen Becky. And then, to cap it all, Becky confessed it wasn't a fox, it was Roy hiding in the rhododendron and that he chased her.' He shook his head helplessly. 'How much of it was lies?' he asked.

'She doesn't have to invent anything about Roy,' Randolph said. 'He's delinquent enough, Heaven knows, without resorting to false accusations.'

'You're both of you on the wrong track,' Laura said suddenly. 'What Becky's trying to do is persuade you that she's terrified of Roy, that she wouldn't touch him with a bargepole. In fact, the truth is just the opposite. That was a rendezvous. He was waiting for her in the woods, and she knew it and was laying a smoke-screen. She laid it on too thick.'

They were silent as they considered this.

'If she was meeting him,' Pharaoh said slowly, 'she had no need to visit me. She could have nipped out from her home and met him. Talking to me took up time when she could have been with him. And why choose me for this ploy? There's no sense in it.'

'Unless she was using you in some way,' Laura suggested.

'We're talking about a little girl!' Randolph was shocked. 'There's no sexual angle in this – is there?' He appealed to Laura. 'Becky's twelve,' he insisted.

'Hell, Dad, that's how people's minds are running at the moment: rape and murder. The kid's been missing since breakfast.'

Randolph sighed heavily and turned back to Pharaoh. 'D'you think this – this chap in the woods, well, if it was Roy – you think he knows something about her disappearance? What do the police think?'

'She didn't go missing *then*,' Pharaoh reminded him. 'Not till after breakfast today. I told the police someone was there. I don't think they believed me.' He drank his coffee and stared at his mug. 'It could have been me,' he pointed out. 'There's a track to the rhododendron and after all, I did go there to look; there's only my word for it that there was a track before I came on the scene. They suspect me anyway.' They made small movements of protest. 'I was the last person outside her family who was known to have talked to her.'

'That's true.' Randolph was gloomy. 'So you think she was having a liaison with young Roy and making an attempt to disguise it . . . So we have to find out where he was, and when?'

'Dad, no crime's been committed.'

The words seemed to repeat themselves like echoes in the kitchen. The night was so quiet that they could hear the house making small settling noises after the heat of the day.

'Are you searching?' Pharaoh asked. 'The police said that Isaac was in the woods.'

'He was. It's dark now.' Randolph looked at Laura. 'Should we do something tonight?'

'No, Dad. She could have run away, or be visiting someone in Kelton. We'll all have a good night's sleep and see what the morning brings.'

'What do other people think?' Pharaoh asked. 'They must have theories. And what about Roy?' he added meaningly.

'Doris telephoned Warthwaite,' Randolph said. 'She contacted everyone she could think of – and the Hartleys hadn't seen Becky today. Anne said she'd ask Roy when he came in, and call back if he'd seen her. Isaac said she hadn't called back. Isaac and I were in the woods but Becky wouldn't have gone there on her own, and Claire was in town with her mother.'

Pharaoh sat up. 'Buckle said Doris Garner passed Marlene on the road and didn't see Claire because she was in the back of the van. Why would Claire be in the back?'

Laura stared at him. 'Because there wouldn't be any room in the front. It was Hugh Mason's van. He's Marlene's' – she grimaced – 'her fellow. Are you suggesting Becky was in the back too?'

'It's a thought.'

'Except that Marlene says—' She stopped. There was another pregnant silence. Laura looked startled.

'Well, why not?' Randolph protested. 'Marlene and Mason take the little girls to town, they know they shouldn't take Becky without her grandmother's permission – and certainly Doris would never let Becky ride in Mason's van – why, she won't even let her go to Starfoot! So when Doris panics about Becky not being home those two keep quiet about it.'

'And they left Becky in town?' Pharaoh asked. 'And Claire kept quiet too?'

'I don't know that anyone's spoken to Claire yet,' Randolph said. 'She wouldn't be with her mother, naturally.'

Laura grinned at Pharaoh's bewilderment. 'Marlene and Mason were drinking in Kelton,' she explained. 'That's the polite way to put it; the fact is Marlene works the bars during the tourist season. You must have realized that she's a prostitute. So the next thing Doris did, once she'd been to Starfoot and found the place locked, was to get Isaac to drive her to town and they went round the bars until they found Marlene. She said she'd brought Claire to town and that she – Claire – had gone to see a friend but she didn't know who, except that it wasn't Becky, and that neither she nor Claire had seen Becky today. So Becky wasn't in the back of the van, not if you believe Marlene.'

'Hugh Mason.' Randolph was shaking his head, having gone off on his own tack. 'I don't think so. He's never shown any preference for little girls.'

'*Dad!*'

'Sorry, just thinking aloud.'

'Don't do that when the police are around. That chief inspector:

82

he's gross and sinister: revolting combination. And he's cunning.'
She shivered.

'What about Armstrong?' Pharaoh asked.

Her jaw dropped. Randolph blinked slowly. 'I'm not with you, old man.'

'What about him?' Laura asked.

'You said Doris had contacted everyone. Did he see anything?'

'Well, he wouldn't see anything up there.' Randolph was puzzled. 'Doris must have phoned him but he knows nothing or Isaac would have said. The child would never go to Hollins . . .' He trailed off, his eyes glazed.

'Are we going to consider every man in turn?' Laura asked with interest.

His attention returned to her. 'If you did I don't think many of us could prove where we were, and that includes me and Pharaoh here.' He shook his head.

'And Mabel?' Pharaoh asked. 'Did she see anything of Becky? Obviously not or you'd have said so. Doesn't she have any ideas? Everyone must have ideas.'

'She's anxious,' Randolph said, without answering the question.

'She would be. The child is exquisite.'

'That's immaterial. Did you say that to the police?' Laura was dry.

'I don't remember that anyone mentioned her beauty.'

'Beautiful?' Randolph was surprised. 'Pretty, yes, but all children are. Mabel was anxious because she says Becky is too trusting.'

'She's immature,' Pharaoh said. 'Except that I don't know how mature—' He winced but recovered quickly. 'She seems young for twelve,' he added flatly, then: 'Who was the last person to see her? Last person *known* to have seen her?'

Laura swallowed. Randolph said, 'Why, Doris. She left her at home and went shopping in Kelton with Joan Bell. Isaac was in . . .' His voice died away.

'Isaac was in the garden,' Laura supplied. 'Or Doris wouldn't have left. She said that since the poaching she didn't like Becky being on her own. She had gone off that one time – when was it? – Sunday morning, but then she was over at Skelgill. That was when she told Mabel she'd seen Roy in the woods, and Mabel went rushing out . . . anyway, that's irrelevant. She didn't leave Becky alone this morning because Isaac – was – there. And then

Isaac left. To patrol the woods, he said.' She stared at her father.

'Don't be ridiculous,' Randolph shouted. 'He's her grand-father!'

At the keeper's cottage Isaac sat in the kitchen without the light on and wondered how far he would get if he left now. Doris was asleep upstairs – heavily sedated – and he had more of the pills to give her when she woke but he knew she wouldn't take them from him; from the doctor, yes, not from her own husband. The bedroom door was open and he could hear her snoring if he went to the foot of the stairs. He dreaded her waking; he longed not to be there when she did – but if he were to take the car he knew he wouldn't be free for more than a few hours. The police would have his registration number and they'd catch him and bring him back, and even if he could afford to hole up in a bed and breakfast, they'd tell Doris where he was. He couldn't go to his niece in Ambleside because she was kin to Becky. He could see no way out and he was terrified. If Doris would only listen, if he could approach her before the effect of the last pills wore off, if she'd even be half-way reasonable, then he could convince her, might convince her that nothing had happened. Becky had run away like they all do – why, thousands of youngsters were living on the streets; if they preferred sleeping on the pavement to a good home it stood to reason Becky wouldn't stay in a keeper's cottage. She'd gone to America to live in a millionaire's mansion, that's what Becky had done. But when he'd tried to tell her Doris had screamed at him that he was out of his mind, and that in the car park in Kelton after they found Marlene Fisher – who knew nothing about Becky and didn't know and didn't care where her own daughter was. Now that, thought Isaac, drowsy with exhaustion, was the kind of woman to have, and he started to dream of Marlene. No one had told Isaac about defence mechanisms.

In the cool caravan that lost its heat so quickly after the sun went down Marlene asked softly, 'Are you awake?'

Mason stirred, releasing a smell of sweat and Brut.

'What's up?'

'You didn't have anything to do with her, did you?'

'Who, for God's sake?'

'With Becky Rudd.'

There was a convulsive movement and she knew that he'd sat

up or – his breath was close to her face – was propped on one elbow.

'You think I go after kids now?'

She tried to identify the sense behind the words: curiosity? A warning? 'It doesn't have to be that,' she said.

'What else would it be – if she's dead?' His voice sank on the last word.

They were both thinking of the open windows. She reached out and pulled his head close. She whispered, 'She could have got in the way or seen something she shouldn't. That's if it's a local guy; if it was sex it had to be a stranger.'

'It wasn't me.' He eased away from her and they lay on their backs, staring into the darkness.

'Are you in the clear?' she asked. 'I have to know.'

'You're wrong. You don't have to know nothing.' He was adamant. 'And I'm in the clear,' he added. 'Go to sleep.'

'Then who—'

'Forget it. She ran away. You haven't seen her for so long you can't remember when. It's nowt to do with us. And now go to sleep.'

Inside the cottage the curtains moved in Claire's room. It was still warm under the slates and the draught from the open window was heady with the scent of resin and lush green growth. A shriek came from Starfoot's roof. Claire's eyes opened sightlessly and closed again. She made no other movement and she slept without dreams. A pale shape dropped from the gable-end as the barn owl pounced on a vole.

Not far from Starfoot, above the escarpment, Hollins showed faint in the starlight beside the silent tarn. Tim Armstrong had finished work for the night and he was leaning against his porch appreciating the fresh air but thinking vaguely of his next home. The States, he thought, somewhere that the sun would shine all through the winter too: California or Arizona, but he'd settle for Australia; it was immaterial, he could work anywhere.

At Skelgill Mabel was awake, sitting on the garden bench, lapped by the scent of roses, aware of dark forms that came and went about her feet, of the cold of the loaded shotgun on her thighs. She had been thinking about Becky, but Becky was basically someone else's problem: her family and the police; Mabel's main concern was immediate: these boneless presences that caressed her ankles, and noises in the woods. She heard a barn owl call and the cry of a startled coot down by Isaac's jetty. She thought that if a pebble was dislodged from Falcon Crag she'd probably hear that too although she could barely make out its bulk against the stars. She wondered how long this would go on: guarding her animals, and she considered, not for the first time, the steps she might take to end it. The final solution, she thought, smiling.

At Warthwaite Stephen Hartley slept like the dead, the window open only a crack to try to dispel the heat without letting in a dangerous amount of night air. Beside him Anne was awake. All the doors in the house were locked but the keys were in the locks. Anne was well aware that Roy could come and go by a window if he chose but she wasn't bothered about Roy. It was Hartley who was concerned about his son. He knew he'd never find another farm in these days and he was scared stiff. So far as Anne was concerned, if Randolph Steel tried to evict them she'd fight every inch of the way, she'd take him to court. She'd had a long talk with Roy and, as she'd told Buckle, lad were innocent as a lamb.

She went over things in her mind. There was never any proof about that bird-nesting lark which was why t'boss couldn't do nothing last year. As for the wallet and the binoculars: that were crap; there were thieves everywhere. And the poaching? She'd questioned Roy, pushing it; she was his mother, he knew he could trust her. He'd laughed at her, not nastily, more like he were teasing his girl. She hoped he'd had nowt to do with t'poaching or at the least, that he'd covered his tracks. She didn't think about Becky Rudd; she'd decided that the kid had run away and hitched a lift to one of them festivals. She didn't want to think about Becky.

In his three-bed semi on a new development with a view up the dale to the central fells Buckle lay and castigated the author of an otherwise accurate book who'd written – he never forgot it – that the mark of the good detective was that he had learned to compartmentalize. When he came home, this paragon, he left the job behind with the closing of his front door. The man who wrote that never knew what it was to be searching for a missing child.

Tomorrow he would be outranked; she'd been gone too long for it not to be foul play – unless she *had* run away – and then there was the possibility of kidnap, the stepfather being a millionaire and all, but there had been no ransom demand. There was abduction – but by tomorrow morning the chief would be in charge. Buckle might welcome the shift of responsibility but he hoped he'd be able to stay with those buggers in Scawdale; he wanted another go at them, shake them down. They knew more than they were telling – not all of them perhaps, some; the bottom line was which ones?

At the head of the dale there was a National Trust camp ground where cars were herded together like cattle while their drivers slept in the woods about a hundred yards distant. The system meant that the campers had the illusion of living rough in sylvan glades without the visual pollution of their vehicles, and their fumes at meal times. The drawback was that the cars, like untended beasts, were vulnerable. There should be a camp guard, thought the marauder, slipping along the metal flanks, soft as a cat, testing door handles, fingers feeling for an open window.

Chapter Nine

Doris woke before sunrise, consumed by a forlorn hope that lured her out of bed to stagger along the landing to Becky's room. The curtains hadn't been closed and the grey dawn filtered into the room to reveal the empty bed and possessions that appeared animate, waiting to be reclaimed by their owner: the mirrored sunglasses, the gaudy trainers, the turquoise bracelet – all sent by Sally from America. Doris caught her breath. Sally on her honeymoon: unconcerned, unaware; what was she to do about Sally?

Pharaoh woke and stared at the grey light, disorientated for a moment, thinking he was hearing a lost child calling, then he heard the name and recognized the voice. He guessed that this would always happen when he identified with someone else's loss, or their dread of loss. Doris was awake and looking for Becky. Through his compassion he felt a twinge of resentment; did the woman think the child was in the vicinity of the Boathouse?

There was no more sleep for him after that. He got up and by the time he'd showered and gone downstairs there was no sign of Doris. He brewed coffee and went out into the garden. The sun was bright on the western fells and its rays had just reached the far edge of the lake. Birds were singing loudly in the woods. He turned and looked at the crags, unable to distinguish the peregrines with the naked eye. He considered the cliffs; if Becky were a climber the first place you'd look would be at the base of them, but even if she were a climber, she'd never have gone up there solo. Why solo? Because she was on her own when she disappeared. He drank some coffee. The police didn't think that, the police suspected him. The suspicion was logical; there was no evidence that she had gone off on her own, only what people said, and people told lies in a case like this. Circumstances, he corrected, it wasn't a case as yet.

Randolph arrived after breakfast. He had twice telephoned the police in Kelton and learned first that Buckle and Fleming were in conference and then that they were on their way. To his question as to whether local people were required for a search, he was told that Buckle would be making arrangements when he arrived. Randolph thought he was being treated in a somewhat cavalier fashion.

'The police can look for the child further afield,' he told Pharaoh, 'but if there's a search in the dale, it's the locals who know the ground. We don't have to wait for permission.'

'Where do you start?' Pharaoh told him about being wakened by Doris.

'I was through these woods last evening,' Randolph said. 'With Isaac and Trudy. We need more dogs: search and rescue, even farm collies. If she's here the dogs will find her.'

'Claire must know something,' Pharaoh pointed out. 'Where was she when her mother was drinking in Kelton? Doesn't that seem odd: a small girl running loose in a busy town from afternoon until – when? Who was she with all that time?'

'Marlene assured Doris that Becky wasn't with them.'

'Not in the van. Becky could have gone to town separately. Marlene could be lying. Becky could have been in the van, but then Mason would have to be lying too, and Claire.'

Randolph was pensive. 'We must go and talk to Claire, not that I think for one moment that Becky was in the van but, as you said last night: best friends and all, Claire must have some idea of what's happened. She'll certainly know the truth about Becky and young Hartley. We'll go along there now.'

'You want me to come?'

'Certainly. We can use your expertise on the search.'

The hawthorn was blooming so lavishly that Starfoot's track was more like a cutting through snowdrifts except that the may was the colour of rich cream and smelled heavenly. Pharaoh's eyes sharpened as they passed a gap.

'Claire's run off.'

'You saw her?'

'Dodged out of the door and raced away to the left.'

'She's gone to the caravan to warn her mother. Marlene doesn't usually get up till late.'

'You mean, she uses the caravan—'

'Laura says she's stopped using the house now Claire's older. No doubt when she's in town she rents a room somewhere.'

'You don't seem bothered.'

'It's not my business, my dear chap. She has to live – and don't forget the little girl.' He came to the cottage and reversed to stop under the gable-end. They got out, taking their time, except for Trudy who leapt out and raced round the corner. They followed and knocked on the open door.

'Come in,' Claire shouted.

She turned from the sink as they entered the kitchen and her lips twitched as if she were trying out a smile, but her eyes were anxious.

'I'm afraid we have no good news, my dear.' Randolph was avuncular. 'I don't suppose you have any?'

She looked blank. 'What kind of news?' Without waiting for a response she stood on tiptoe to reach mugs in a cupboard. She put them on the draining board and fetched sugar and coffee. She went back to the cupboard for a fourth mug. 'Mummy won't be long,' she said, glancing uncertainly at Randolph as if wondering if she were behaving correctly, saying the right thing.

'That's fine,' Randolph said. 'We wanted to— What I'm interested in, and Mr Pharaoh here – is whether Becky said anything to you about taking off or – er – running away?'

'No, she didn't say anything.'

The kettle boiled. She switched it off and spooned coffee into the mugs.

'When was the last time you saw her?' Pharaoh asked.

'Sunday.'

She picked up the kettle, using both hands, and filled the mugs with great care. Pharaoh waited until she'd brought them to the table, obviously concerned not to spill a drop.

'Do you know what she was doing yesterday?' he asked.

She stared at him in surprise. 'I didn't see her.'

'What do you think she was doing?'

She turned to Randolph, appealing to him. 'Her gran would know. Why don't you ask her? I was in town.'

'Who were you with?' Pharaoh asked.

She gave a snort of indignation at this impertinence but before she could protest there was a commotion in the passage. Trudy came bouncing into the kitchen as Marlene called gaily: 'Hi,

90

everyone! Be with you in a jiffy!' They heard her go upstairs. A
door slammed.

'I was with a school friend,' came Claire's voice: cool, almost
adult. 'Why?'

'Becky's your best friend,' Randolph said. 'You know her as
well as anyone does. It stands to reason you must have some idea
where she's gone. She could be in danger, Claire.'

'What kind of danger?'

'Suppose she had an accident—'

'Or was attacked,' Pharaoh put in.

'Who would attack her?'

'Oh, come on,' Randolph exclaimed. 'Surely you're told at
school not to accept lifts from strangers, or sweets—'

'Oh, that kind of attack. But I wouldn't know about anything
like that when I was in town. I wouldn't know if she met someone
in the dale, would I?'

Randolph looked at Pharaoh who hesitated, then asked curiously, 'Where does Roy come into it?'

Claire sat down, and they followed suit. She studied his face as
if trying to read his meaning from his expression. 'Come into
what?' she asked.

'Becky's disappearance.'

'Does he come into it?'

'I'm asking you.'

Randolph stirred uneasily, throwing a glance at the doorway,
intending Pharaoh to catch the warning.

'I don't know what you want me to say,' Claire said.

'Has he threatened her?'

'I don't know.'

'Do they meet?'

'Does who meet?'

Marlene stood in the doorway, bare footed, her face shining,
her hair unkempt, a man's shirt thrown on over a shabby skirt.
'Make me a coffee, sweetie,' she said, coming into the room,
taking the chair that Claire vacated. She addressed Pharaoh. 'Who
are we discussing?' There was an edge to her tone.

'Roy and Becky.' Pharaoh returned her gaze and saw the
sudden amazement before she looked away.

'Roy and Becky?' she repeated. 'What *is* this?'

'Nothing.' Claire was sulky, watching the kettle. 'He's trying to
put the blame on Roy.'

There was a long silence before Marlene asked, 'Is there any news?' Her eyes were speculative.

Randolph shook his head. 'It's early days yet.'

Pharaoh was amazed. 'She's been gone nearly twenty-four hours!'

'Yes, but she's just run away,' Marlene said absently. 'That's what you think, isn't it, sweetie? And you should know. Claire and Becky are like sisters,' she assured them. The men looked at Claire who placed a mug of coffee in front of her mother and said loudly, 'I don't know what she did or where she went. I haven't seen her since Sunday.'

'And that's all of three days ago,' Marlene said brightly, picking at a crumb on the table, hesitating. 'What makes you think Roy's involved?' she asked.

'Because someone was spying on her in the woods on Monday evening,' Pharaoh said. 'And she said he'd threatened to get her one dark night.'

Marlene turned slowly. Claire was expressionless, leaning against the sink. 'Did you know this?'

'Not really.'

'What d'you mean: "not really"? Did you or didn't you?'

'Some of it.'

'Come and sit down.' She couldn't, there was no chair, so Marlene put her arm round the child and became maternal, even cloying. 'You haven't done anything wrong, ducky; tell us what that animal said to Becky. He threatened her?'

'She didn't tell me that.' Claire slid sideways and stood in the doorway. 'He must have said that since Sunday.'

'She also said that Roy was involved in poaching our deer,' Randolph said.

'She knows something I don't then.' Claire sounded resentful. 'I didn't know Roy was poaching. I know he took the hawks' eggs. Everyone knows that.'

'And Laura's binoculars, and he broke into Miss Cooper's cottage twice.'

'Oh, wow!' she breathed.

'All villages have problem families,' Marlene said, looking fondly at her own daughter – and then she caught on. 'You don't really think he had something to do with – oh no!'

Claire licked her lips and looked from one to the other of the men. There was a soft crunch of tyres outside and a low whine as an engine reversed.

92

'Now who's that?' Marlene asked, exasperated. 'I'm going to clean up, sweetie; see to the visitors, will you?'

She rushed out and ran up the stairs. Claire went to the door, dragging her feet. Pharaoh and Randolph exchanged glances and came to the same conclusion. Police, mouthed Randolph. Claire returned, looking very small in front of the new arrivals. 'It's the police,' she said, watching their faces.

'Your dad's up to High Row,' Anne said as Roy came in the kitchen for his breakfast. 'Joe Postlethwaite's strained his back so Dad's cutting his twenty-acre. You want black pudden with your bacon?'

He sat at the table like a young pasha as she poured his tea, made fresh when she heard him in the bathroom. 'Becky didn't come home all night,' she told him. 'I spoke to Isaac and he says her gran is going spare, think's something dreadful happened.'

'Such as?'

'She got picked up by someone and carried off.'

Roy looked interested. 'Someone we know, like, or a stranger?'

'How would I know, son? Doris thinks the worst. Isaac now, he's playing it down; he reckons she's on her way to America.'

'He's daft.'

'Not when you think about it. There's nothing for a young girl to do here – why, Doris wouldn't even let her go to town on her own. America must seem like a dream, particularly if your mam's married a millionaire. Becky'll be frantic to join up with Sally and her new husband.'

'Mam, America's on the other side of the world! Where'd Becky get the money for the plane ticket?'

Anne looked blank. 'Kids are always running away; they live in those cardboard cities.'

'Yeah, they don't run off to America. That costs.'

'So where do you think she is?'

He shrugged. 'Not my business, is it?'

Mabel was hoeing her asparagus bed and she didn't stop while Randolph was bringing her up to date on the curiously amorphous situation. 'Fact is,' he was saying, 'we have no idea what's happened, and the more we learn the more confusing it appears to be.'

'Except that circumstances seem to point to Roy,' Pharaoh put in.

'Everything *does* point to Roy.' Mabel chopped viciously at a

93

thistle. 'And as for Becky' – she stepped off the raised bed – 'I find myself wondering if she ever left the dale.' She regarded them defiantly, as if challenging them to contradict her. 'We have to look for her, Randolph; it's the least we can do.'

'Oh, I agree. We were intending to do just that. I suggest we divide the woods between us: you work south, we come north from the quarry.'

'What about your leg?' she asked Pharaoh.

'I can manage.'

'You won't stop him.' Randolph grinned. 'The chief inspector, Buckle, has him tagged as the last man to have seen her – sorry, bad taste' – as Mabel turned disapproving eyes on him – 'but it's true! They've yet to find who saw her after Doris left to go shopping. Buckle was pretty short with you at Starfoot, eh, Pharaoh? With both of us, come to that; d'you think he resents me questioning my own tenants, is that it?'

Pharaoh ignored this, harping resentfully on his own problem: 'Buckle's suspicious of me because he can't work out why Becky should have come to visit me the night before she disappeared. I think Laura could be right: that there was something going between those two: Becky and Roy.'

'I can't believe that,' Mabel said. 'But how fortunate for you that she was alive and well after she was at the Boathouse.' She nodded gravely at them. 'There's a lot of pressure on the police,' she added ambiguously as she led the way to the tool-shed. She replaced the hoe and snapped the padlock on the door. The padlock was new. 'Seventy years I've lived in this dale,' she said. 'And now I have to secure even my garden shed because of just one boy, and a local at that.'

'Are you sleeping with that shotgun?' Randolph asked.

She didn't answer that directly but he had started a train of thought. 'If he could threaten my cats,' she said, 'how big is the step to threatening people?'

'Becky says he did.' But Pharaoh was doubtful.

'There could have been an accident,' Randolph said.

'With an air gun?' Mabel asked. 'Is it possible?'

'At close range, through the eye? It wouldn't kill—'

'But if she were blinded she could fall—'

They turned and regarded the face of Falcon Crag. Randolph shook his head as if to rid it of something nasty that clung. 'Well now,' he exclaimed on a high note, 'what d'you say, my dear?

You take the woods to the north and we'll go down to the quarry and work up to meet you. How's that?'

'I should do the quarry end,' Mabel said. 'Because the first thing that would happen there is that Trudy will go straight to where you buried the remains of the deer and you'll have difficulty getting her to concentrate after that. You take this end.'

'You don't need me,' Pharaoh told Randolph. 'You've got the dog. I'll go with Mabel.'

So that was what they did: Randolph and Trudy going straight into the woods at the back of Skelgill, Mabel driving Pharaoh up the dale to park in the quarry.

'Does your experience help on this kind of search?' she asked as she locked the car.

'Not specifically. It's a matter of common sense really; the first places to look would be below waterfalls, in gorges—' He glanced in the direction of the escarpment which was now hidden by trees.

'Below cliffs,' Mabel said.

He didn't respond to that. 'But an accident with an air gun . . .' he began, and left it hanging. He sighed. 'We just have to do what we can. I think Randolph will have to come down here with the dog because there's no way we can search properly, just the two of us.'

'We have eyes,' she said stoutly.

But the bluebells were thick and the ferns already tall while the paths, such as they were, worn by deer and sheep, never went in the right direction, however, they utilized them where they could, doggedly working northwards, far apart but retaining visual contact. Pharaoh was down the slope with the road below him, Mabel – who was amazingly agile – clambering over mossy boulders above.

Randolph had made such a good job of burying the fawn and the deer guts that neither of them stumbled on the sites. They came to the beck that descended from the tarn where Armstrong lived. Mabel started down the bank towards Pharaoh and as she did so a peregrine called harshly.

'Damn,' she exclaimed, slipping in the mud. 'We're disturbing them.'

Pharaoh halted, his face streaming sweat, and craned his neck at the tower which was not quite masked by young foliage. His glance travelled down the line of fall but the foot of the cliff was over a hundred yards away and hidden by the undergrowth.

'She'd never have gone up there,' Mabel said, and he couldn't tell whether she meant the base of the cliff or its summit. He did know she wanted him to agree with her.

'We have to look,' he said.

They toiled up the slope which was composed of block scree, every depression lush with ferns. Immediately below the cliff they found a faint track and they followed it, keeping together but in single file, Mabel in the lead.

Unlike Grey Buttress this cliff had no sweep of clean rock; it was damp, vegetated and loose: "dirty" was the jargon word, and climbers avoided it. Pharaoh surveyed it with grim interest; basically it was the same as any low-altitude cliff: vertical gullies and walls, but the gullies were choked by a hanging jungle of green plants and the walls were scored by cracks and interspersed with ledges and rakes, the lower pitches draped with ivy. No wonder the falcons had chosen to nest here. They were silent now, hundreds of feet above and apparently unbothered, as if aware that their nest was unassailable.

They crossed the foot of the gully below the nest, rounded a shattered prow and tramped up a gentle slope as the crag fell back. They came to another gully that was deep in shadow with globe flowers shining in the gloom. It took them a moment for their eyes to adapt to the change from bright sunlight and when they did they saw, hanging in space above eye-level, a pair of binoculars.

They stared without speaking and it was Pharaoh who recovered first – because he was more accustomed to coming on objects which had fallen from a height, or objects that had fallen and been arrested. Binoculars didn't remain unsupported in space, they were suspended. And so, knowing it had to be there but obscured by the vegetation, he assumed the presence of a strap and his eyes rose unwillingly and slowly to the gully above the glasses. There was a step, like the tread of a staircase, and the lip was covered with honeysuckle. Below this the glasses dangled surreally.

'The strap's caught,' Mabel said, too loudly. 'Someone dropped them off the top of the cliff.'

'I didn't think of that,' he said, and stepped forward.

'Are you sure—' She bit her lip. He was the expert.

There were plenty of holds but the rock was friable and in the back of the gully water trickled over slime. However, by straddling

96

wide and carefully testing every hold before he put his weight on it, he managed to advance to the lip of the platform. He pulled himself up carefully, turning his head to the back of the recess, and then he stopped moving. Mabel closed her eyes.

'She's here,' he said.

Chapter Ten

'I don't believe this,' Buckle said, sitting in the car outside Warthwaite. 'Here's the father disappeared on the tractor, the son away to the woods, and the mother so busy with the washing she won't stop to talk to us. We should have got here earlier. That bloody conference!'

'We caught the other child at home,' Fleming pointed out. 'Claire.'

'And a fat lot we learned from her that we didn't know already. I want to find that lad.'

They drove slowly down Warthwaite's track. 'Where to now?' Fleming asked, stopping at the cattle grid.

Buckle pondered. 'We'll go to the village,' he said. 'Hartley's somewhere in that direction, and we can call on Hugh Mason – Marlene's boyfriend or pimp according to who's talking.'

'She works the bars in town. She's known.'

'So he's her pimp. Pull over, you're blocking the track.'

A battered Fiesta had turned off the main road and stopped, its indicator still winking. Fleming started to reverse on to the grass. The Fiesta advanced and slowed and they saw that the driver was Miss Cooper. She looked past Fleming to Buckle.

'She's been found,' she called, and drove on.

'Here, wait!' shouted Fleming, but she'd moved only to get room to open her door. Buckle got out and approached her.

'Alive?' he asked, but he knew the answer from her expression.

'No – and the only comfort is that it must have been instantaneous. She fell from the top of Falcon Crag.' She dismounted and pointed to where the tower showed beyond Warthwaite and the woods.

'How close can you get a vehicle?'

'You park in the quarry and walk half a mile. And you're going to need a rope.'

98

'She didn't fall to the bottom?'

'The body's about fifteen feet above the ground but you can't see it until you climb up to it. We guessed it might be there because there's a pair of binoculars dangling in full view. She didn't leave go of them.'

'So you climbed up.'

'Pharaoh did. He said you'd need a rope.'

'Let's get this straight. Pharaoh climbed up to the body, right? Then so can we.'

'No.' He blinked at her, his anger rising. 'Pharaoh's lame,' she said coldly, 'but he's still an experienced climber. Do you want to break a leg, or worse? You're going to need a rope so either we take it up with us now or I descend again to fetch it when you realize the position – and I'm not doing that.' She walked to her car and started the engine.

'She could be right,' Fleming said.

Buckle swore. 'It's just she's so bloody arrogant. Still thinks of herself as gentry.'

'She is gentry,' Fleming said.

Following the Fiesta down the dale, Buckle stared at the crag until the trees closed in at the end of the pastures. 'She fell, or was pushed?' he asked. 'A twelve-year-old on top of that precipice on her own: highly unlikely.'

'Or thrown over,' Fleming suggested. 'Killed first and the body pushed over the edge.'

'And she was clutching binoculars. What was she watching?'

'Or who. But we don't know about the binoculars; only what Miss Cooper says.'

'And she got there first.'

'No. Pharaoh got there first.'

Buckle grinned. 'Working together? Doesn't sound like guilty behaviour though, does it – going back to the scene of the crime?'

'Unless they – or he – wanted to remove something.'

'He'd have done it before. On the other hand a clever chap would know he'd leave traces, and they could date, so he wouldn't approach the body before it was found, but he'd see to it that he got there first. They knew exactly where it was— Now where's she going—' as Mabel indicated she was turning left. 'Ah, to the Boathouse – to fetch the rope. His rope. He's a climber – Mountain Rescue; I suppose he'd know the first place to look is under the cliffs.'

99

Mabel had the keys to Pharaoh's Transit. The detectives stood at the open door and surveyed the interior with interest. She handed them a purple rope and metal objects which they handled circumspectly. Buckle cursed under his breath. He'd heard of this happening, the CID constrained to view a body *in situ* on a cliff before it could be moved, but he'd never had the experience himself, and neither he nor Fleming had the remotest idea how to utilize this specialist equipment.

Mabel emerged carrying a chunky little hammer and locked the van. They were silent as they followed her back to the road until Buckle asked suddenly, 'Are there any trainers in the back?'

'There are some wellies.' Fleming was laconic. This was one time Buckle would be on the sharp end.

Half an hour later they struggled up the last few feet to find first his spaniel then Randolph Steel at the foot of a gully. Looking up, Buckle could see Pharaoh's face above a screen of vegetation below which dangled a pair of binoculars, just as Mabel had said. He wondered why Pharaoh had gone up there again but that was a question which could wait. He looked at the rock and thought that if a cripple could shin up that it must be easy. It looked easy; it couldn't be much more than ten feet. He stepped forward.

'Rock's loose,' Randolph warned then, seeing the other's incomprehension: 'It comes away in your hand. That's why Pharaoh didn't come down. He's been up there waiting all this time.'

'We didn't hang about.' Buckle was intimidated by the situation.

'Let's have the rope,' Randolph said.

He uncoiled it and with a sailor's throw managed to get one end to Pharaoh who hauled up the gear and the hammer, then turned and busied himself with some activity screened by the plants.

'Where's the body?' Buckle asked.

'There,' Randolph said. 'She's still holding the binoculars.' There came a sound of hammering: metal on metal. 'Securing himself,' he explained.

Mabel was nudging him. 'Lift your arms,' she ordered. 'I'm going to tie you on.' She was holding the other end of the rope.

He raised his arms, feeling ridiculous. Fleming caught his eye and looked away. It was fantastic to think that there was a body a few feet above them and it crossed his mind that this was an elaborate practical joke. If it were he'd have every one of them

100

in court – but he knew it wasn't. He jumped. The purple rope was snaking fast up the rock. The police stared at it, fascinated. It tightened at his waist.

'Right,' Pharaoh said, his face appearing again. 'Take your time.'

He stepped forward but when he was actually touching the rock he couldn't see where he should put his hands, let alone his feet. The rock was much steeper than he'd thought and below the binoculars it was covered with slime.

'You straddle.' Mabel moved up beside him and pointed out the holds. 'A bit difficult in wellies but you've got the rope.'

'I pull up on that?'

'No, but it will hold you if you fall.'

He put one foot on the rock. 'I can't do this,' he said.

'Here.' Randolph edged Mabel out of the way. 'Stand on my shoulders.' He crouched down. Then Fleming came forward and he climbed up their bodies somehow, on their knees first, then their shoulders, the rope so tight he felt he'd be asphyxiated by the constriction on his lungs. He pawed at the rock, sending the binoculars swinging, and finally he stepped off their shoulders to be hauled over the lip, clawing and gasping, lunging forward. One hand gripped Pharaoh's boot, the other his bare leg – and that yielded alarmingly.

'I've got you,' Pharaoh said calmly. 'Get your breath back.'

'Jesus!' Buckle gasped. 'Jesus!' He stared at the man's legs close to his face, denim covered. Still prone he turned his head and saw that the leg he'd grasped was near her neck, and that was twisted too. The body looked like a small broken manikin.

He pulled himself to the wall of the gully. Pharaoh held the rope tight and waited. Buckle started to relax as the fear of falling was replaced by a familiar confidence. Pharaoh was the expert on his own ground but the situation had changed. The rope and the gear, even the job of safeguarding the layman, was Pharaoh's responsibility still, but the body was Buckle's concern.

'Have you touched her?' he asked.

'No.'

'How far did I move her?'

'You rolled it towards you. It's gone back to where it was.'

Buckle thought suddenly that Pharaoh could have seen as many bodies as himself, and probably in worse condition if this one was anything to go by. He was familiar with photographs of people who had fallen or jumped from tall buildings but they landed flat, like starfish. This one was contorted. There were wounds but not much blood. He looked up but he could see nothing beyond a long overhang draped, surprisingly, with honeysuckle that smelled like a perfume counter. The foliage was undisturbed.

'I take it she bounced,' he said. 'She couldn't have fallen free all the way.'

Pharaoh nodded. 'It's not as steep as it looks, and in a gully people hit ledges and ricochet; every impact means more damage. At least it was quick; she was dead before she reached here. Sorry, that's your job.'

Buckle held his eye. 'She could have been dead before she went off the top.'

Pharaoh sketched a shrug. 'That's still your job.' He looked at the body. 'God knows how you're going to find out. Do you propose to bring the doctor up here, and photographers?'

Buckle knew what was implied: every man would have to be hauled up by the expert, and that was Pharaoh, and if there had been foul play Pharaoh was a suspect.

'One thing's for sure,' he said, 'if a crime has been committed, then how she's lying now doesn't have any bearing on it, so she can be moved.'

'Good. I'll be glad to get down.'

'Why didn't you go before?'

'It's easier to climb up – and I had the incentive – but climbing down is awkward at the best of times with a game leg. On this rock I wouldn't risk it without a rope.'

Buckle glowered at him; he hadn't missed that bit about incentive. 'Can you get a camera up here without smashing it?' he asked.

On the ground they padded the police Nikon with a sweater and Pharaoh hauled it up inside Mabel's day-sack.

'Are you going to keep a tight hold on that rope?' Buckle asked, struggling to his feet. He started to take pictures, beginning at the back of the gully and working forward.

The body lay with its head towards the drop, the legs splintered and awry, one arm under the torso, the other extended above the head. Although she was lying on her back the neck was broken and her face was downwards, the skull like a broken egg-shell, but the worst of the horror obscured by the dark hair. For Pharaoh the most touching feature was her braid, the pattern still visible

102

as she must have plaited it a few hours before. More significant, tacitly noted by both of them and carefully photographed by Buckle, was the state of her clothing: shorts and shirt in the condition that his report would describe as 'fully clothed' although stained by rock and plants and the inevitable blood – but not much of that compared with the amount you'd have with a stabbing. Buckle photographed everything, from every angle, held tight on the rope, finally parting the vegetation and weighting it with stones in order to get pictures of the hand tightly closed on the strap of the binoculars.

Roy had spent an interesting morning. From his secret place on the rock pinnacle above the farm he had watched the police car climb the track to Warthwaite to leave after a brief interval. His mother had sent them packing quickly enough. They might have meant to go after his dad, but he saw them meet Mabel Cooper at the cattle grid and his eyes had sharpened when he realized she was directing their attention to Falcon Crag. For one moment he'd thought that she was actually pointing at him and wondered if she'd caught a glint from his binoculars, but they'd piled in the cars and cleared off down the dale.

He was intrigued and just a little disturbed. He decided to abandon that hiding place, at least temporarily, and move the big rucksack deeper into the woods. Having concealed it in a crevice masked by ferns he climbed a gully that was one of his chosen routes to the top of the escarpment and worked along the edge to a point that overlooked the face and the near side of Falcon Crag. The lower section was hidden in the trees but he could hear voices down there although there was no way of telling whether they were trippers, or climbers, or Mabel and the police. In any event his main interest was the peregrines – not the nest, because it wasn't visible from this angle, but the behaviour of the birds.

By midday he decided that the female was still sitting on eggs and he faded back from the edge, careful not to show himself to anyone who might be watching from below. Even among the trees he had to be circumspect because there was only a narrow strip of ground between the escarpment and the road. He was close to the place where the public highway ended at the entrance to Hollins' drive, he could see the notice at the open gate. No cars were parked in the space outside the gateway and there seemed to be no one about until he saw a flash of colour in the trees on the other side of the road. He dropped down behind some brambles and, careless of the thorns, parted the leaves.

Claire was coming through the trees pushing her bike. She was walking towards him but she hadn't seen him because she was having to watch the ground. There was no path at that point. When she reached the road, instead of going down towards the dale and her home, she mounted and pedalled along the drive to Hollins. As soon as she was out of sight he ran across the road to the place where he'd first seen her and started to work backwards, following the marks of her tyres.

'No!' Tim Armstrong was shocked out of his wits. 'No way can you come in my house!' He threw an anguished glance past the child planted so firmly on his doorstep.

'I'm not saying she's here,' Claire persisted. 'It's just that we've got to look everywhere, and she did say you'd asked her to come and see you.'

'*I what!*'

She nodded earnestly. 'Because she wants to be a writer too, and you said you'd be happy to give her some tips.'

'Shut up!' Claire took a step back. She was wide-eyed and her lower lip trembled. Armstrong drew a deep breath. 'Look, I haven't the remotest idea what you're on about. Someone's been pulling your leg. This is private land,' he added wildly, seeing he wasn't getting anywhere. 'It belongs to Mr Steel.'

'Oh, I know who it belongs to all right. Mr Steel's searching too. She's been missing all night. They didn't send me, don't worry; I haven't told anyone else that you said she was to come here on her own.'

'Christ!' He wiped his forehead. 'How many times— Are you telling me this kid actually told you she was coming here?'

'She's not a kid. She's twelve but she looks older. She's very pretty. I don't blame you. I mean, it's not the first time, is it? She's been here before.'

Armstrong studied her face. He was breathing hard. He said shakily, 'Maybe she came here when I was out – with you perhaps?'

She licked her lips, unable to interpret his reaction; she thought he looked hopeful and yet she knew he was frightened. 'I've never been here,' she said.

'And you never told anyone that she came – said she came here alone?'

She was anxious to co-operate. 'I didn't, but she told her boyfriend. She tells him everything.'

'She told him she came here?'

'Must have done because she told me.' Her tone lightened. 'But if she's not here you haven't got nothing to worry about.' Her eyes wandered to the skyline and focused. 'I have to go now. Bye!'

She danced out of the gate, picked up her bicycle and sped along the drive.

There was no sign of anyone on the skyline so far as he could see. He went indoors and eyed his telephone.

The next visitor arrived not long afterwards. Armstrong was sitting on a boulder outside the porch when he became aware that he was being watched. He'd heard no one approach. He looked up to see a threatening figure, dark and glowering, even sinister. A closer look showed him that this was only a youth. He opened the gate and entered the garden. Armstrong watched him intently. He didn't stand up. He guessed what was coming, and he was right.

'Becky inside?' The tone was laconic.

'You know she isn't.'

'Mind if I look?'

'I do mind.' Armstrong got to his feet and went to stand in the porch, barring entrance.

Roy grinned broadly, the grin transforming his heavy features. He was happy. He stopped wondering why Claire should have been so willing to explain her visit to Hollins when he'd accosted her. Now he knew that, for a change, she'd been telling the truth. This guy definitely had something to hide.

'These kids,' Roy said airily. 'They run wild in the woods. It's not safe.' Armstrong said nothing, he couldn't decide what he should say. The situation was unprecedented – and the lad was young but dauntingly powerful. 'They get bored,' Roy went on. 'All they got to do is spy on their neighbours. That Becky, she knew too much.'

'Like – about the burglaries,' Armstrong said, feeling his way.

'And other things.' Roy too was gauging his man. 'Young Claire reckons it's a sex crime: some guy took Becky home. Me, I think she saw something as she shouldn't.'

'Why are you telling me?'

'Why am I telling you? Because Claire' – he gestured as if she were just round the corner – 'she reckons Becky's here.'

'She's not.'

'All right. So you want me to go away.' There was a fractional pause. 'So that you can get on with your – work.'

'If you don't mind.' The sarcasm was venomous. 'Shut the gate behind you.'

Roy eyed him without expression, measuring degrees of humiliation. 'The police could be your next visitors,' he said. 'The CID is in the dale.'

'Hardly your business, is it?'

'It could be because it's down to me whether I tell them to look for her here, tell them what she told me. You can't bar your door to them.'

'I see. You're looking for a hand-out.'

'I didn't say that.' His eyes widened in a travesty of innocence. 'What I was thinking was that you must have some jobs need doing. Clean your car? Deliver some logs.'

'How would you deliver logs?'

'You're right; I haven't got a car and I'd rather not bring anyone else in on this. There's no call for it. Yet. I'll bring a couple of bags up tomorrow on my bike, OK? I'll take the money now because I have to get them from the yard. Nothing comes free.'

Armstrong's jaw was set. 'How much?'

'Fifteen quid a bag.'

'Who d'you think keeps thirty quid on him?'

'Most folk.'

Sweet Jesus, Roy crowed, trotting along the drive, the notes snug in his back pocket, what *is* it? He can't, surely he can't have Becky in there – can he? But there's something going on, has to be; he paid up like a lamb.

Behind him, Armstrong retreated to his kitchen and dropped into a chair. He knew he'd done wrong to pay but it could have been worse to refuse, and there was no other option. Well, there was but he had to have advice. And at that moment the telephone rang.

'I can't make head nor tail of those binoculars,' Randolph said, opening the gate at Skelgill, waiting while Pharaoh latched it. '*Becky* stole them? Laura was so sure it was Roy.'

'There is a connection—' Pharaoh began, and stopped as Mabel came down the path.

'We brought your rucksack,' Randolph said. 'How's Doris?'

106

'As you might expect. Very quiet now, poor soul; the shock will hit her later. As for Isaac, he seems resentful: a defence mechanism, no doubt. He can't cope with Doris. Joan Bell is there: such a good steady soul,' she told Pharaoh: 'far better than a man in this kind of situation. I tried to get hold of Sally, but there's no reply from the number she gave Doris. The operator couldn't get an answer either. Joan said she'd keep trying. I'm so sorry for Sally.' Randolph said nothing and it was as if she read his mind. 'It's a dreadful thing to have happened,' she said, 'but we can't be sorry for Becky, not now. It's the ones who are left behind who are suffering. What's the position up there now?' She indicated the cliff.

'They've taken her away,' Randolph said. 'You couldn't manage a pot of tea, my dear?'

'What am I thinking of? You must be dying of thirst. I'll put the kettle on – and some sandwiches wouldn't come amiss, I'm sure.'

She bustled indoors and Randolph started to stroll aimlessly about the garden. Pharaoh made for a seat and collapsed, closing his eyes. After a while he opened them to see Randolph staring at a clump of lupins. Beyond him the crag rose above the tree canopy: inanimate and apparently deserted except for the falcons. A half-grown white cat leapt on the seat, purring loudly. It had one blue eye and one amber. It interpreted his interest as affection and, rearing on Pharaoh's thighs, placed delicate paws on his chest and butted his chin. The huge eyes glowed at him. Pharaoh sighed.

Mabel emerged from the cottage with a tray of tea and sand-wiches. She smiled at the cat and Randolph hurried over to place a table in position.

Pharaoh was ravenous, but he was always hungry after rescues; presumably the ebb of adrenalin left an empty gut behind. Nothing was said until they'd taken the edge off their hunger when Mabel, stiff with impatience, said pointedly, 'They were Laura's binocu-lars, weren't they?'

'Yes.' Randolph looked at Pharaoh. 'What connection?' he asked.

'He was reminding me that Laura said all along that Roy stole them,' Pharaoh explained to Mabel. 'But there's a connection between Roy and Becky, so he could have passed them on to her.'

'I'd thought of that,' Mabel said. 'Isaac's mystified as to what she was doing on top of Falcon. She had no interest in birds. Why else should she be using binoculars?'

'Oh, my God!' Randolph breathed. 'Is it possible that she was acting as a look-out for young Roy?'

They thought about it. After a few moments Mabel said, 'Not in daylight. Remember, she went missing after breakfast.'

'We don't know when she fell,' Pharaoh pointed out. 'The stomach contents may give us the answer, although not if she fell a long time after breakfast.'

'Depends whether she had something else to eat after breakfast,' Randolph said. 'Suppose she fell last night, in the dark? But look: Roy can't go after those eggs since we cut down the trees. Anyway, the birds are still at the nest, I looked; so the eggs are safe. And Becky wouldn't be using binoculars in the dark; those aren't night glasses. What d'you say, Pharaoh?'

'I'd like to go up there.'

'Good idea. What about the police?'

'We haven't been told not to, and it's your land.'

'Did Buckle give you any clue as to what he's thinking?' Mabel asked. 'Did you tell him they were Laura's binoculars?'

'I didn't,' Randolph admitted. 'When they're identified I shall say I wasn't certain. As for his theory concerning why she fell, he didn't say, and I didn't ask.'

'When he was alone with me,' Pharaoh said, 'he suggested she could have been dead before she fell.'

'Or was pushed,' Randolph murmured, and they all looked at the crag.

'Ah!' Mabel exclaimed as a peregrine shot out from the vicinity of the nest. 'They don't seem to have been bothered by all the activity. So what's the next move, Randolph?'

'There's the autopsy, and the police are going to need statements, at least from you two. I suggest we go up to the top before it occurs to Buckle to restrict our movements.'

'I shall stay here and plant out my leeks.' Mabel got to her feet. 'Incidentally, what happened to the binoculars? Have you seen Laura?'

'I haven't been home yet. In any case she intends being away all day: some business in Carlisle.' He smiled vaguely. 'I suppose one should tell Buckle that they might be hers, otherwise it looks as if I'm trying to conceal the fact. What *could* Becky have been doing up there?' He stood up. 'Let's go and see if we can discover anything.'

There were no vehicles on top of Falcon Crag, there had been none at Grey Crag either. People were probably dubious about the weather. The afternoon had grown increasingly humid and when they left the car they found that it wasn't only the trees making it dark but a cloud that had obscured the sun. Cumulus was piling ominously in the west.

'Going to have a storm,' Randolph remarked. 'Good. We can do with some rain.'

They crossed the road to the cleared space where all that remained of the larches was five stumps. Randolph looked around and then at Pharaoh.

'I don't know what I expected to find. How about you?'

'If Roy roped down from this spot then I take it the nest is directly below.'

'That's right. We won't go any nearer the edge; I don't want to worry the birds. You see the break: that's the top of their gully; it fines down to a crack at this point.'

Pharaoh moved away, Randolph following, both of them studying the ground, which was bedrock. The larches had been rooted in fissures.

'It's more broken to this side.' Pharaoh had gone out to the edge. 'It looks like a way down.'

'There can't be; it's still hundreds of feet to the bottom. A climber might rope down—'

'Someone's been here.'

'I can't see anything.'

'This rock's polished. See: smooth and shiny, the lichen's been worn off. Rubber soles did that.'

'Oh come, my dear chap! Well, you're the expert.' Randolph was grudging.

'What about that?' Pharaoh pointed. In a pocket of dust there was part of a footprint with a zigzag design. 'You'd expect that,' he said. 'Becky's soles were the same pattern, and I reckon she fell from around here.'

Below them was a riot of ferns and honeysuckle where a gully fanned out at its top to form a small hanging amphitheatre.

'She didn't fall on that lot,' Randolph said. 'It would be crushed flat. Now where are you going?'

'Just looking.'

109

He was clambering down broken rock, pausing here and there. After about ten feet and still above the vegetation a ragged ledge went off to the right with a kind of natural parapet that afforded some protection. As he moved along this traverse a clap of thunder rolled round the fells and Randolph glanced uneasily at the sky.

The ledge ran into a platform at a corner and at that point the parapet ended. 'This is a bit exposed,' Pharaoh called, peering over the edge. 'Nasty.' He turned and froze.

'What is it?' Randolph shouted.

Pharaoh stepped out of sight.

Randolph stared and swallowed then, his eyes widening at the thought of the hundreds of feet of air below, he started down the rock.

'Ah!' Pharaoh reappeared at the corner. 'I thought you'd follow. Come and look at this.'

At the corner was a shallow cave. Hugging the rock, keeping well back from the unprotected edge, Randolph crabbed sideways and squatted, looking round the confined space, then at the floor which was of bare rock. Baffled, his eyes returned to Pharaoh who was intent on the view.

'Your house is obvious,' he said. 'And the Boathouse, and Skelgill. There's Mabel planting out her leeks.' He glanced to the left. 'Not a vantage point for the peregrines though. But well hidden from any adults.'

'You think they met here: Roy and Becky?'

'I don't know, but I do know that anyone going over this edge would end where she did; a falling body would be funnelled into the fall-line of that gully.'

'There's nothing to show that anyone was ever here. This rock's as clean as a whistle.'

'I thought that myself: just as if someone had cleaned it.'

Chapter Eleven

Armstrong came round the corner of his cottage carrying a large carton. 'Hope we're not intruding,' Randolph said.

Armstrong hesitated. 'Of course not.' He put the box in his car and lowered the hatchback. 'Just finished here anyway.' He dusted his hands. 'Old jars for recycling,' he explained, nodding to Pharaoh.

'We *are* interrupting,' Randolph stated, not apologizing. 'But this isn't a social visit. May we come in?'

The man turned without a word and they followed him. Armstrong hadn't looked particularly fit the first time Pharaoh met him but today he looked positively seedy. Randolph had noticed it too.

'Are you feeling all right?' he asked.

'I'm fine.' He ushered them into the parlour where a window looked out on the tarn. 'Take a seat. Coffee, or something stronger?'

'We could all do with a Scotch,' Randolph said.

There were bottles on a cupboard in one corner. While Armstrong found glasses Pharaoh glanced round the room but the focus of attention was on the table. Like Mabel, Armstrong used a typewriter: a small portable; he didn't even run to an electric model, let alone a word processor. This chap was supposed to be an author – and there was the proof: stacks of paper either side of the typewriter, carbons, a pottery jar with pens and pencils. There were books with paper markers: guide books (to the Caribbean), a thesaurus, a dictionary.

Randolph asked for water with his whisky and as soon as Armstrong left the room Pharaoh rose and turned the top sheet of each pile of paper. That on the left was blank. The reverse side of the top page on the right was numbered 147 and the first lines read:

"got eyes like chocolate-brown velvet. They say his great-grandmother was a slave. Who cares? He's the dishiest thing in Martinique.'

'I'm not looking for a husband, Tracey.'

Sharon pouted. 'I didn't say—' "

'Don't look at that,' came Armstrong's voice: not angry, rather resigned. It threw Pharaoh into confusion and he blundered back to his chair.

'You've got to admit,' Randolph began easily, pouring oil, 'that everyone's been dying to discover what you write. You've been so secretive.'

'We had to assume it was pornography,' Pharaoh said. 'I'm sorry. It was unpardonable to pry.'

Armstrong sat down. He glanced at the typescript and shrugged. 'Nothing criminal about it, but you owe me now. Just keep quiet about it, will you? Even in the family?' He addressed Randolph who nodded acquiescence although he didn't know what Pharaoh had seen. Armstrong's lips stretched but there was no amusement in his eyes. 'It's more than my life's worth – well, my livelihood – if my publishers find out. Even they only know my pen name – and I'm not telling you what that is.'

'Well—' Randolph looked meaningly at the typescript. 'Will it hurt to tell us what it's about?'

'It's romantic fiction.'

They were surprised, but more because it was such an anti-climax than at the nature of it. 'I don't see—' Randolph began, then, noting the other's frown, 'It's your business, my dear chap. We'll keep quiet, eh, Pharaoh?' He took a gulp of his whisky.

'You suggested this wasn't a social visit,' Armstrong said.

'The police haven't been here?' Pharaoh asked.

'Why should they?' He looked amazed.

'A girl's been found dead,' Randolph told him. 'At the foot of Falcon Crag as a matter of fact; she'd fallen from the top. You ought to be told because the police will be coming to see you.'

Pharaoh watched the man's face. He saw no horror, only astonishment. 'Was she climbing?' he asked.

'Oh, no, this child— We don't know what she was doing.'

'Child?' Now he was horrified.

'She was twelve,' Pharaoh said. 'Becky Rudd. Did you know her?'

'Of course not; I don't know anybody. But another kid was here earlier, looking for her.'

'A boy,' Randolph stated heavily.

'No. A small girl: a stocky kid, very sure of herself, on a bike.'

'Claire,' Pharaoh said. 'Why did she come here?'

'She said you were searching everywhere.'

'I don't like that,' Randolph told Pharaoh. 'Claire should stay at home. It's not safe to be out.' He saw Armstrong's expression. 'There's a possibility of foul play.'

'You don't mean— Is that why you warned me about the police?' Armstrong was flabbergasted. 'Was it a sexual attack?'

'They're doing the autopsy now,' Pharaoh said. 'We'll know more this evening, that is, if the police see fit to tell us.'

'I can get word unofficially.' Randolph checked, startled. 'You don't mean they wouldn't tell *me*?'

'If it was foul play we'd all be under suspicion,' Pharaoh said.

There was a strong and spicy smell of meat in Marlene's kitchen. Laura sniffed ostentatiously. 'You're having venison for supper.'

'Right first time,' Marlene said brightly. 'The last of a Christmas present. How about a beer?'

'No thanks, I'm not staying.' But Laura pulled out a chair and sat down. 'Did you hear about Becky?'

'God, yes.' Marlene was stricken. 'I can't believe it.' She sat opposite Laura and glanced towards the passage. She leaned forward. 'She's very subdued,' she whispered. 'She's up in her room; she should come down, not stay up there moping.'

'Did you know Becky was holding my binoculars when she fell?'

'Those were yours?' Her eyes caught a movement on the stairs and she raised her voice. 'Come on down, sweetie; Laura's here – and supper will soon be ready.'

Claire crept down the stairs and stood in the doorway, looking wary and sullen.

'Hi.' Laura was casual. The child sketched a shrug by way of greeting.

Marlene's lips tightened. 'Like a Coke?' she asked, on too high a note.

Without a word Claire went to the fridge. Marlene raised her eyebrows at Laura who asked, 'How did Becky come to have my binoculars, Claire?'

The child turned, lifting the tab on a can. She kicked the fridge

113

door to close it. 'You should ask her gran,' she said. 'Or maybe not.'

'I can't ask her gran at this time,' Laura protested. 'Or any other time, come to that. And why "maybe not"?'

The girl looked at her mother. Marlene said angrily, 'So why ask Claire? How would she know?'

'They were friends,' Laura said. 'She probably knew Becky better than anyone.'

Claire pursed her mouth and said nothing. Marlene continued defiantly, 'She wasn't Becky's keeper. I'm sure she has absolutely no idea how your binoculars came to be in Becky's possession, have you, love?'

Claire started to fidget under the combined scrutiny. 'Everyone thought Roy stole 'em,' she muttered.

'That's what you told me,' Marlene reminded her.

'Had to be him.' Claire glanced at Laura. 'He's a thief; everyone knows. He took the hawks' eggs and broke into Miss Cooper's place.'

'I'm not arguing.' Laura was impatient. 'But how did *Becky* come to have my glasses?'

'He gave them to her, of course!' Claire's tone implied that all grown-ups were thick.

'They did know each other, Laura,' Marlene pointed out.

'Well, I suppose it's obvious,' Laura said. 'I didn't realize they knew each other that well.'

Claire blinked, apparently trying to decipher her meaning. Marlene said comfortably, 'Easy come, easy go. There doesn't have to be a close relationship between children for them to give things away, particularly when they're not yours to give away in the first place.'

'How right you are.'

Laura stood up and Marlene accompanied her to the door. 'I didn't mean to be rude,' she said quietly, 'but I did feel you were – you know – badgering her a bit? She's only eleven. It was a ghastly thing to happen—' She glanced over her shoulder as Claire slipped upstairs, and shook her head in exasperation.

'I'll leave my car here,' Laura said. 'I have to go to Warthwaite.'

'That's right, you go and interrogate that yob.' Marlene was vicious. 'If anyone's the bad apple in this dale it's Roy Hartley but then, like Claire says, that never was a secret, was it?'

*

114

Laura caught the Hartleys in the middle of supper, coming so silently to the back door that Roy had no chance to slip away. She wondered if he'd considered escape but, observing him help himself to another slice of bread, concluded that, after his first surprise at her appearance, he'd decided to brazen it out.

She declined the tea which Anne offered distractedly. 'This won't take long,' she said, addressing Hartley, not sitting down. 'Did you know that Becky was holding binoculars when she fell?'

Hartley's face rose so slowly from his food that it verged on the ridiculous, but no one smiled. He looked from Laura to his wife, then at his son. Roy continued eating. Anne was still.

'You come here to tell us that?' Hartley asked.

'Not only you,' Laura said pleasantly. 'Everyone. I've just come from Starfoot.'

Anne's eyes narrowed. 'And what did they have to say?'

'Claire couldn't explain it.'

'You think we can?' Hartley's voice rose.

'Roy might be able to.'

Roy put down his fork politely. 'I don't see how I can help you,' he said. 'I didn't know her that well.'

'At their age boys and girls don't mix,' Anne pointed out.

'They were my binoculars,' Laura said.

'Oh.' Hartley gaped. 'How did she come by 'em?'

'They were stolen from my car a few weeks ago.'

'Were they now?' Hartley's face started to redden. Anne watched him tensely. Roy was eating again. They all knew his father was struggling between fury and the fear of antagonizing his landlord. Fear won. 'They were stolen,' he growled. 'And they turns up with Becky. So she stole 'em.'

'Or someone else did and gave them to her.'

'Why—' he began, but was overridden by his wife: 'Why would anyone want to give Becky Rudd a pair of binoculars?'

'That's what I'm wondering,' Laura said.

'You think my boy's mixed up in this. He's got his own glasses, what would he want with—'

'Give over, Mam!' Roy stood up, a menacing figure with his black looks and the hair falling over his forehead. Powerful young lout, Laura thought. 'I didn't take your binoculars,' he told her. 'And I don't know how Becky come to have 'em. Maybe she did take 'em, did you think of that?' He grinned then. 'Or were you thinking I had summat to do with pushing her off the top? It's all

115

right, Mam' – as she gasped – 'I were nowhere near the crag, you know that. Of course,' he added thoughtfully, and then he stopped.

'Go on.' Laura was encouraging.

'Nothing. Just, of course you would put blame on me. Give a dog a bad name.'

That was true – but she was certain that wasn't what he'd been about to say. He could have been going to remind her that there were others in the dale: men, not boys. He knew how to shift responsibility.

At Burnbank Randolph called the pathologist, with whom he shot pheasants in his younger days. He replaced the telephone as Pharaoh came in from the yard. 'Result of the autopsy,' he said. 'One relief: there was no sexual assault. She was a virgin.'

'It doesn't mean it wasn't a sexual crime,' Pharaoh countered. 'She could have been resisting. There'd be no way of telling – and presumably there's no way of telling how she died: whether she fell or was pushed.'

Randolph nodded agreement. 'Or if she was dead beforehand. No bullet was found, nor a track, no pellets, and the injuries could be masking a stab wound. But she wasn't throttled or strangled; apparently there are indications, and they'd still show. I didn't ask what they were. It looks as if she was alive when she fell.'

'She could still have been pushed.'

'I gather the police thinking is that it was an accident. By the way, it appears that she died some time after breakfast, late morning perhaps. They got that from the stomach contents.'

'Doesn't it seem a little unethical,' Pharaoh asked, 'that your pal should be allowed to tell you so much?'

'Allowed? You mean, usually they don't want people to know how the police mind is working?'

'Not just people: suspects. This seems more like a deliberate leak; they want us to think they're treating it as an accident.'

'I've known the pathologist for decades.' But Randolph was doubtful now. He brightened at the sound of an engine. 'Here's Laura, I wonder if she discovered anything. She was here when I came home from Hollins so she knows we found Becky. She left again when I told her I recognized the binoculars. I think she went to Starfoot.'

Laura came in the kitchen, switching on the light. 'It's dark out there,' she said. 'We're going to have a storm.'

116

'It keeps trying,' Randolph said. 'Doesn't come to much. Did you find out anything?'

They were surprised when she grinned. 'Marlene's stewing venison; she's tried to disguise it with spices but you can tell. She says it was a Christmas present. But you meant the binoculars, of course. Claire says Roy gave them to Becky. I went to Warthwaite and Roy denied it. Incidentally he also denies pushing Becky off the cliff but that was unsolicited; it hadn't crossed my mind until that moment that she might have been pushed, let alone that he was responsible. Anne was climbing the wall; you can be sure she'll give him an alibi whatever happened.'

'It was to be expected,' Randolph said. 'I mean, she'll alibi his movements no matter what he gets up to.'

Laura took off her jacket, put on a butcher's apron and opened the fridge.

'We got the results of the autopsy,' Randolph went on, and told her about them while she started to prepare a meal.

A bantam rooster advanced to the doorway and Trudy made her dashing charge along the passage. There was a flash of lightning and big dark spots appeared on the step. Laura glanced out of the window then went back to dicing lamb. 'But if it was an accident,' she said, 'what was she doing on Falcon Crag? And what made her go so near the edge?'

'You were in and out so quickly at tea time,' Randolph said, 'you didn't hear the rest of the news. We must call Buckle first thing in the morning,' he told Pharaoh, and went on to tell Laura about the cave and their visit to Hollins. 'We discovered Armstrong's secret!' he said, smiling.

She was dribbling oil into a saucepan and there was a sudden golden surge. 'Shit!' she exclaimed, and rummaged in a drawer. She found a funnel and poured surplus oil back in the can. '*Armstrong* has a secret?' she asked.

'He writes romantic novels under an assumed name. Would you believe it?'

'Why does he do that? I mean, why the secret?'

Pharaoh said, 'Probably women writers sell better. I don't know. Could it be that he also writes serious stuff which doesn't sell, or he means to one day . . . but if it were known that he wrote romances it would damage his image' – he was thinking it through – 'also this women's magazine type of thing is a way of buying time.'

'This is what he told you.'

'Oh, no,' Randolph butted in. 'The manuscript was there. Pharaoh got a look at it – when Armstrong was out of the room.'

'Only a bit of it,' Pharaoh protested. 'It was enough though: about a dishy number with eyes like velvet chocolate whose great-grandmother was a slave. Reminds me of something.'

'Pornography,' Randolph said, and chuckled.

'What's his pen name?' Laura asked. 'I must read this.'

'He wouldn't tell us.'

She was measuring spices into the pan on the stove. 'What's this?' Randolph craned his neck, intrigued.

'A goulash. Just a little spice: not enough to bother you nor to kill the lamb – like Marlene's venison. That's going to be like old boots, it can't have hung more than three days. In May!'

'It would be pretty cool in Mason's cellar,' Randolph said thoughtfully. 'I think I'll pay him a visit tomorrow.'

'It's not our house,' she reminded him. 'What excuse will you have for asking to see his cellar? There's no point anyway. If there was any deer meat in it there won't be any now, you can be sure of that.'

Lightning flashed and the bulb flickered. They waited for the thunder. After a few moments there was a muffled crash and a long roll. Trudy trotted in and stood up with her forepaws on Randolph's thighs. He fondled her ears.

'Funny thing,' he mused. 'We go for years without anything much happening and then we have an outbreak of crime: petty theft, break-ins, poaching, and now – this.'

'Dad, you don't know that Becky's wasn't an accident.'

'Can you explain what she was doing up there? And then there's that cave.'

There was no answer. He was frowning and Trudy, unable to hold his attention, dropped back to the floor and sniffed round the stove for crumbs. Laura nudged her out of the way. Pharaoh wondered who, if it hadn't been Roy, might have been meeting Becky on top of Falcon Crag.

He was still wondering when he reached the Boathouse and went out to his garden. Night had come early with a low cloud ceiling above the dale and the thunder still growling in distant ranges: the Pennines, High Street, beyond Scafell. Scarcely any rain had fallen and the air was stagnant. The lake was invisible except where lights on the far shore were duplicated in a surface like oil. There was a soft splash at the mouth of the inlet and he felt the hairs rise on the back of his neck.

He sat on the veranda without a light, thinking that the air should be less oppressive out here than indoors but the difference was minimal. Lightning flashed across the water, throwing trees into quick relief: black on silver, silver on black; and the thunder crashed some ten seconds later. The air was leaden, and gathering weight.

The storm came quickly, the intervals between flash and crash decreasing. Suddenly the trees joined the tumult, bowing before a charge of wind. The next flash showed petals driving like snow across the garden. Twigs rattled on the roof of the veranda, a branch cracked like a shot. The gust passed and, across the woodland canopy he heard the rain approaching with a soft soughing like the wind. It struck and the world turned liquid. The veranda filled with spray.

He went inside and closed the windows and stood at the open door listening to the rain and thinking how much he had changed: to be able to enjoy it. Five years ago rain was hell; rock turned slimy and dangerous, ropes became sodden, clothes were a clammy burden. He had hated rain. And lightning, that most dangerous of hazards: worse than avalanches or stone-falls, worse than blizzards. Now he wandered to his kitchen window as the storm passed and regretted that he'd been on the veranda when it was at its height. He'd missed seeing the crags lit by lightning. He opened the window and the residual sounds of the storm invaded the kitchen. The rain was easing, had probably stopped, but it was impossible to tell because the trees were shedding water and the gutters were flooded. Something dripped loudly on metal. The sounds continued long after he'd gone to bed.

He had opened all the windows again in order to bring the fresh green smell of the woods into his house. The last thing he heard before he slept was the tap of water on the veranda roof which receded and advanced with his consciousness, to merge with the tapping of a hammer as his second man retrieved a piton on a Dolomite wall.

Chapter Twelve

'Storm brought that old elm down back o' quarry,' Hartley announced, coming into the kitchen for his breakfast. 'Have to get Roy to give me a hand, get fence back afore cows is into woods. Isn't he down yet?'

'Give him a shout,' Anne said, breaking eggs in the pan. 'Haven't heard him go in bathroom.'

Hartley tramped to the inner door and shouted, then again. He started forward. 'Take your boots off!' Anne cried. He was plastered with mud to his knees. 'Wait!' She pulled the pan to the side of the stove.

She didn't shout as she hurried up the stairs. Behind her Hartley went to the sink. He was drying his hands when she came back. He stared at her face.

'His bed's not been slept in.' It was almost a whisper.

'Young bugger! Out all night. I'll speak to un.' But the words were only a formula. He sat down heavily.

'He went to town,' she said. 'I told you. He didn't say who it was rang. Who could it have been?'

'Any one of his mates. What's the last name of that Neil? Try him.'

'They're not real close—'

'We got to do summat, woman. Out all night—'

'You're going to need a rope,' Pharaoh said, and frowned, remembering the last time he'd put Buckle on a rope.

'No, we won't,' Buckle said. 'Leastways not your rope. We've got our own experts today.'

The police had found him inspecting his property for storm damage. He hadn't been sure that they would come in response to Randolph's telephone call, he wasn't sure himself that the cave on Falcon Crag had any significance in Becky's death. It was obvious she had been on top so did it matter exactly where she'd fallen from? Only if she was pushed.

'But you think it was an accident,' he said now.

'Do we?' Buckle turned to Fleming who blinked owlishly.

'So Mr Steel was given to understand last night,' Pharaoh said, feeling silly.

'But I didn't speak to him last night,' Buckle said in astonishment, over-reacting, then seriously, watching Pharaoh: 'And that was last night. Since then we've had this call from Mr Steel saying there's a cave on top where someone's removed all traces of occupation. He says you reached the cave first.'

Pharaoh suppressed a sigh. 'He didn't need to report it.'

'You'd have preferred it if he hadn't?'

'I didn't have to call Steel along to the cave and show it to him. I could have climbed back and not mentioned it. No one would have been any the wiser.'

'We'll go and see, shall we?' Buckle beamed and his tone was sprightly.

You sod, Pharaoh thought, a good thing you're not going to be on my rope.

He locked up and went out to his van. A second police car was parked in his drive. The occupants weren't introduced and he assumed these were the 'experts'. He hoped they were competent. He was developing a jaundiced view of the police which, he supposed wryly, was to be expected if there was a possibility of murder, if he was a suspect, however ridiculous that was. He climbed in his van and led the way up the drive, crashing through the puddles.

It was a glorious morning, everything sparkling fresh in the sunshine and, although the vegetation was still soaking wet, the rock should be drying rapidly, which was a good thing considering the exposed nature of that platform outside the cave.

Once on the road he remembered the peregrines and wondered if he could prevail on Buckle to keep his men quiet. He was resentful that Randolph should have left this task to him but he needn't have worried; when he arrived at the top of the crag both Randolph and Mabel were waiting for him. The police cars drew up and Buckle approached Randolph, obviously annoyed.

'This isn't necessary, sir; Mr Pharaoh can show us the cave.'

'We shan't intrude.' Randolph was cool. 'Miss Cooper and I are here to see that the peregrines aren't disturbed. The cave is close to the top so there won't be any need for you to shout. Try not to kick any stones down.'

Buckle stared. 'Why should I do that?'

Randolph looked past him. Mabel said: 'Inadvertently, of course. We hope the female will stay on the nest; we don't want the eggs exposed for long even if it is a nice morning.'

Buckle said tightly: 'A child was killed here, ma'am.'

'We're not interfering with your job.' Mabel was not unfriendly. 'We're merely asking that you go about it quietly.'

Pharaoh, with only part of his attention on this exchange, was quartering the ground looking for the imprint of Becky's shoe but the rain had removed all traces. He ranged wider, as far as the stumps of the felled larches. Randolph watched him uneasily while Mabel lectured the police on the importance of conservation and the climbers uncoiled the rope and waited to see where it would be needed.

Pharaoh's eye was caught by something just as Buckle said, 'So, if you're ready?' He went across to show them the route down to the cave. Mabel and Randolph moved to where he'd been standing. 'What was he interested in?' Randolph murmured. 'I can't see any prints, can you?' She shook her head.

The climbers and Pharaoh went down to the cave unroped. Buckle watched their progress from the top, having been warned not to go near the edge. When his men returned, confirming that there was indeed a kind of cave, he went down himself: roped and safeguarded by his own people.

The going was easy until the parapet came to an end and he looked over the exposed corner. He shrank back against the wall, his mouth dry. It took a moment for him to recover and concentrate on the cave.

He returned to the top and regarded Pharaoh balefully. 'You saw young Hartley here: firing at Miss Cooper.'

'No, he was on Grey Buttress.' Pharaoh pointed to the other cliff, half a mile to the north, Skelgill brilliant in sunshine at its foot.

Buckle looked then glanced away to the lake and the Boathouse. 'You could see he was wearing a balaclava from your place?'

'Through the binoculars. I'd been watching the peregrines.'

'Ah. Those – birds. And Becky was holding binoculars when she died. And she could have fallen from that cave.' He turned to Fleming. 'You can see everything from here.'

122

'The Boathouse,' Fleming said. 'The keeper's cottage, Miss Cooper's, the Steels' big house, Roy's—'

'Not Roy's,' Pharaoh cut in. 'The cave looks west and north. The corner cuts off everything to the south. The view from there is more restricted than what we can see from here.'

'Oh, yes.' But Buckle had noticed that himself. 'All the same, Roy was here,' he pointed out. 'Once at the very least, when he stole the eggs.'

Pharaoh glanced at him uncertainly but Buckle was moving back from the edge, followed by his men. Randolph and Mabel came across to join them at the cars.

'I hope we haven't disturbed the birds.' Buckle was only faintly ironic.

'The male is on Grey Buttress waiting to come in.' Mabel was reproving. 'He'll have brought food for the female.'

'But we didn't make her leave the nest?'

'I hope she's still on it—'

'She was sitting snugly enough at seven thirty,' Pharaoh said. 'I looked to make sure she hadn't been washed out.'

They knew he was implying that if she had gone it was Buckle's fault. Mabel's lips were compressed. 'We'll go down to the Boathouse,' she said. 'We have a good view of the nest from there. We can see that everything's all right.'

'Don't give a damn, do they?' Buckle said as they drove away. 'A child's been killed and all they can think about is a pair of bloody birds.'

Fleming picked out the salient statement. 'You've got no evidence. Only the word of another child and that at third or fourth hand: what she told Laura and what Laura told her father.'

'We'll see her later on. Right now I need a word with young Hartley before he learns we were in the cave, if he doesn't know it already. And if he's disappeared again we'll know what to think. We're not going to find any evidence on top. If he did push her we'll be far more likely to find something down below.'

'At his place?'

'We need more than we've got at the moment to apply for a warrant. It's a big jump to murder from frightening old women with an air rifle.'

'There's a lot of thieving that kind of bridges the gap.'

'Eggs – and no proof even of that: just what Steel says, and he's biased. As for the rest: Laura's binoculars, Mabel's wallet –

even less proof. The Lakes are full of thieves this time of year. How many cars are broken into every week? Why, only a couple of nights since there was one right here.'

'Climbers. Climbers are always stealing equipment. It's valuable stuff; that haul on Tuesday night was worth five hundred quid.'

'As much as that? You're kidding.'

'No, he took the rucksack as well. That cost an arm and a leg.'

'If it's young Roy he's moving into the big time, comparatively speaking. It's still a big jump to murder. It'll be interesting to see his face when we turn up.'

At Warthwaite Hartley met them in the porch, staring as if he were in shock. He knows what we've come for, Fleming thought; it *was* Roy who pushed her. Hartley said nothing but his eyes were asking questions he couldn't articulate.

'Something wrong, Mr Hartley?' Buckle asked genially.

'You – come – about my boy?' It was a whisper.

Fleming moved up, uncertain whether the man was going to attack his boss or collapse.

'Perhaps we might have a word with him,' Buckle suggested, in a tone that was really a demand. He was watching Hartley's eyes while Fleming watched his hands.

'Have a word with un? With Roy?' Hartley was shrill. 'You haven't got un, you didn't find un? He's all right?'

'Take it easy,' Fleming said, pushing past, taking his arm. 'We'll go and sit down, shall we? Where's the wife? Where's Mrs Hartley?' Raising his voice to let her know they were coming.

The kitchen was empty. Hartley sank into a chair, breathing hard. Fleming went looking for some kind of spirits. Hartley grabbed at a pack of cigarettes, missed, finally hit them and spilled them across the table. He got one in his mouth but his hands were shaking so much that Buckle took the matches and lit it for him. He inhaled deeply.

'Wife's gone to look for un,' he said at last. 'Been out all night – the boy has, not her. I thought you'd come to say there'd been an accident.'

'What about his friends?' Buckle asked.

'She phoned all as she could think of.'

'When did you see him last?'

'In the evening.'

'Exactly when, Mr Hartley?'

Either the insistence or the courtesy stiffened him and at that moment Fleming came back with a bottle of Scotch and a glass. Hartley tossed off a small measure and exhaled gustily.

'Supper time,' he said. 'No, that were when Miss Laura come. After supper then. I were outside but wife were in here. You'll have to ask her exactly when. Someone telephoned un.' He glared at Buckle, a suspicion crossing his mind, but it was too late to retract. Buckle thought that he was torn between resentment at the caller and betrayal of his son.

'Who called him?'

Hartley shook his head. 'He didn't say.'

'What did Miss Laura come about?'

He blinked in surprise. 'Her? Ah, I remember.' And then he remembered all of it and shut up.

'Yes?' Buckle was encouraging.

Hartley stared at the table. 'She accused lad of stealing her binoculars. Them as *she* were holding.'

Buckle glanced at Fleming. Randolph had told him this morning that he'd recognized the binoculars.

'Go on.'

'Well, he didna! 'Twas Becky Rudd had Laura's glasses, not my lad.'

'How did Miss Laura explain that?'

'Said he give 'em to Becky.'

'Did he?'

'My lad never saw them glasses! He's got his own, how many times do I have to tell folk as how he got his own glasses? He gets blamed for everything.'

'Where did your wife go?'

'Why, to Kelton of course.'

'Did you call the hospital?' It was brutal but necessary. Hartley said they hadn't called the hospital. Fleming went to the telephone.

'And you haven't contacted the police.' It was a statement, not a question.

Hartley poured himself more whisky and stared at the bottle while Fleming conducted a one-sided conversation on the telephone. Buckle was thirsty but he didn't want to break the tension by making tea, let alone asking Hartley to make it. He waited silently, looking out of the window at the green wall of the wood, his face expressionless as Fleming dialled again and spoke to the

125

police. The sergeant replaced the receiver and shook his head behind Hartley's back.

Buckle came to life. 'He hasn't had an accident,' he said. 'Isn't that reassuring?' He was demanding a response.

'Why should he? He rides well.' It was half grudging, half truculent. 'Wanna drink?' And that was defiant. Buckle declined for both of them. Fleming leaned against the dresser.

'He went on his bike,' Buckle said carelessly.

'O' course. He can't take a car on roads. He's only fourteen.'

'Who picked him up?'

Hartley blinked. 'How would I know? I thought he went all the way on his bike. It's not at the road-end or she'd have come back and told me.'

'So he rode to Kelton.'

'He *went* to Kelton. That's why she went.'

'Because the phone call came from Kelton. Who was it phoned?'

Hartley gaped, then turned angry. 'What're you trying to make me say? I told you, we don't know. If we'd known we'd have got in touch with t'chap first, not gone rushing into Kelton to try to find un. I got better things to do with my time than chasing after lad what stayed out all night . . .' He trailed off. He was shaking again. Buckle nodded to Fleming who slipped into a chair on the other side of the table. 'Why didn't you call the hospital, Mr Hartley?'

'You don't.' The voice was flat, like an automaton. 'Lads spend a night with their mates, forget to call home.' His gaze came back to the whisky bottle. 'Could even be drinking.' Something flickered at the back of his eyes. 'Glue,' he said, with feeling: 'or that cannabis. They get into bad company, go to parties, smoke that there drug. She's terrified he's done something as he shouldn't and he'll be caught. Better to tell you,' he muttered, glancing at Fleming. 'Don't let on I told you. She'll kill me.'

Fleming nodded carelessly. 'A rucksack was stolen on Tuesday night,' he said. 'From the Trust camp ground along the road. Five hundred quid's worth of equipment all told.'

Hartley swallowed. 'So?'

'And there was Miss Cooper's wallet and money from her purse, Miss Steel's binoculars found in a dead child's—'

'No, no!' It was a wild shout. He lunged to his feet, knocking over his chair. Buckle had been ready for it and was up before

126

him as Fleming came round the table. Hemmed in, backed against the dresser, Hartley continued to shout.

'It's got nowt to do with him! It's all a put-up job. He were never out at night; we know when he's out – *she* does. She locks doors. Bird-nesting is all. Lads allus go bird-nesting. *I* did. You did if you was country-born. He's just mischievious. You go an' look in his bedroom. There isn't nowt as shouldn't be there. I'm telling you. Go and look!'

'You're asking us to look in his room?' Buckle was gentle.

'I'll come with you! I'll show you. Come on!'

He blundered out of the kitchen, along the passage and up the stairs.

Roy's was a corner room with windows in two walls, that at the side being immediately above the roof of a shed. The room was large and spoke eloquently of two people; the neatly made bed showed a mother's hand, but the possessions were a boy's, and not particularly remarkable except that there were no posters. There was a cassette player and a pile of tapes on a chest of drawers along with some bird books (one called *The Peregrine Falcon*), a pair of binoculars, several large-scale maps, a denim cap and mirror sunglasses.

The furniture was old-fashioned: a huge wardrobe, a smaller chest of drawers beside the bed with a lamp and a travelling clock in a pigskin case, several ugly chairs with shiny padded seats and a dressing table which bore only a comb and several T-shirts neatly folded. All this the detectives considered thoughtfully while Hartley stood irresolute beside the bed, glowering, finally almost spitting at them: 'There! Satisfied? Where's the rucksack? Where's the wallet? Where's the binoculars? Them's his' – as their eyes went to the pair on the chest of drawers – 'we give 'em to un last birthday. Wife's got the receipt.'

'I see nothing out of line,' Buckle said dubiously, 'but how many hiding places are there?'

'What! Hiding places?' Hartley started pulling out drawers at random. He threw open the wardrobe, gesturing at the contents (an air rifle stood in one corner); he flicked aside rugs exposing the floorboards. The detectives watched with the interest of terriers at a rabbit hole.

'Well?' Hartley exclaimed.

'The bed?' Fleming suggested, smiling, making a joke of it.

'Bloody hell! He's hidden a rucksack under the bed? Is that what you're saying?'

He seized the candlewick spread and tossed it up on the bed. The floor was innocent even of dust.

'I suppose you want to look under the mattress,' Hartley cried. Buckle raised his eyebrows.

With a heave the man threw mattress and bedding off the springs, knocking the lamp to the floor, smashing the bulb. The mattress crashed back against the wardrobe's open doors.

They all stared at the wallet on the mesh base of the bed.

In the silence they heard the telephone start to ring.

'You'd better answer it,' Buckle said.

They trooped downstairs, Hartley lowering himself on the banister as if it were a life-line. In the kitchen he picked up the phone. He made some kind of exclamation and listened.

'Where?' It was a gasp and, after a few moments: 'They're here now – them detectives—'

'If that's Roy—' Buckle began, moving forward, but Hartley had dropped the phone on its cradle.

'She rung off,' he said. He looked terrified.

'She found Roy,' Buckle stated.

'She found his bike.'

'Where?'

'In car park in Botchergate. Chained to railings outside toilets.'

'What was that about the police?'

'She said she was going to 'em. I said as how you was here.'

The detectives went back upstairs and talked quietly in the bedroom, their hands in their pockets, careful not to touch anything.

'You stay here until Forensics arrive,' Buckle said. 'I'm going to see the wife. I don't think there'll be anything in that room connecting him with Becky; he wouldn't have dared bring her here, but you never know. We'll go over it with a tooth-comb. At least we've got something to hold him on now.'

'If it was a spur of the moment thing, a quick push during a quarrel, or her trying to get away from him, we may never find anything to nail him on.'

'He's only fourteen, he might confess – eventually.'

'When we find him,' Fleming said.

Chapter Thirteen

'That was a nasty business in your woods at the weekend,' said Wilf Wharton, the paunchy landlord of the Stag at High Row. He pulled a pint of bitter and passed it across the bar. 'Do the police have any leads?'

'They wouldn't tell me.' Randolph was morose, realizing that he was referring to the poaching, not to Becky.

'It were a bloody shame,' came a voice from one of two old men in a window seat. 'Wicked, that were. Them dogs'll kill anything as runs.'

'It couldn't have been anyone local,' Wharton said, wiping the bar. 'No one's got lurchers, have they, Aaron?'

'No one round 'ere's got lurchers.'

'Aye, no one round 'ere.'

'You sound like a bloody Greek chorus,' Randolph snapped. He had known Aaron Bell and old Pinfold all his life. Wharton, who had been in the dale only twenty-two years, was a foreigner from Keswick.

'You can't keep a dog without neighbours knowing,' Bell protested, as if he'd been challenged.

'Can't do nothing 'ere.' Pinfold leered. 'Nothing private. And what were that girl doing on top? Did police find owt?'

Old foxes, thought Randolph, and inquisitive as cats; they'd been leading up to Becky.

'They wanted to see where she fell,' he said.

No one looked surprised, only interested, but no one spoke either; they were waiting for him to elaborate. He had come here with the forlorn hope that he might learn something about the poachers – not their identity but some way in which he might guard against future depredations – and he found himself viewed as the repository of information concerning Becky's death. Well, it was to be expected.

'It's a mystery,' he confessed.

'Was she alone up there?' Wharton asked, and the old men sat like immobile shadow-figures against the light.

'No one has any idea,' Randolph said, and addressed Aaron, who was Joan Bell's father-in-law. 'Hasn't Doris said anything to Joan?'

'Not 'bout that,' old Bell said. 'Fact, Doris she keeps asking that same question. The girl never went nowhere on her own.'

'She weren't alone,' Pinfold muttered, shifting his position on the bench.

'We don't know that,' Wharton said, trying to keep the conversation smooth. 'Like Mr Steel says, it's a mystery.'

'Nothing mysterious 'bout young folk,' Pinfold growled. 'No harm neither, 'cept from stealing birds' eggs.' He threw a wary glance at Randolph, everyone knew he was touchy about them hawks. 'Boys will be boys,' he muttered.

A figure appeared in the doorway, black against the sunshine. 'Morning all,' Hugh Mason said, approaching the bar and digging in his pocket. 'Morning, Mr Steel.'

'Have that one with me.' Randolph was expressionless. He ordered drinks all round.

They lifted their glasses to him and drank, and no one referred to Becky nor to poaching. In fact, the remarkable feature of the conversation once Mason interrupted it, was the skill with which it was kept flowing without any reference to the presence of police in the dale.

After a quarter of an hour Mason sauntered outside followed by Randolph. They moved away from the open door and halted. Mason's cottage was directly opposite.

The village of High Row was little more than a hamlet; it had no church or post office, and no shop. It had a village hall, relic of palmy days when the quarries were operating, but otherwise there was only the Stag and a handful of cottages on a road which, a hundred yards above, ran into a track that would in its turn become a path to the open fell. At either end of the hamlet was a farm: that of Bell's son down the hill, Postlethwaite's place at "top end". The cottages were mostly detached, standing in their own gardens; several below Mason's were second homes with ceramic name-plates and ruched curtains. In contrast Mason's was uncompromising and shabby: brown curtains, whitewash dropping off in flakes, the garden a riot of dandelion heads and grass.

Beside the cottage was a shed, the van visible inside with its back doors open.

Randolph regarded the interior of the van. 'Having a clean-out?'

'No.' Mason considered. 'It's an idea, house could do with it; never been touched properly since me auntie died. You seen inside this place, Mr Steel?'

'I can't say I have.' A lie, he knew every cottage in the dale.

'It's a fine roomy house: worth a packet if I decided to sell to a townie. It's got a loft – could have a spare bedroom there with one of them plastic windows in the roof – and there's a cellar. Like to see over?' He took a step forward, his face inviting and ingenuous.

'A cellar?' Randolph didn't budge. 'That's unusual; you've only got to go down a few inches and you hit rock.'

'Ah, but this cellar musta been dug out before they built the house. Me folk were all quarrymen. Come and see for yourself.'

'Another time. I must go home now; got an appointment with the police.'

Mason nodded, his eyes understanding, even sympathetic. Randolph was very thoughtful as he drove home.

Pharaoh was watching the peregrines from the island, doing it in comfort and privacy (he thought), the boat hidden from the shore and himself in drab clothing, lounging on cushions. The male had just driven off a buzzard with a breathtaking display when Randolph hailed from the shore. Pharaoh sighed, collected his cushions and rowed home.

'They should be hatching at any time,' Randolph announced as he approached. 'Any sign?'

'How would I tell? The male's just chased a buzzard away, but the female sat tight.'

'Good. That's excellent – because I've just had some disturbing news. Fleming tells me that not only did young Roy take Mabel's wallet, but Tuesday night someone stole a rope and pitons from a car in the National Trust camp ground. If that was Roy . . .' Randolph turned and stared at the crag in consternation.

'Now that's funny.' Pharaoh knotted the painter and straightened. 'There were marks in a crack on top. Someone could have used a peg there – a piton.'

'If Roy did steal that rope he hasn't used it yet. The birds are quite safe? You did see both at the same time?'

'No doubt about it; I've been watching them on and off for an hour.'

'We'd do well to keep a watch on the nest though – but he's not going to try anything in the daylight. Is that what's happened: he's gone to ground, holed up, and he's waiting for nightfall? What went wrong last night then?'

'What are you talking about?'

'Sorry. Things have been moving. Roy's vanished and the police have been called off! It appears some suspect terrorists could have joined up with Irish travellers arriving for the horse fair at Appleby. Buckle and Fleming have gone over there. I was at Warthwaite when the patrol car came to pick Fleming up. Buckle was there earlier and he found Mabel's wallet under Roy's mattress. He went back to Kelton for the forensic people and got caught for this other job. Fleming too. They're off the case.'

'Why did he have to go back? Why didn't he send for the rest of the team?'

'The focus shifted. They found Roy's bike. What happened was that someone phoned Roy from Kelton last night and he rode there on his bike but he didn't come back. Anne went there looking for him this morning and found the bike chained to railings in Botchergate. Presumably Buckle went chasing after Roy and got nobbled for this other thing.'

'Terrorists being more important than Mabel's wallet. They're right, of course.'

'Oh, no doubt. Here's Isaac. I must go and call on the Garners but I don't like to—'

Isaac approached from the direction of the stepping stones.

'Good afternoon, Isaac.' Randolph was sombre. 'How's Doris?'

'Bearing up, Mr Steel.'

'Have you spoken to Sally yet?'

'Joan Bell spoke to someone at their house in Texas and left a message. Seems they're somewhere on a river boat, I can't call the place to mind. It's in the jungle and this chap's going to try and contact them so she can be told.'

'Bad for Sally,' Randolph said.

Pharaoh looked out across the lake, wincing at the recollection of how it felt to be told that the person you loved most had been killed. You could never go back to where you were before; you had to change direction and that took time. Poor Sally: honeymooning in the jungle with this horror waiting for her.

'—came to ask you about her bike, Mr Pharaoh,' Isaac was saying. 'Doris keeps asking.'

'I never thought,' Randolph said in surprise. 'Did you, Pharaoh? Becky took her bike. Where is it?'

Pharaoh seized on the diversion. 'Where did you look?' he asked, but Isaac hadn't searched for the bike at all; he'd gone into the woods to escape from his house and the women, not to look for Becky's bike. It held no significance for him.

'I didn't see it when we were on the top,' Randolph said. 'Tell you what: I have to go to Hollins and I'll bring the bike down when I come back. We'll take your truck, Pharaoh, a bike won't fit in the Volvo. Feel like a run to Hollins?'

'I was going to ask you to come with me anyway,' he said as they drove away from the Boathouse. 'If someone has been trying to get down to the peregrines, you can tell, can't you? I want you to show me.'

'There's no way of telling when it happened,' Pharaoh said. 'Although it must be since you felled the trees because no one's going to bother with a peg when he can put the rope round a tree trunk. But it needn't have anything to do with Roy; it could be climbers prospecting for a new route: abseiling down the top pitches to see if the line was feasible.'

'Why couldn't they see that from the bottom?'

'The lower pitches are covered with ivy. They're not going to waste energy tearing that off if the top isn't worth doing.' Pharaoh frowned. 'But they could study the rock from the shore.' He shook his head. 'No, I don't think it's climbers.'

They reached the top of the crag and parked. There were a few cars there today and the sound of people in the woods. There was no sign of a bicycle.

'We'd have seen it before – or you would,' Randolph said. 'It could well have been stolen.'

'Or taken away,' Pharaoh suggested.

'What's the difference—' Randolph began, but Pharaoh was crossing the road towards the top of the crag.

'These birds are too close to the road,' Randolph grumbled, catching up. 'The most likely hazard for them is some tripper throwing stones over the edge.'

'You can't guard against everything,' Pharaoh muttered, going straight to the crack which had claimed his attention this morning. He squatted, gasped, and sat down clumsily. Randolph remained standing.

'Leg acting up?'

'The joints are a bit stiff after the rain. I forget I'm not young any longer.' He traced the line of the crack with sensitive fingers. 'A peg has been here, definitely. Nothing else could make a mark like that.'

The grey crack, deep but no more than half a centimetre wide, had cream scratches on both sides.

Pharaoh stood up and stared at the lake. 'Impossible,' he said incredulously.

'What's that?'

'Nothing. Just, last night, before I dropped off to sleep . . . no, it was a dream. I dreamt I was climbing and someone was removing a peg, tapping it free with a hammer . . . but this didn't happen last night.' He gestured at the crack.

'How can you tell?'

'Because climbers wouldn't be out in that storm, and no one was after the eggs because the birds are safe on the nest. Of course, it could be that climbers came here, meaning to abseil to look at the top pitches and changed their minds. Then they'd have taken the peg out and left. That must be it.'

They walked away slowly. Pharaoh looked back once, puzzled despite what he'd said.

'Forget it,' Randolph chided. 'No harm's been done – but we'll keep a close eye on the nest all the same. Now I have to see Armstrong; I want to refresh my memory about the lay-out at Hollins. We're thinking of putting in a proper bathroom; there's only a small lavatory at the moment, and a makeshift shower.'

'How's the water supply?'

'Ah, another problem. We'll need to enlarge the reservoir and install new pipes, a septic tank and so on; going to be quite a job excavating the rock but worth it when it's done. Good investment.' He looked a trifle embarrassed.

More cars were parked at the start of Hollins' drive, one blocking the entrance. There was no one in it but the windows were open. They got out and looked inside, watched by two women sitting on the grass. 'It must be their car,' Pharaoh muttered as the women conferred.

Randolph walked across. 'If it's your car,' he said politely, 'I wonder if you'd mind moving it.'

The older woman was a bottle blonde who had been out too long in the sun, and she did mind. 'It's doing no harm where it is. You got plenty of room to park.'

'People live here,' Randolph informed her. 'The drive is blocked.'

'No one lives here,' the woman said. 'We was along at the house. It's empty.'

Her younger companion was growing alarmed. She nudged the other and whispered something. The first one gaped. 'You don't live there!' she stated indignantly.

'We own it,' Randolph said mildly.

'Well, I'm sorry' – furiously – 'but there's nothing we can do. We haven't got the keys.'

Frantic now, the younger woman looked towards the woods and brightened. 'Here they come now—'

'How was we to know—' the other began.

'What *have* they found?' her companion exclaimed, fighting to create a diversion but stopping suddenly as if anticipating further friction.

A boy on a bicycle came speeding towards them, shrieking with glee and followed by two other children and a man. The first boy skidded to a halt.

'Look what we found, Mum! Thrown out as junk, chucked in the blackberries. There's nothing wrong with it! It's mine, I saw it first!'

'It's a girl's bike, Gary.'

'I know but I can sell—'

Randolph advanced, followed by Pharaoh. The other children came up shouting, laying claim to the bike. The man arrived and was taken aside by the younger woman.

'Where did you find this?' Randolph asked the boy, more sternly than he'd intended.

'Dad!' It was a wail.

'What business is it of yours?' the man began, blustering.

Pharaoh ignored him. 'Do you recognize it?' he asked.

'Could be,' Randolph said. 'Girl's bike. I'm not sure.' He addressed the man. 'I want you to show me exactly where you found this—'

Pharaoh saw panic flare in the man's face. He said quietly, 'If we could have a word—' leading the fellow away from his family.

He took them to the small quarry which, said Randolph, was where the stone was taken from to build Hollins. Unused for

135

centuries, to a layman the miniature face looked natural, but the rock was too sharp and the spoil heap still showed as a heap under thin grass. Between the spoil and the face was a low forest of brambles, beaten down at one side where the man had forced his way in to recover the bicycle.

'We saw it from the top,' he said. 'Someone dropped it over the edge because I had a hell of a job getting to it. I'd have let it lay if I'd known it was stolen.' No way was he going to hang on to the machine after Pharaoh had voiced the dread phrase: "receiving stolen property".

Once the drive was clear they continued to Hollins. 'What d'you make of it?' Randolph asked, glancing over the back of his seat at the bike as if it might tell him something.

'One thing's for sure: Becky didn't throw it off the top. Assuming that it *is* her bike.'

'But this is appalling! If someone else put it there, *hid* it . . .' He was too horrified to continue, and Pharaoh wouldn't help him. They completed the short drive in silence.

There was no car at Hollins and the door was locked. All the windows were closed. Randolph peered into the parlour, shading the glass with his hand. 'Nothing on the table,' he said. 'Typewriter, manuscript, books: all gone.'

The other room at the front held little more than a table, four chairs and a cupboard. Nowhere could they see anything personal, anything that might belong to Armstrong.

At the rear the kitchen window was still draped with the tacky nylon net.

'It looks as if he's done a flit,' Randolph said thoughtfully. 'He doesn't owe me anything; he's paid up to the end of the month, but it would have been good manners to give me some notice. However, we could be misjudging him; perhaps he's just gone away on a visit, to see his publisher in London for instance. Why not? The fellow's a bit of a recluse but he was never rude. You're quiet. What are you thinking, eh?'

'That bike,' Pharaoh said.

'Hell!' Randolph was off on the other tack. 'Now I have to take it to the Garners and ask them if it's Becky's. I don't fancy that one bit, but someone has to do it.'

They heard iron strike stone and looked up to see Laura coming down the fell path on her black mare. 'Dad, you're snooping,' she called as she came up to the garden gate.

136

'Armstrong seems to have gone away,' he told her.

'Why not?' She was amazed. 'He doesn't have to report to you.'

'Not if he's coming back, but there's none of his stuff inside.'

She slid down and fastened the halter to the gatepost. She peered through the ground-floor windows then stood back, and looked up. 'He's taken his possessions upstairs,' she said, 'where they can't be seen by nosy people peering through windows. A word processor's valuable.'

'He uses a typewriter,' Pharaoh said. 'A cheap portable.'

'A *typewriter*! I don't believe it.'

'I told you,' Randolph said. 'We were inside. I think he's probably taken his manuscript to London.'

'Does he owe you anything?'

'No, he pays in advance.'

'You're all right then.' She went back to the mare and untied her.

'Becky's bike's been found,' Randolph called.

'Really?' This did interest her. 'Where?'

He told her. 'We've got it here: in Pharaoh's van.'

'That's weird.' She led the mare round the back and they joined her at the Transit. She stared at the bike. 'If it's not hers, why would anyone throw a perfectly good bike in a quarry?'

'Why would they if it is hers?' Randolph asked.

'Yes, why should – what?' Her jaw dropped. 'You're not suggesting that her – that she really was pushed?'

'It was a possibility all along.' Randolph was phlegmatic.

'If it is her bike, this clinches matters,' Pharaoh pointed out.

'It's a long way from the crag,' Randolph mused.

'Is it?' Pharaoh was dubious.

'No, not when you think about it. A quarter of a mile? What I meant was it's a long way to push a bike, because you certainly can't ride through the trees from the crag to the quarry: too rough.'

'He'd ride along the road and then go into the woods at the nearest point,' Laura said. 'That old quarry is only a hundred yards from the road.'

'Two hundred,' Randolph corrected.

'No matter. It's close enough – if you've got the incentive.'

'Roy's done a flit too,' Randolph said.

No one spoke for a moment then, haltingly, he elaborated. Laura wasn't at all surprised that Mabel's wallet should have been concealed in Roy's bedroom, she was concerned with the basic question.

'Why would he kill Becky?' she asked. 'They're only kids. Surely passions don't run that high, do they?' She looked at Pharaoh, then away; people were embarrassed when they recalled that he'd had a young daughter. 'I don't remember raging passion at twelve years old,' she added quickly.

'Roy is fourteen,' Pharaoh said. 'There could have been a struggle and they were too close to the edge: horse-play perhaps. And then he panicked. Poor kid, you almost feel sorry for him.'

'But if he hid the bike?' Randolph demurred.

'It could still be panic. And now he's scarpered. It makes sense. His prints will be on the bike. Well, would have been.' The men exchanged guilty looks, remembering how many people had handled it, including themselves.

Laura rode gently through the woods keeping close to the road but avoiding the hard surface. She was thinking about Pharaoh: a guy who would repay further investigation, she thought, surprised at herself, wondering why she should find him so fascinating when her usual reaction to an attractive man was masculine: a flare of desire and a brief affair, even a one-night stand. Yet she didn't *desire* Pharaoh; she wanted to know him better, to discover how he could appear hard and yet be so soft he could feel sorry for a yob. An affinity? There but for the grace of God? If the guy had criminal tendencies, he was exciting and, more to the point, he was dangerous.

His van was in the yard at Burnbank. The men were in the kitchen drinking tea and conducting a post-mortem on the day's events.

'Still no sign of Roy,' Randolph told her as she filled a mug. 'The police told me when I reported finding the bike. That *is* Becky's; Isaac identified it. Roy's in London now, you may be sure of it.'

'I suppose so.' Pharaoh was thoughtful and Laura pricked up her ears.

'You don't think he's hanging around?' she asked.

He frowned, but not at her. 'He's got an idea about the crag,' Randolph explained. 'He feels he ought to go and look underneath it again.'

'Again?'

138

'The first time was when Becky's body was found,' Pharaoh reminded her.

'I see. You think you missed something.'

He hesitated. 'It's possible.'

'No one's stopping you,' Randolph said. 'I must talk to Buckle, if I can find him. His superintendent otherwise – and goodness knows how long it'll take to find anyone. Better leave the bike here; you don't want to be carrying that around; it's vital evidence.'

'You're going up there now?' Laura asked. 'I'll come with you. Two pairs of eyes are better than one.'

In the woods she noticed that Pharaoh's limp had become pronounced but she didn't remark on it, he'd had a strenuous day and the ground was steep. It was late afternoon now and the heat had built up until it had become oppressive. The sun was intermittently obscured by clouds and the sky was slate-grey to the south, over the central fells. The trees were quite still, even the birch leaves motionless. Sounds didn't carry but were absorbed by the heavy air. They spoke quietly as if there were people listening.

'The peregrines are quiet,' he murmured as the crag loomed above, more sensed than seen, a towering presence.

'It's hot. She'll be shading the eggs and the male will be dozing in some cool corner if he has any sense.'

'It seems late for a bird to be sitting on eggs.'

'Not really. They're probably hatching right now – and it is an early heat wave.'

'It's a heat wave all right.' He stopped and wiped his forehead. 'How do you keep so fit when you live in London?'

'I jog, and I work out. I'm careful what I eat.'

'That must take a lot of self-control in your job.' She shrugged. 'Who runs the business when you're away?' he asked curiously.

She shifted her feet, anxious to be off. 'I have a partner: business partner. She's very efficient.'

'You must be doing well.'

She stiffened. 'So-so. Why the sudden interest?'

He gave an embarrassed laugh. 'I was thinking aloud. Sorry.'

'Dad's been talking.'

'Actually yes. He looks as if he's mortgaged to the hilt and yet he's putting in a new bathroom at Hollins and bringing in experts to devise a management plan. That can't be a free service.'

139

'There are grants,' she said vaguely. 'But I contribute my share. It's an investment; after all, I'm the heir. My mother ran off with a racing man when I was young so she don't count. This will be all mine eventually.' She waved at the trees.

'Do you have the same affection for it as Randolph has?'

'My God, you don't wrap it up! Affection? I never thought about it. The land is ours, and that's it.'

'What would happen if you had to sell—'

'We wouldn't—'

'—like Mabel?'

'But Mabel never left. It's still her land, or rather, her dale.' She grinned. 'She doesn't have title but in her mind she belongs to the dale – I mean the other way round, of course; the dale is hers.'

'I see that, but Mabel had Randolph; he made it possible for her to stay. If you had to sell who would stand in as your benefactor?'

'So that's what you're getting at. There are several options. I could marry a rich man – plenty of those in the City – or I could make my own fortune, invest it carefully and run the estate on the profits. Or we could have a theme park.' She smiled engagingly. 'How would you like to be the estate manager?' She held his eye and after a moment he looked away. 'You have to find something to do,' she said lightly. 'You can't eat the lotus for the rest of your life.'

'Something will turn up.' He flexed his stiff leg and sighed. They resumed their plod up the slope.

Laura started to zigzag, smooth as a guide. He looked up to gauge their distance from the base of the crag and caught her sideways glance. Automatically he followed the direction of her gaze and stopped. He peered, then plunged downhill.

'What is it?' she called as he stopped and picked something up.

He struggled back. 'It's a peg hammer: for pitons. Someone' – he craned his neck – 'someone must have dropped it.'

'Useful?'

'Yes.' He was studying it: a chunky little tool. 'Very useful,' he murmured.

'What's eating you?'

'You don't drop a hammer without knowing. It's heavy, you'd miss the weight. You drop slings and pegs, crabs even, but not hammers. If you were climbing and you did let it fall you'd come down and look for it.'

140

'Maybe they did and couldn't find it.'

He stared at her. 'Why didn't I think of that?'

They jumped as a peregrine started to scold.

'We're too near the nest,' she said. 'Time we backed off. What was it you were expecting to find here?' She was trying to locate the nest through the foliage. 'It's an old raven's nest, you should be able to see the sticks projecting over the edge—' It dawned on her that she was getting no response from Pharaoh. She glanced at him and saw the strangest expression; she thought he looked lost, hopeless – and then she sensed that what she was looking at was resignation.

She turned to see what claimed his attention. Above them were huge, moss-covered boulders with ferns in their crevices and a leafless creeper like the slimmest of green snakes, but they had no creepers in the Lakes and nothing that curious shade of green, with gold flecks, which wasn't growing anyway but festooned in wide loops among the boulders. And hanging over the top of one of the boulders like a schoolboy's practical joke was a shabby trainer – a shoe – and a leg.

Chapter Fourteen

Laura didn't want to see the thing on the rocks but she knew she should, this was family land and Pharaoh was an incomer; to go and look was the correct course: politically correct, she thought hysterically, deploring Pharaoh for being so slow clambering over the boulders, his slipping on the moss which was still damp in the shade. Then she slipped herself and cracked her shin so hard that she felt a wave of nausea. Tears of pain filled her eyes. She started to say, 'I can't do this,' but he had pulled himself over the edge and was looking down, his face relaxed and empty. In a moment he would tell her to stay where she was. She swallowed and climbed up to him. He heard her coming and inhaled deeply, letting it out with a sigh. She edged up close, holding to him.

It wasn't so terrible after all; no blood was visible because he had fallen on the jumbled rocks and if there had been any blood it had drained down the fissures. He didn't look human any longer, the limbs and even the torso having conformed to the angles of the rocks. He was lying on his back and staring at the new spring leaves. Chequered sunshine played across the face which was unmarked but askew like a Picasso portrait. The skull was compressed.

'Let's sit down,' Pharaoh said, and she realized she was clutching his wrist. He turned her to face away from the body and they sat on a boulder and stared into the depths of the wood.

'What happened?' she asked and then, to show that it wasn't rhetorical, that she had herself in hand, 'Can you tell?'

'I think so. He wasn't abseiling because he's not attached to the rope; it looks as if he was just sliding down it – and the peg came out, the piton. You hammer a peg into a crack, clip a crab to it, run the rope through the crab. That's a carabiner. He was pumping me for information but I didn't tell him that part so he

142

most likely watched some climbers to find out how it was done. Are you all right?'

'Oh yes; quite all right, thank you.'

He stood up and coiled the green and gold rope, pausing as something came to hand that clinked, laying the coils neatly beside the body.

'I was right,' he said, returning to her. 'The peg came out. He couldn't have hammered it home securely. The crab's still attached, and the rope's through the crab.'

'So when he put his weight on it—'

'It could have happened as soon as he went over the edge.' He stared morosely at the slope below. 'Now we have the hard part: telling the family.'

'The police will do that.' He didn't respond. 'Or I could,' she added diffidently. He turned to her in surprise.

'Oh no, you can't do it.'

'Someone has to.'

He thought how like her father she was. 'Let's go down,' he said. 'Forget it for the moment. Watch your footing; you could sprain your ankle here.'

This time there was no speculation, no mystery as to what Roy had been doing on Falcon Crag nor how he had fallen. He had gone after the peregrines' eggs and the piton had come out of the crack when his weight came on the rope. A couple of uniformed policemen toiled up the slope behind the rescue team that recovered the body, the team doctor certified death and the police had no questions. Pharaoh had led the team to the site and shown the police where he found the hammer. They asked the team leader about its significance and were told that Roy would have dropped it when he fell. There was a flicker of doubt in the leader's eyes at this point but there were more pressing problems clamouring for attention and it was left to Pharaoh to wonder how the hammer came to be some thirty or forty feet from the body and not on the same fall-line. And whoever heard of someone carrying a hammer without its being attached to his person? But Roy wasn't a climber; he'd probably tucked it in his belt. He wasn't wearing a belt. Why did he take the hammer down with him anyway? Once he'd placed the peg he wasn't going to need the hammer again until he removed the peg. The hammer would have been left on top, beside the peg.

A flurry of excitement ran through the group round the body.

'I'll take it,' the uniformed sergeant said firmly.

'Sure nothing stuck to your fingers?' someone asked.

'That's in deplorable taste, my man.'

'How much is there?'

'Thirty quid. You think that's what he was getting for the eggs?'

'Don't be daft. They wouldn't pay before he delivered, would they?'

'Thirty quid,' the sergeant confirmed, pocketing the notes with a grimace.

'Where were they?' Pharaoh asked of the man closest to him.

'In his hip pocket. Is that all he had on him?'

Pharaoh looked at him coldly. Black humour was common on rescues but that remark was over the top.

'Where's the rest of it?' Randolph asked. 'There were a hundred pounds in Mabel's wallet. There were only ten in it when they found it at Warthwaite.'

'It could be anywhere,' Pharaoh said. 'He must have had caches all over the place. Where's the rucksack that contained the climbing gear? It's not on top of the crag.'

The police had contacted the climber whose equipment had been stolen and although he hadn't seen the rope yet he had confirmed that his was green and gold.

'I bet Trudy could find that rucksack,' Randolph boasted. 'We'll try for it tomorrow, although if it rains it might take the scent.'

They were in the garden at Burnbank. The evening was cool, as if it had rained already, but the ground was still dry after the day's heat. The lake, ruffled here and there by a light breeze, was ashen under a sky of pigeon tones. Even the trees were sombre without sunshine to bring up their shades of green. Inside the house they could hear Mabel and Laura in the kitchen.

'They're happy,' Randolph said, and shook his head ruefully. 'So am I, although relieved is a better word. That lad was a threat. A brood of peregrines is more worthy.'

'Of survival?'

'Naturally.'

'And Mabel values her cats more than a yob.'

'Do I detect a vein of disapproval?'

'No. A warning.' Randolph turned and stared. 'The police wouldn't understand your attitudes,' Pharaoh explained.

144

'Ha! And you do?'

'I understand but I can see the law's point of view. Your attitudes – yours and Mabel's – give you motives.'

'For what, for God's sake?'

'Murder. For knocking out that piton.' Randolph was flabbergasted. 'The hammer wasn't in the right place,' Pharaoh pointed out. 'It shouldn't have been there at all. He would have left it on top.'

'What – are you saying – happened?'

'That someone else was there, and knocked the piton out as Roy went over the edge, or as he was going down the top pitch.'

'I don't believe it!' But that was rhetorical. Randolph stared at the water with wide eyes and after a while he said, 'Are you sure?'

'Of course I'm not. I'm just telling you not to let the police know that you value the peregrines more than the boy, that's all.'

'Pharaoh says it would be prudent to keep our feelings to ourselves,' Randolph announced as they came to the table.

'Feelings of relief?' Mabel nodded. 'Naturally; one has to consider the Hartleys.'

'Was that what you meant?' Laura asked Pharaoh, pouring wine in his frosty glass.

'Smoked salmon,' exclaimed Randolph, pleased as a child. 'We *are* celebrating! Pharaoh says we have motives for murdering Roy.'

'For Christ's sake, Dad!' Laura glanced at the open windows.

'You put the peregrines first too,' he said.

'Not quite so indiscreetly.' She took the bottle to the kitchen and returned. 'Is that your private opinion, Pharaoh, or do the police think that way?'

'Just a thought,' Pharaoh said. 'The hammer could have been thrown down.'

'Could it?' She sipped her wine. 'I thought you were puzzled when you picked it up.' She was thoughtful, elbows on the table, her chin on her hands. She frowned. 'Becky!' she exclaimed. 'Can there be a connection? Two deaths – in the same place, virtually. Both accidents – apparently. How odd.'

'We thought Roy could have been involved in Becky's death.' Randolph was choosing his words.

'She was terrified of him,' Mabel recalled. 'Sunday morning, when she saw him in the woods, she was quite pale when she reached my place.'

'You're right.' Pharaoh remembered Becky's expression. 'I thought I'd frightened her but she told me afterwards that she never even saw me. It was Roy she'd seen.'

'The morning after the deer were killed,' Randolph said. He addressed Pharaoh: 'Could it be that Roy was working with the poachers and one of *them* knocked the piton out and then threw the hammer down?'

'Don't rock the boat,' Mabel said. 'As things stand now we're far better off than we were this time yesterday. A violent threat has been eliminated; we shouldn't question how it happened. And if it was a case of thieves falling out, then that will be the last we'll see of the poachers. They're not going to come back to a dale where they've been involved in murder. Perhaps double murder.'

'Double?' Laura echoed. 'They were involved with Becky?'

'Why not? Perhaps she saw something she shouldn't and that was why she was pushed over the edge. After all' – Mabel looked round the table – 'we suspected Roy, and now you think he was one of the poaching gang. It all ties in; the others could have told him to get rid of Becky.'

Marlene was exasperated. She was dressed to go to town, Mason was over an hour late and she was filling the time by drinking and smoking and picking on Claire.

'I can't see how you couldn't have known,' she exclaimed, not for the first time. 'You were closer than sisters. She must have told you something about their relationship. For God's sake, they're both *dead*! You can tell the truth now.'

'I keep telling you: I never saw her after Sunday morning. She were all right when I left her.'

'She couldn't have been if you'd quarrelled – and don't give me that bit about the Boathouse. Listen. You were always the leader; if you said you didn't want to play round the Boathouse, she'd have given in straight away, she'd never have argued. So what did you really quarrel about?'

Claire was slumped on the sofa in front of the television. Marlene switched it off and faced her daughter. Claire regarded the empty screen sullenly.

'Was it about Roy?' Marlene demanded.

'I don't give a toss about Roy.'

'Well then, is that what it was: she wanted to spend time with him? She's older than you – was older; did she say she'd rather be with him, was that it?'

Claire looked up, no longer sullen. There was a flicker of calculation in her eyes. 'I don't think it was that way,' she said. 'She was scared of him.'

'But you've been saying they were friends.'

'Not like that. Only sort of. And you can be frightened of a boyfriend.' Claire's eyes were candid. 'Women get beaten up by their fellows, even killed sometimes.'

Marlene swallowed and turned to stare out of the window. She whirled back. 'You changed the subject! We all know she was – Roy could have . . . We *know* this. I asked you why you quarrelled. You never answered me.'

Claire licked her lips and sighed. 'We found the deer guts,' she confessed. 'She panicked, said she was going to tell her grandad. I told her not to. We argued and I called her names. That's it.'

Marlene absorbed this in silence. At last she said carefully, 'Hughie didn't have anything to do with those deer, sweetie.'

'I know he hasn't got a lurcher.'

'And doesn't know anyone who has.'

'Laura was here when you were cooking venison stew.'

Marlene held her daughter's eye and said clearly, 'That venison came out of the deep-freeze and we'd had it since Christmas.'

'I know; I heard you tell her. What do you say when that Buckle comes and asks to see the deep-freeze we haven't got? Venison wouldn't last a week in our old fridge.'

'We'll cross that bridge when we get to it. You'll think of something.' The tone was dry. Marlene hesitated, then went on emphatically, 'We're in the clear, sweetie; if someone gave us some venison, who are we to know when the season ended, that there was anything illegal about it?'

Claire looked down at her hands and smiled but the smile was missed by her mother who had turned back to the window. 'Here he is!' she cried. 'An hour and a half late. You'll be all right, lovey? There's the chicken and the ice cream and some cans of 7-Up. I wish you had someone to keep you company – or a dog . . .' She paused uncertainly. 'Maybe one day . . .' She trailed off in the face of that attentive stare.

Mason appeared in the doorway, blocking it as Marlene picked

147

up her handbag. 'We're not going,' he said. 'We'll stay in the village tonight.'

She was amazed. Claire's attention refocused and sharpened.

Mason was excited. 'Police are back. That Buckle and his sidekick: they've just gone up to Warthwaite. And the Mountain Rescue were in the Stag earlier, they was kidding as Roy were pushed.'

'Like Becky,' Marlene murmured.

'Hell, Becky were an accident, they was both accidents!' He looked at Claire. 'Weren't they?'

'Of course.' She was wide-eyed. Marlene regarded her dubiously.

Mason was saying, 'I was here last night. You and me' – he looked at Marlene – 'were in the caravan. Did you know that, Claire?' His tone was soft.

'I know now,' she said obediently.

Marlene was horrified. Mason put his arm round her shoulders. 'I had nowt to do with Roy's death,' he said, his fingers digging into her flesh, 'and what I was doing don't matter. So far as you're concerned I could have a lady somewhere else, but you're going to tell the police I were in the caravan with you, right?' A thought struck him. 'You were alone last night?' She nodded. 'That's fine.' He looked back at Claire. 'And you were tucked up alone in your little bed.' Marlene gasped and started to protest. He held up both hands. 'All right, all right. Just so we're straight: me and you were in the caravan.'

'When?' Claire asked.

His eyes narrowed. He asked silkily, 'When do you think?'

'When did he fall?' Claire asked.

'Jesus!' He glowered, and Claire waited for the question to be answered while Marlene stared from one to the other in bewilderment.

Buckle's tone was benign but his comment was barbed even though it was addressed to the bereaved father. 'What I can't understand,' he confessed, 'is why you didn't know Roy hadn't been home all night until he didn't come down to breakfast.'

Hartley glanced at his wife. Anne was haggard but she had herself well in hand. 'We don't wait up for him,' she said, and set her jaw, seeing the mistake but refusing to change the tense.

'You left the door unlocked?' She stared at him. 'I thought you locked up since the poaching business.' The tone was insinuating and her eyes glittered. 'You weren't bothered,' Buckle persisted, and saw that that had struck home, but still she wouldn't respond. Hartley shifted as if his chair were uncomfortable and the detective regarded him thoughtfully. 'A fourteen-year-old boy,' he mused.

'He were big for his age,' Hartley grunted: 'Clever lad.'

Anne inhaled sharply. The detectives exchanged looks. Fleming said, 'He was with Hugh Mason.'

'No!' It was jerked out of Anne.

'Oh, yes.' Buckle was calm. 'They were seen together.'

'Why not?' Hartley was belligerent. 'They knows each other.'

'Not—' Anne began, then quickly: 'Course they'd *speak*. We've known Hughie Mason all his life, we knew his family; course Roy would speak to Hughie.'

'It was Mason who telephoned him last night,' Fleming said, 'and arranged to meet in Kelton.'

Her eyes blazed and she started to shake her head. As suddenly she was still. The detectives waited patiently. She swallowed and made to turn to her husband but checked. 'You know this,' she stated.

Buckle said, as if continuing an idle conversation, 'They met in Botchergate, Roy chained his bike to the railings outside the toilets . . . Why didn't he put his bike in Mason's van?'

Anne was shaking her head again. Hartley said, 'He didn't have nothing to do with Mason, that I'll swear. It were no more than the eggs – never – just bird-nesting—'

'Shut your big mouth!' Anne spat out, then sighed. What was the use? 'There was Miss Cooper's wallet,' she admitted. 'He got into bad company.' It was a mother's eternal plaint and Buckle was used to it. 'Mason's got a record,' she went on, as if they didn't know. 'But we couldn't keep t' lad in a cage, could we?'

'No,' Buckle said. 'I'm sorry. You did your best, Mrs Hartley.'

'Which is more than we did,' Fleming complained as he drove down the track. 'No one *said* anything in there. She didn't say it was Mason who rang last night; she thought I was telling her it was when actually I was just asking her a question.'

'You could have fooled me. So either it was Mason telephoned or she thinks it was because the caller disguised his voice.'

'But you didn't tell her that Mason was seen talking to Roy in Botchergate.'

'By a car park attendant who knows Mason but not Roy: just a dark threatening lad, he said.'

'Who chained his bike where Roy's was found. That was Roy all right.'

'That lad was out more nights than I've had hot dinners.' Buckle was incensed. 'House locked, my arse! May have been, but he could have come and gone through his bedroom window: shed right below and the lad was built like a gymnast.'

'You reckon they knew all along?'

'One of those things, isn't it? They knew and turned a blind eye; probably didn't even discuss it between themselves. Remember when we found the wallet: Hartley going on about cannabis and such? That was to put us off the track of something heavy – like murder. Hartley was out of his mind with worry and she'd gone racing off to Kelton to find the lad. You don't behave like that because your boy was at an all-night party smoking a few joints with his mates *and* when you're accustomed to him staying out, because they were, you know; locking doors was just a pretence. No, they panicked this morning because they thought Roy had done a runner and that would be because they think he killed Becky.'

'You reckon Becky knew about the poaching?'

'Ah, now, was that the connection between Roy and Mason?'

Fleming braked at the cattle grid but he didn't pull out on the road. 'I thought back there you might have been hinting they were gay.'

'It's an angle.' Buckle was phlegmatic. 'Mason's Marlene's pimp, he don't have to be her lover.'

'Then there couldn't be anything sexual between Becky and Roy.'

'We know there wasn't – well—' Buckle turned to the sergeant. 'It could have happened like this: they were watching the peregrines from that cave, she made a pass at Roy, he was disgusted and pushed her.'

Fleming stroked the steering-wheel with stubby fingers. 'Sounds reasonable, but only if Roy was gay. But Mason as well? They don't behave like it.'

'We never saw much of the lad; he always made himself scarce when we were around.' Buckle sighed and turned to the road. 'Let's go and find Mason, see what he's got to say about that meeting with young Roy last night.'

150

They glanced up at Starfoot as they passed below it. No vehicles were outside but the front door was open.

'Marlene will know where he is,' Fleming said. 'She could know a lot more than that, if she'd only talk.'

'And there's the little girl.'

But the little girl was alone in the house and plainly in awe of them. Her mother, she said, had gone to town and yes, she had gone with Uncle Hughie and she didn't know what time they'd be back. Buckle pondered; you didn't question a young person without an adult being present, relative or social worker, but what an opportunity! He stepped back and addressed Fleming.

'So *were* they mates?' he asked loudly. 'Roy and Hugh Mason?'

Fleming eyed Claire and answered his boss. 'Big age difference,' he mused. 'Boy of fourteen, man in his twenties?'

Claire stared at him as if mesmerized, then shifted her gaze to Buckle as he responded.

'A big boy,' he said. 'A clever boy.'

They looked down and she blinked under the concerted stare.

'They went to town,' she whispered. 'Can I go now?'

While the police were at Starfoot Anne Hartley passed on her way to High Row. She parked outside the Stag. Mason's shed was open, the van inside. She walked to the cottage, depressed the thumb latch on the front door and found it locked. She turned and strode across the road to the inn.

Mason had observed her trying his door and he was waiting for her. He was smiling, but she knew he had to be uneasy; they weren't on visiting terms.

Marlene, in a green skirt and a top like a man's singlet, had her back to the door and was talking animatedly to Wharton behind the bar, giving the effect of distancing herself from her companion.

Anne crossed the room, vaguely aware of other customers, probably people she knew but she didn't look. She stood at the bar on the other side of Mason from Marlene. Wharton moved to serve her, producing the landlord's welcoming smile, his eyes as jumpy as if lager louts were squaring up to each other. Anne ordered a Babycham.

'On the house,' Wharton said, overdoing the sympathetic tone. The woman's son had just been found splattered below a cliff, for Heaven's sake! What did she *want* here?

151

Anne turned to Mason. 'What did you and Roy talk about last evening?' she asked loudly.

There was a lull in the talk, even the tourists turning to see why the locals had fallen silent.

Mason took a pull of his beer. 'I didn't see Roy last evening,' he said. 'Did we, Marlene?' He sounded the slightest bit doubtful.

Anne didn't miss Marlene's hesitation but the girl was on her best behaviour. 'Good evening, Anne. Roy? No, we didn't see him.' She was thoughtful. 'Where would this be?'

'You telephoned him,' Anne said to Mason.

'I *what*?' That shook him.

'And told him to meet you in Kelton,' she added, a catch in her voice.

'Don't be daft, woman! I never telephoned Roy. I never spoke to un on telephone in me life!'

Now the only person who appeared cool was Anne. Marlene was gaping, Mason intense and indignant, Wharton was pleading: 'Now, now, Hughie, get a grip on yourself, she's hyster—'

'And you met him in Botchergate,' Anne said, facing him squarely, her hands free, her face reddening, 'and then you brought him back here and took him up to crag and pushed him off' – Wharton had lifted the flap in the counter and was squeezing through the gap – 'like Becky Rudd!' Anne shouted. 'Both of 'em! You're a fucking murderer!'

And as Wharton moved to intercept her she threw herself at Mason, her strong hands clamped on his throat, bearing him back under her weight, crashing into Marlene who staggered against old Pinfold and knocked him off his feet.

They all fell. Marlene was screaming, men were shouting, stools and glasses broke, and above it all rose Anne's roars of rage and grief. It was the noise she was making that daunted people as much as her actions. No one would go to Wharton's aid as he grabbed ineffectually at her meaty shoulders, her hands fastened on Mason's throat as tight as a pit bull's jaws.

Wharton threw a wild glance sideways. 'Help me!' he shouted. 'Pull 'er off! She's choking him!'

Two figures advanced, pulled Wharton away, and then Anne – not easily but with a degree of expertise. Anne slumped on the floor, her back against the bar, watching Mason without expression. Marlene, gasping, was crawling towards him. He was doubled up, retching, pawing at his throat, his shoulders heaving.

152

'Wait till I get you alone,' Anne said, and made a movement. Fleming pushed her back.

'We arrived just in time,' Buckle observed genially. 'You'd better come with us, Mason.'

'For your own protection,' Fleming said.

Anne's smile was like a dog's snarl. 'You're going to hang,' she said.

A tourist, determined to be included in a spectacle with which he would entertain his cronies for years to come ('our holiday in the Lake District') observed shakily, 'There's no capital punishment any longer – more's the—'

Anne's eyes hadn't left Mason. 'I'll be waiting when they let you out,' she assured him. 'And you're right' – responding to the tourist but not looking at him – 'hanging's too quick anyway. You're going to die slow, Hughie Mason.'

'Christ!' he whispered painfully. 'Get me out of here. She's gone mad.'

Chapter Fifteen

Mason refused to talk to the police in his own house or anywhere else that was accessible for Anne. Buckle said that she was over it now but he remained unconvinced so they took him to Kelton. In an interview room at the police station he denied that he had seen Roy last night, even that he had been in Kelton; he maintained that he was with Marlene at Starfoot.

The car park attendant was brought in and identified Mason as the man he'd seen talking to the youth who was chaining a bike to railings outside the lavatories; the attendant knew Mason by sight and by name. A lot of people in Kelton knew Marlene and her fellow.

'So what was the point of denying you were in town?' Buckle asked. 'You knew we'd find out.'

Mason was amazed. 'You saw her! If you hadn't come along at that minute she'd have choked the life outa me! Jesus, me throat's sore as hell. Was I going to tell her I met Roy last evening, even by chance – which it was? You have to be joking. So once I told her I didn't, I kept it up with you. Had to, didn't I?'

'Why?' It was Buckle's turn to register surprise. 'We're not going to throttle you just because you talked to the lad where everyone could see.'

Mason hesitated, then, 'And only for a moment.' They watched him carefully. The attendant had told them more. They waited for it from Mason. 'I just asked him if there were a rave on somewhere – joking like – and he said he were going to a party in town, and that was it.' He looked from one to the other, his face shining with sincerity.

'Then what?' Buckle prompted.

'I went for a drink – to the Royal Oak. I've no idea where he went. I didn't watch him go.'

'You both went in the toilets,' Fleming said.

Mason stared at him and then he laughed. 'You think I'm gay?'

'And then you brought him back to the dale.'

To their surprise he seemed to relax. He smiled. 'I had a drink and I went home.'

'Taking Roy with you.'

He said nothing. He was still relaxed.

'You were seen leaving the car park with him,' Fleming said. 'In your van.'

Mason's eyes dropped to the table and his lips moved fractionally, otherwise he was quite still. He refused to say anything more. He didn't even ask to see a solicitor.

There was more rain in the night and the dale was sparkling fresh when the sun came up. Pharaoh surveyed his larder, ate some cereal, looked at the peregrines and walked over to Mabel, ostensibly for eggs. He found her thinning seedlings.

'I was coming down to you when I'd finished this chervil,' she told him. 'The peregrines are hatching.'

'I know. I've been watching them.'

'One anyway. It's occurred to me that the reason Roy had to risk going down to the nest in the storm, apart from the fact that thunder would drown the noise of hammering, was that he guessed the eggs would hatch soon and he had to steal them before they did.' He frowned and would have spoken but she was continuing, 'Did you hear about Anne and Hugh Mason? She attacked him in the Stag last evening – and then the police took him away. The night Roy died he met Mason in Kelton, so apparently Mason was involved in Roy's death.'

'How?' Pharaoh was puzzled.

Mabel straightened her back. 'You explained it very effectively last evening,' she said drily. 'When you were attributing motive to Randolph and me.'

'Method actually.' He grinned. 'I didn't have to attribute motives. You admit them: peregrines and cats have priority over yobs. I was talking method last night: the peg being knocked out by the killer. But when I asked how Mason could be responsible for Roy's death I meant where's the connection between them meeting in Kelton and the two of them together on top of Falcon Crag?'

'I don't know what goes on in criminals' minds.' She was leading the way to the house. 'No doubt everything will be explained eventually.'

He followed her into the kitchen. The shotgun was no longer on view and in its place on the dresser was the typewriter and stacks of paper.

She filled the kettle. As she waited for it to boil she said thoughtfully, 'I can see Roy Hartley as a member of a poaching gang but I can't see Mason stealing peregrine eggs. Roy doesn't – didn't need an accomplice; he managed very well on his own last spring, and he'd want to keep the money to himself.'

'That puzzles me. What would he have done with the eggs? They must be kept warm. What's the system?'

'It's all very professional. Someone is waiting with an incubator. They use vehicles with a power supply. No expense is spared, but you have to remember that the final value of a peregrine to a falconer can be in five figures. It's worth the initial outlay.'

'So there had to be a vehicle close to the top of the cliff.'

'Probably on the spot: to take delivery immediately Roy – oh, I see what you're driving at. But if there was foul play it wasn't those men: the middle men. How could it be? They hadn't got the eggs, and you don't kill your supplier.'

'But if it wasn't them and they were waiting for him to climb back to the top, how could someone else get past them to knock the peg out? Unless they weren't right there, or had to go away because—'

'Because the killer saw their vehicle! I always said you were sharp.'

'You weren't so interested last evening; you said it was immaterial how the threat had been eliminated.'

'Last evening I didn't know that Anne was so certain that Roy and Mason were in cahoots that she'd try to kill Mason.'

She made coffee while Pharaoh watched her absently. 'They didn't have to be in cahoots,' he said. 'Roy could have been a threat to him.'

'How?'

Pharaoh shrugged. 'Blackmail? Roy had something on Mason? Becky was scared stiff—' He stopped.

'When she came here on Sunday morning,' Mabel supplied, placing a mug in front of him, and a tin of homemade biscuits.

'Why did she come to you?' Pharaoh asked.

'Because she'd just seen Roy in the woods. You know that.'

'Not "just". She was terrified when she passed me – but then she went home. It must have been later that she came to you. Why didn't she tell Isaac?'

156

'I suppose she thought I'd be more concerned about the peregrines than Isaac – although they were at risk only if Roy was on top of the cliff. I know: she was thinking of the cats!'

'In that case she'd have come straight to you instead of going home and thinking about it.' He stared at the typewriter. 'What did she do when you went to look for Roy?'

'I have no idea. I was so concerned . . . two of the cats were missing, d'you see; I ran out, calling to them. She cycled home presumably; she wasn't here when I came back. Why?'

'It fits.' He nodded. 'Some of it fits. You remember: it was that morning the note was dropped inside Randolph's car, the typed note saying there were dead deer in the woods. Becky typed it on your typewriter. It was finding the remains of the deer that terrified her because then she'd realize that grown men were involved. Saying Roy was in the woods was just a ruse to get you out of the cottage.'

'And she couldn't tell anyone directly, neither Isaac nor me, because of the fear of retaliation. So she did it anonymously. Handwriting can be identified, so she typed it.'

'Not knowing that type can be identified too. Give me a sample and I'll compare it with the note about the deer.'

'That's hardly necessary. The "a" is out of alignment.' But she put a sheet of paper in her machine and typed: "The quick brown fox jumped over the lazy dog."

She handed it to him. 'If she was killed because she knew the identity of the poachers,' she said, 'you do realize that Claire must know too?'

Randolph was sitting on the mounting block in the yard, splicing a halter. He listened with interest to Pharaoh's account of his visit to Mabel but at the end he was shaking his head. 'No one will touch Claire,' he said firmly. 'She'll do as her mother tells her, and since they're eating the venison Marlene's as bad as the poachers. Hypocritical of her to pretend to feel sorry for the fawn.'

'She could have been sincere. Until then she might have thought the poachers were expert marksmen who shot only adult animals.'

'Huh! Or she could have turned a blind eye. To be frank I'm undecided what to do about Marlene. Prostitution's one thing but taking deer with dogs is obscene. If I had proof it was Mason – but there, if I evict Marlene, Claire suffers. And Marlene's a good mother; I can't be responsible for putting them out on the street.'

'Talk to Marlene,' Pharaoh suggested. 'Warn her. And Claire, but she'll be more difficult.'

Randolph's eyebrows shot up. 'She's not important – in the context; she's only a child.'

'I'm not so sure about that. I think she was behind Becky's curious behaviour. The afternoon before she died, when she showed me the short-cut from the keeper's cottage, she wasn't bothered about Roy. An hour or two later he was every kind of villain—'

'We've been over all this, including the fabrication about the Jack Russell—'

'Which gave her the peg for a tirade against Roy. What we didn't consider was that it was Claire hiding behind the rhododendron, Claire who persuaded Becky to come back to me and put the blame for all the crimes on Roy, and most particularly the poaching. Claire wanted attention shifted from Mason.'

Randolph stood up and went in the stable. He hung the halter on a peg and came back to stare at the Chinese gander stalking across the cobbles.

'If Claire's protecting Mason,' he said, 'it's further evidence that he's poaching. And he's got a cellar. Yesterday he was insistent I go inside his cottage so obviously the meat's been moved.'

'Do you still have that anonymous note?'

'Should have somewhere. Why?'

He couldn't remember if the 'a' had been out of alignment. He searched but he couldn't find the note, neither in his pockets nor the Volvo, and they both agreed that to look for it in the house was hopeless. 'Probably burned,' Randolph said. 'Is it really important?'

Pharaoh thought about it. 'I don't know,' he confessed. 'It would point to Becky having typed it on Mabel's machine but I'm inclined to take that as read.' He snapped alert. 'I'm going up to the top.'

'Hang on. We'll take Trudy and look for that rucksack Roy stole. It has to be somewhere near the top of Falcon.'

'I'll see you there. I want to take another look— We'll divide our forces, get more done that way. Division of labour.' And he was gone in a hurry.

'Doesn't want us,' Randolph muttered. 'What's he up to then?'

*

158

Pharaoh drove to the top of the escarpment and through the woods, not stopping until he reached Hollins. There were no vehicles outside the cottage and the garden gates were closed. The front door was locked and the windows shut; in short the place looked no different from when he was here yesterday.

He stood outside the porch and looked across the tarn to a rocky slope that was set with hawthorns and the hollies that gave the cottage its name. Tim Armstrong didn't look like an outdoor man, he thought, and the fellow certainly wasn't a mountaineer. Even fell walkers sense a bond when meeting each other but Pharaoh had no feeling of empathy with Armstrong. The chap was a writer of course, and writers are solitary creatures – and Randolph charged low rents; maybe that was enough to explain the seclusion. He opened the other gate and strolled round the cottage.

The window in that gable-end was open and a pane was broken. It was the small window that was draped with tacky net.

His first thought was walkers. Someone without a tent had intended sleeping out, had been caught by last night's rain and broken in for shelter. With luck the only damage was the broken window.

There was a sound from inside but he couldn't identify it. 'Armstrong!' he shouted, moving to the window, pushing the curtain aside. He heard a scuffle, then silence. 'You there, Armstrong?' he cried, but there was no response.

He listened for a few moments and then went along the back of the cottage to come out by his van. There was a flash of alien colour on the drive where someone was running fast – too fast for him to have a hope of catching them. He went back to the open window and climbed into the kitchen. He went quickly to the front and found the parlour window open.

Yesterday, when they'd looked through the windows, there had been no sign of Armstrong's personal possessions. Laura had suggested he'd put them upstairs. There were two bedrooms. On one mattress the blankets were neatly folded; the other bed was made up but not even indented. If the intruder had been looking for shelter he hadn't slept on a bed, or if so, he'd made it afterwards. But walkers with backpacks could never run as fast nor as lightly as the figure he'd seen flashing up the drive.

There was no sign of Armstrong: no clothes in the two wardrobes or the drawers; that was obvious immediately because the wardrobes gaped wide and all the drawers had been pulled out.

He went downstairs. There were ashes in the grates of both the parlour and the room opposite, ashes of paper some of which had retained its shape. In the parlour he stirred the black sheets with a poker and saw that the brick at the back of the fireplace was cracked. There was a glimpse of cinnamon brown. He eased the brick apart and, caught in the crack and unburned except for a scorch mark on one side, was a triangle of paper: merely a scrap, a corner of typescript with the ends of three lines. The first read: "day, and", the second: "a distin – ", the third: "tty malice". The fragmented words meant nothing but the 'a' was out of alignment.

The light changed and he swung round to see Laura at the open window. She eyed him bleakly, waiting for an explanation.

'You saw the broken window?' he asked. 'I didn't break it. I got here about ten minutes ago. Someone was inside then. Presumably the person who broke the window. You must have seen him jump out of this one and run.'

'Not really. I wasn't looking. I was coming down from the Roman road and this is a rough old track for a horse. I did see someone on the drive but there are always hikers about. Who was it?'

'I only got a glimpse.'

'Have they done any damage?'

'Nothing that I can see apart from the pane. Armstrong's gone though; everything personal has been taken.'

'Let me in the front door, will you?'

He went out, and came back. 'It's locked and there's no key.'

'Great! Now we have to put a new lock on too.' She was morose. 'I suppose I must come in and see for myself. Dad will want a full report.'

She climbed over the window sill and Pharaoh went out the same way and left her to it. She wasn't long. He could hear her banging doors, going upstairs, thrusting drawers back in place, coming downstairs again – a pause while she inspected the ground-floor rooms.

'We'll come up this afternoon and glaze that window,' she said as she rejoined him. 'Can't leave it like that or hikers will be in and starting fires. Armstrong seems to have burned papers before he left. Thank God he didn't set a chimney on fire.' Her face clouded. 'Who could the intruder have been? It wasn't a hiker: no rucksack. What do you think?'

'I wondered about Claire. Elimination, you see. It wasn't a walker or a motorist – there are no cars at the end of the drive – and Claire was here two days ago, looking for Becky. Did she suspect he might have something to do with Becky's death?'

'And broke in looking for evidence that he held her here? Possibly.' She thought about it. 'Of course he didn't,' she added, jeering at herself. 'There was no rape – nor any other sexual act according to the post-mortem. What have you got there?'

He had taken the fragment of paper from his pocket. 'This is what he was burning: old typescripts presumably.'

'So what?'

'This was typed on Mabel's machine.'

She took it from him and studied the fractured words.

'I don't understand.'

He told her about the defective letter and she shook her head and returned the paper scrap.

'Aren't you curious?' he asked.

She shrugged. 'Not really. If Mabel and Armstrong are – some-how – connected, it's not my business. We respect each other's privacy in Scawdale.' She smiled to show she wasn't being heavy about it, just dropping a gentle hint.

'Prove it,' Mason said.

'We have eye-witnesses,' Buckle told him. 'You didn't even buy a ticket. You drove into the car park, met the lad, went in the toilets and drove out again. With him. We have a statement.'

'Then the chap as made it is blind. I never had Roy Hartley in my van. Go over it; you won't find his prints.'

He was right there; they had gone over it and had failed to find one print of Roy's. And it hadn't been wiped.

'Surfaces can be wiped,' Buckle said. 'Like they were on Becky Rudd's bike. But you forgot to clean up your cottage, didn't you?'

It was the second time they'd got under his skin. The first time was last night when he was relaxed until told that he was seen leaving the car park with a passenger in his van. He'd had eight hours' sleep since then and he'd eaten a good breakfast. Brought to the interview room for his second session with Buckle and Fleming he was jaunty again – until his cottage was mentioned.

'I never clean my house,' he said tightly.

'You should,' Fleming said. 'There are a child's prints everywhere.'

161

Mason looked puzzled but he was overdoing it. They knew his brain was racing. 'I don't remember Roy ever being in my place,' he said.

'You'll have to do better than that.' Fleming looked bored.

'He wasn't referring to Roy's prints,' Buckle said genially. 'Roy had large hands. He was referring to a little girl's prints.'

Mason was silent for too long, staring at the table. He knew they were waiting for him and he screwed up his eyes nervously. 'Claire,' he said. 'Marlene's kid. That's who them prints belong to.'

'And Becky?' Fleming asked.

'No.' Mason was firm but he was tense too. 'Becky was never in my cottage.' Suddenly he grinned. 'You can't pin that on me, she weren't interfered with.'

'Kids have been killed because they knew too much,' Fleming said. 'Like who was poaching, and when.'

'Them's Claire's prints,' he said stubbornly.

After he was taken back to the cells Buckle said, 'We need young Claire's prints. That shook him. He didn't know a child had been in his cottage – and no wonder, seeing as how she climbed in through the back window. It was Claire sure enough, and she didn't want him to know, no more'n she wanted to be seen by folk in the Stag. Now why did she go there?'

'Why not ask her?' Fleming suggested.

Pharaoh met Randolph on the road on top of the escarpment and they exchanged news. Randolph wasn't greatly surprised that Armstrong appeared to have left for good, nor even that Hollins had been broken into, and he was only mildly curious. He had seen no one running down the road either but then he'd been directing Trudy, who hadn't needed much direction when it came to it; the rucksack was quite close to the top of the crag. It was in the back of the Volvo now: a large blue pack being guarded by the officious springer.

'There are some carabiners in it,' Randolph said, 'and those wire loops with aluminium things—'

'Nuts. They're called nuts.'

'Oh, yes? And the black balaclava's there too, but no money. What d'you think he did with Mabel's hundred pounds?'

'He had thirty on him when they picked him up. He'll have hidden the rest somewhere else. Where was the rucksack?'

162

'Behind a rock, not hidden at all really, just not visible to us when we were on top of the crag. I'm surprised it wasn't picked up by tourists but presumably they thought it belonged to people who were climbing. Which way did Laura go?'

'I thought she was following me.' Pharaoh took the scrap of paper from his shirt pocket and handed it across. 'This seems to have been typed on Mabel's machine.'

'There's that wonky "a". Where did you find this? It's been burned.'

'It was in Armstrong's grate.'

'I'm not with you, dear chap. She wrote to him and he burned old letters when he left. There's nothing sinister about that. You're starting to see bogeys. I'm off, I have to measure that pane and find a new lock somewhere.'

Mabel was removing a sheep tick from the white cat, pressing a whisky-soaked swab to his nose.

'How does it work?' Pharaoh asked.

'Suffocates the tick and it drops off. What is it this time?'

He held the fragment of paper so that she could see it. 'Was this typed on your machine?'

'It looks like it. Where did you find it?'

'In a grate at Hollins.' He told her about the break-in.

'What did Laura think?' she asked, more interested in the cat which was now supine on her thighs. She relaxed her pressure on the swab and grimaced at the bloated tick caught in the threads. She ground it under her heel and fanned the cat's face. 'The fumes won't hurt him,' she said. 'Not like sniffing solvents.'

'Laura' – Pharaoh began, staring at the cat which was blinking its bicoloured eyes – 'Laura says it's your business.'

'What is, dear boy?' She retrieved the cotton wool and stood up, smoothing her trousers.

'If there was something between you and Armstrong.'

She smiled indulgently. 'Dear Laura. Such good manners. I'll wash my hands and we'll have coffee.'

'You must excuse me.' He returned the smile. 'I have a date.'

'Look who's here,' Marlene said without enthusiasm, not getting up from the plank seat as Pharaoh stopped the Transit on the track to avoid covering them with dust. Claire was expressionless. 'Is there any news?' her mother asked.

'About what?'

'About Hugh. You know the police arrested him?'

'I didn't know that. What's the charge?'

'I – can't say.' Marlene was disconcerted. She glanced at Claire whose face hadn't changed.

Pharaoh approached them but he remained standing because his leg wouldn't allow him to squat, and although there was room on the seat he wanted to watch Claire's face.

'What were you looking for?' he asked her.

Marlene glanced uncertainly at her daughter. 'When?' she asked.

Pharaoh waited.

Claire came to life. 'Like Mum says: when?'

'In Hollins just now.' He was patient. 'Laura saw you as she came down from the Roman road, and Randolph was on top of Falcon Crag.' Of course she wouldn't have gone past Falcon, the locals would have their secret ways up and down the escarpment.

'I didn't' – she began quickly, paused, then – 'go in Hollins.'

'What were you—'

'When was this?' Marlene asked, shocked. 'This morning? What were you doing up there in Tim Armstrong's place?'

Claire scuffed her trainers in the dust. 'Looking,' she said sullenly. She glanced at her mother. 'He's not there. He's split. Since Becky died, see? I went to find out if he'd been keeping her a prisoner.'

'For God's sake,' Marlene exclaimed. 'He had nothing to do with Becky. That was an accident.' Hadn't she realized the significance of the bicycle?

'It wasn't your first visit,' Pharaoh persisted, still addressing Claire. 'What made you suspect him?'

She looked at him from under her eyebrows. 'Becky said he told her to go there. He would show her how to write.'

Marlene gasped. 'You never told me that! You should have. Did she tell her grandma? Did she tell anyone – oh!' Her hands flew to her mouth and she stared at Pharaoh. '*Was* it him?'

He ignored her and concentrated on Claire who looked frightened. 'The note about poaching,' he said, 'the one Becky dropped through the window of Mr Randolph's car on Sunday morning' – her eyes widened – 'we know Becky typed that . . .'

She nodded and then she winced as if she would have liked to retract the gesture. 'I did wonder whether Becky typed that note,' she said.

164

'It was after you found the deer guts.' Claire's face went blank but Marlene stiffened. 'And it was Becky typed the note,' he went on, 'not you. It wouldn't be you; that would be telling tales.'

Claire said, 'I didn't know she was going to tell.'

Marlene said carefully, as if she were a child interrupting adults, 'Poaching isn't a very serious offence in these parts. Everybody does it.' She looked to see what had attracted Claire. 'Oh, my God!' A car was coming up the track. 'It's all right,' she added breathlessly, but it was clear that she was the one who needed reassurance.

The car stopped behind the Transit. Buckle and Fleming approached with all the leisurely deliberation of executioners. Buckle smiled broadly at everyone but he addressed Claire.

'And why,' he said ponderously, 'are a certain young lady's fingerprints on Hugh Mason's kitchen window sill where she left them when she climbed in?'

'Never!' Marlene exclaimed. 'She doesn't—' She stopped and stared at Pharaoh, remembering her daughter had virtually admitted breaking in to Armstrong's cottage.

Claire said earnestly, 'Someone was poaching, and we get presents of venison. I wanted to make sure it wasn't Hugh doing the poaching. So I went to his house to find out.'

'And what did you decide?' Buckle's tone was like treacle.

'Nothing,' she said in surprise. 'There was no meat in the fridge at all 'cept some bacon.'

'You didn't go down in the cellar?'

'Wouldn't be in the cellar. Dirty old place.'

'So why are your fingerprints on the cellar door?'

'I opened it but I couldn't find the light.'

'And on the rail beside the steps?'

'I went down a few steps in the dark but it was spooky so I came back.'

'Your prints are on the light switch, Claire.'

'I saw it when I came back up. I switched it on but I didn't go down again.'

They regarded her with mixed feelings: relief, speculation, admiration.

'So you had your suspicions,' Buckle mused, and Marlene shifted restlessly while Pharaoh thought what a superb advantage children had in that they could stare without expression at their inquisitor and no one had the remotest idea of the emotion or the thought behind the stare.

165

'About Becky's bike,' Buckle said, and the child's gaze didn't waver. 'It had been wiped clear of fingerprints, and being in the place where it was found, hidden, that showed the person who hid it knew what had happened to Becky.'

Claire frowned and he was on it like a flash. 'Yes?'

'Someone said she fell before dinner time?' It was a query – and for Becky dinner was eaten at midday. 'It couldn't have been Hugh,' she told them earnestly, including Pharaoh and her mother. 'Because we were in town; we were there all day. Remember, Mum? You were with Hugh in the pubs, I went to Dawn Reid's house. So it wasn't Hugh. We were in Kelton.'

'So who put Becky's bike in the old quarry?' Buckle asked.

'I thought that was Roy,' Claire said innocently.

'Why would he want to harm Becky?'

'I don't think he meant to.' She was earnest again. 'Just they were playing too near the edge – and then he got scared that he'd be blamed for it so he hid the bike and pretended it hadn't happened. Or she could've said something nasty about him stealing. Everyone knew about that. Like Laura's binoculars and Miss Cooper's money and her trifle. He even stole food.'

'When did he steal that?' Pharaoh asked, and the detectives stared at him.

'What?' Claire asked.

'The trifle.'

'Oh.' She was flustered. 'I dunno. The day Miss Cooper's cat died. He was always breaking into cottages and stealing.'

'And poaching,' Buckle said.

Claire thought about that, then said carefully, 'You can't say a thing happened unless you saw it, can you?'

Fleming smiled, which was a surprise, he was usually dour. 'And were you there when the thefts happened?' he asked.

Claire was shocked. 'He was grown up,' she told him. 'Roy wouldn't take a girl along on his break-ins. He despised us. 'Sides, he was a loner. He never took anyone even when he stole the eggs.'

'What about Becky?'

'Not when he was thieving, I mean. Other times was different. Then he'd meet Becky.'

Laura was cleaning the chestnut's hoofs. 'They've taken Claire to the police station?' she repeated incredulously. 'What's she done?'

'Only to be fingerprinted,' Pharaoh said. 'Marlene's with her, of course.' He told her about the child's prints in Mason's cottage. 'Buckle was bluffing. He couldn't know they were Claire's but he made her admit it. He needs to make sure that Becky wasn't there as well. But he *has* Becky's prints so he knows already whether she visited Mason. Why does he want Claire's prints?'

'Elimination somewhere else?' Laura put the hoof down gently. 'If the police were building a case against Mason, they'd want to know if Becky had been in his van.' She ran her hand down the chestnut's rear leg.

'He has an alibi,' Pharaoh said. 'He was in Kelton when she died – although nothing was said about times, not specifically. She died late in the morning and if he didn't go to town until, say, twelve thirty, he could have pushed her. But Claire says they were in Kelton all day. It looks as if Roy was involved. Someone had to be because her bike was hidden. As for Roy's death: Mason's denying everything.'

'Why would Mason kill Roy anyway?'

'If everything else fits, the police don't ask for motives.' Randolph had approached the stable unnoticed. 'And if Mason's not talking they suspect the worst. The car park attendant saw him turning into Botchergate with Roy in his van, so there you are! Someone brought Roy back, that's obvious.'

Laura released the chestnut's leg and straightened her back. 'How d'you know all this?'

'Buckle's opening up,' Randolph told her. 'It's all starting to fit together.'

'It *was* Claire at Hollins,' Pharaoh told them. 'She says she was looking for traces of Becky there. She said Armstrong asked Becky to visit him.'

'Rubbish!' Randolph exclaimed. 'I don't believe it. Do you, Laura?'

She was examining the horse's ears. 'Claire's a young monkey,' she said: 'into everything. She was probably looking to see if there was anything left lying around that we wouldn't miss.'

Chapter Sixteen

'We've got that straight,' Buckle confided to Mason as if they were conspirators. 'It was young Claire in your cottage; she climbed in the window to find out if you'd hung the deer in the cellar.' Mason's eyes were shifty. 'Were they blackmailing you?' Buckle asked. 'The banknotes in Roy's pocket when he died: originally they came from the sale of the venison.' It was a statement, not a question. Either way it brought no reaction from Mason.

'Claire talked,' Fleming said. 'She's worried about her own skin.' Buckle turned lazy eyes on the sergeant. 'You weren't with Marlene Wednesday night,' Fleming said.

They waited, well aware that he could have gone to Marlene after Roy was killed; the landlord of the Stag had said that he hadn't heard Mason come home that night. They were on edge, waiting to see if he would spot the loophole.

'I were in Kelton,' he said, and swallowed. All the stuffing had been knocked out of him. He glanced helplessly at the tape-recorder and gave a heavy sigh. 'I were with George Townsend. I spent the night at his place in Gibson's Yard. Him and his woman: they'll tell you.'

Buckle smiled. Fleming looked disgusted. Townsend had a record as long as your arm, and the offences included poaching.

'What's your connection with Townsend?' Buckle asked.

'I have a drink with him when we meet.'

Fleming coughed. Buckle sat back. Fleming was turning the pages of his notebook. 'There were deer meat in your cellar on the Sunday,' he said thoughtfully, 'and none yesterday when you asked Mr Steel to enter your cottage. So you took the carcasses to George Townsend on Wednesday night.'

Mason was the picture of dejection. 'Wednesday evening,' he corrected. 'Met him in Botchergate. He had a customer for the meat.' He closed his eyes as if the next question would be in the

168

form of a blow but they didn't ask who the customer was, instead Buckle murmured, 'And Roy?'

'I did meet him but like I said: just by chance. He were seeing some people. I went off with George. That's who were in van with me: George Townsend.'

'You went in the toilets with Roy.'

'That's a lie. I went in toilet. If he followed me it were coincidence. His mates were outside – and them weren't boys!' His voice rose and he glared at them. 'It were tourists, see! Two German fellas in a Volks bus with a foreign number plate and the big "D" on back.' He grinned then. 'They'd have an incubator in a secret compartment.'

'Oh, yes.' Buckle looked at him as if he were a fly he was about to swat. 'And you're going to tell me Roy got in the bus and left Botchergate in the direction of Scawdale and it was the Germans who threw him off the cliff.'

'Knocked out—' Fleming began and stopped, but he hadn't broken the thread.

'No.' Mason ignored him and answered Buckle. 'It were too early. It were broad daylight. They musta gone somewhere first. We drank in Kelton, George and me.'

'With the deer meat in the back?' Buckle was laughing.

'We flogged it.' Mason's shoulders slumped. 'Took it to the Old Swan, didn't we. And when pubs closed we went back to George's place an' I slept on his settee. I had a hell of a hangover, didn't get back to High Row till gone opening time.'

The detectives held a post-mortem on the interview.

'The phone call Roy's mum said he got could have come from the Germans,' Buckle said. 'Since he was after the eggs there had to be someone close by to take delivery, and that means an incubator and a largish vehicle. It fits.'

'Too glib,' Fleming grated. 'Too convenient for Mason.'

'Not necessarily. He had an alibi all the time – he didn't want to use it because it meant admitting the poaching. The risk of a murder charge changed his perspective, that's all. But what kind of alibi is it: a villain and his woman? And if there were a couple of Germans in a bus, they could have taken Roy to the top of the cliff and then retired to a discreet distance to wait. Now that would have given Mason his chance to slip by them and knock out that piton thing.'

'Not if Mason *was* asleep in Townsend's house. And what were

Roy and the Germans doing all evening? Surely the boy never risked going after the eggs in the daylight, but it was early on when Mason says he saw the lad meet the Germans.'

'It was a stormy night so it got dark early. All the same, not that dark. But Roy told Mason he was going to a party. Now if that's so he could have taken the Germans—'

'To a kids' party?'

'Never mind that for the moment. Get someone on to finding his mates in town and we'll go and see George Townsend.'

Gibson's Yard was approached by a spray-painted alley between shops in Finkle Street. The alley led into a kind of flagged well enclosed by sandstone buildings with high barred windows. Littered steps led down to basements with scarred doors, and flights of steps went up to entrances framed with worn red blocks, where the doors looked as if they might still be secured on the inside by draw-bars. There was a smell of tom cats and dustbins. The detectives mounted steps and knocked on a door.

Townsend's current partner was a plain powerful girl who looked as if she'd be more at home on a farm. George was away, she said, and didn't invite them in.

'When did he leave?' Fleming asked.

He had left that morning and she thought he had gone to Appleby. Who was he with Wednesday evening? Her eyes wandered. He was out, she said. Doing what? Drinking. Who with? His mates. Which ones? She shook her head.

'Who else besides Hughie Mason?' Buckle asked, at his most avuncular.

She looked grateful. Here was something she could answer without doing anyone any harm. 'Just Hughie,' she said.

'And what happened?'

'Hughie come back here and slept on the settee. He were too drunk to drive home. He couldn't even get up steps on his own.'

'I see. And earlier on they sold the deer meat at the Old Swan.'

She gaped. 'What deer meat?'

Buckle turned and surveyed the yard. 'Took the lurchers with him, did he? To Appleby?'

'I – I dunno.'

'Oh, come on!' Fleming jeered. 'They're not ordinary dogs, them's highly trained . . .'

'They're not here,' she whispered then, gathering strength: 'We don't have no lurchers.'

'Dad keeps 'em, does he?'

'Not my dad—'

'*His* dad.'

She shook her head and took a step back, grasping the door.

'We won't trouble you any more.' Buckle beamed at her. 'Good day to you.'

'Put someone to finding the father,' he ordered as they returned to the station. 'Probably he keeps the lurchers outside town, but that's a side-issue. We know Mason and Townsend were poaching; it's immaterial where they kept the dogs. Someone else can look after that problem. Our concern is to find Roy's mates; the most likely place he was on Wednesday evening was at that party.'

'Your mother will go spare,' Pharaoh said.

Claire shook her head. 'I left a note on Hugh's windscreen. She's bringing the van home if the police won't let him go. I said I'd come home on the bus.'

'But you hitched!' Pharaoh was appalled. 'Don't you know—' His shoulders sagged. What was the use? 'Someone's going to have to teach you the facts of life,' he said, and castigated himself. How often had that statement been a prelude to the seduction of little girls? Claire observed him with interest. He had the sudden thought that she knew what he was thinking.

'I'm not going to tell anybody,' she assured him.

'We'll sit outside,' he said, leading the way from his kitchen to the veranda. 'And I don't have any Coke,' he added roughly, sitting down. 'Now what are you not going to tell anybody?'

'That I was here of course.' She looked very small in the garden chair. He deplored the position she'd put him in and he frowned as more half-formed thoughts wriggled in murky depths: not personal memories but sensations at one or two removes. The kind of thoughts other men had when alone with Claire?

'Roy was murdered, wasn't he?' she said.

He hesitated.

'Of course he was,' she said impatiently. 'The police was saying Hugh did it but he couldn't have because he got drunk and spent the night in town.'

Pharaoh was amazed. 'You know more than I do.'

'They let Mam talk to him. Hugh's only a poacher. Mam's trying to get some cash together to get him out of prison.'

'You mean bail?'

She shrugged, it wasn't important. 'I know who killed Roy.'

Pharaoh sketched a nod. 'You must tell Mr Buckle.'

She tightened her lips. Bloody grown-ups. 'I wasn't the only visitor to Hollins Wednesday afternoon; Roy went there too. He stopped me when I was coming away and made me tell him what Armstrong said.'

'What did he say to you?'

'Nothing really, but he was frightened. It's funny for a grown-up to be frightened of a little girl, isn't it?'

'What are you trying to tell me?'

'Roy asked Armstrong why he was frightened of me. Roy said he reckoned Armstrong could have thrown Becky down the cliff. And her bike were found close to Hollins.'

Pharaoh sat still. Birch leaves rustled. An aircraft murmured overhead, spinning its trail of fluff across the blue ceiling. 'He's got away,' he observed. 'Why didn't you tell Mr Buckle that Roy went to Hollins?'

'He wouldn't believe me. He says the money was Miss Cooper's.'

'What money?'

'What was in Roy's pocket when he fell. Now someone's said Hugh gave him that after the venison was sold, but Hugh and Roy weren't mates, and Roy wasn't poaching. The money came from Armstrong, I reckon.'

Pharaoh was awed. 'You know more about what's going on than an adult! Why did Armstrong give Roy money?'

'Because he killed Becky of course.' She regarded him candidly.

'And?'

She blinked at such obtuseness. 'So Armstrong had to kill Roy.'

Pharaoh closed his eyes in an effort to conceal his astonishment, not at what she said but at the way it fitted together.

'You ask Laura,' she persisted. 'She'll tell you.'

'You're telling me— How would she know?'

'They got a relationship.'

He sucked in his cheeks and held her eye. 'Do you know what that means?'

'Yeah, he's her feller. She's always there; I seen them heaps of times.'

'At Hollins?'

'No–o. Coming away from there – along the top road.'

They glanced up automatically as if they could see the

escarpment through the walls of the Boathouse. Pharaoh had gone very still. He forced himself to relax.

'You were – kind of watchers,' he said, with a hint of admiration. Her expression didn't change. 'You used to watch people from your cave.'

'What cave?'

'I saw you there with Becky.'

'In a cave?' She was puzzled. 'Maybe. We were always on top, and there are lots of caves.'

'You could see everything that happened. It was far better than a tree-house. From the top you could keep an eye on Laura riding through the woods, in front you could see everybody's house—' He waited for her to say, 'Not everybody's,' but she was silent, watching him attentively. He smiled. 'You'll tell me next that Miss Cooper had a secret life.'

'She did?' She seized on that.

He stopped smiling. 'You manipulated people,' he said angrily, then caught himself. 'You made them do what you wanted.' She stared at him. 'You told lies,' he said, on firmer ground.

She shrugged. 'We played games. It was fun.'

'Oh, yes?'

'We made up stories about people. Like Randolph, how he buried his wife in the woods and had to move the body before the bulldozers uncovered the bones when he made a theme park. Which was how we come on the deer's guts. I saw lights at night.'

'I knew that bit.' It wasn't a lie; she'd confirmed a theory. 'And then you typed the note in Miss Cooper's cottage—'

'Not me' – quickly – 'Becky did that.'

'Fingerprints?' he murmured.

There was a pause. He sensed cogs meshing. 'We'd been in her place before,' she admitted.

'Ah yes, the trifle.'

'It wasn't a crime,' she muttered.

She'd just been fingerprinted and her mind would be full of the thought of prints but he didn't refer to skylights and illegal entry. 'And Miss Cooper's wallet?' he asked.

She didn't hesitate. 'Roy stole that. It were in his bedroom.'

'Where's the rest of the money?'

'How would I know? He hid it of course.'

'And he's not here to tell his side of the story.'

'That's how it is,' she said coldly. 'He were a villain and he come to a bad end.'

Pharaoh found Laura picking lilac in the garden at Burnbank. She listened wide-eyed to his account of Claire's fantasy concerning her father's homicidal exploit, astonishment giving way to hilarity. 'And that was how they got on to the poachers,' he told her. 'Claire saw lights in the wood and they went looking and found the deer guts.'

'And what was Claire doing out in the dark?' she asked drily, no longer amused, but then her tone lightened. 'All little girls have fantasies. I used to dream about being on the Olympic equestrian team; Claire's probably influenced by the telly. Poor old Dad. Mum ran off before these kids were born but they've heard gossip and invented their own murder story. What other stories did she entertain you with? Come inside and tell me while we have tea.'

He followed her to the kitchen. She switched on the kettle and found a bowl for the lilac. 'Dad's glazing the window at Hollins,' she said, arranging the flowers, standing back to admire them. She made the tea and put a plate of gingerbread on the table. 'Were there more stories?' she prompted as she sat down.

He smiled ruefully. 'There were several. That child has an amazing vocabulary for her age. She says you have a relationship with Armstrong.'

'A – relationship!' She gave a bark of laughter. 'Does she know what that means?'

'I asked. She said he was your fellow.'

She leaned back in her chair and her eyes moved at the sound of an engine in the yard. A car door slammed. Trudy came pattering into the kitchen followed by Randolph.

'Ah, good, I'm ready for tea,' he announced as Laura got up to fetch another mug. 'Had to padlock the door,' he told Pharaoh. 'Most thoughtless of the fellow: going away with the key.' He sat down heavily. 'You're quiet, you two; have I interrupted something?'

'I've been having a heart-to-heart with Claire,' Pharaoh said.

'Have you indeed! You learned something too by the look of you both. Something unpleasant? Not more villainy on the part of Mason, surely?'

'I'm looking for answers,' Pharaoh said. 'Claire says that Laura might answer a question.'

'Claire and Becky invented fantasies,' Laura told her father. 'She says you murdered Mum and buried her in the woods.'

'Well?' Randolph looked from one to the other, unperturbed. 'Children hear snatches of gossip and they fill the gaps. Fertile little minds. Doesn't bother me.' He stiffened. 'Has she come up with something more – apposite?'

Laura stared at Pharaoh. He said, 'She told me that Laura knows that Armstrong paid Roy thirty pounds.'

'*Did* he indeed.'

Laura said coldly, 'She also says Armstrong's my lover.' She turned to Pharaoh. 'He paid Roy thirty quid to keep his mouth shut, is that it?'

'No doubt children pair everyone off in their imaginations,' Randolph said comfortably. 'Nature and little girls abhor a vacuum.' He beamed at them. 'Who am I linked with? Mabel of course. No, not exciting enough for 'em.'

Pharaoh sighed, his mind a long way from fantasy. 'The curious thing is that both deaths could have passed for accidents except that someone had hidden Becky's bike; sure, she could have hidden it herself if she'd been meeting Roy on the quiet, but she wouldn't have dropped it over the lip of a quarry. And then – the piton hammer: that had been thrown over the edge too . . . There are some basic questions. Who hid Becky's bike? Who threw the hammer down Falcon? How did a scrap of typing from Mabel's machine come to be burned at Hollins?'

They were both staring at him. 'You're not suggesting that bit of paper had something to do with the deaths?' Randolph asked weakly.

'Mabel told me she doesn't know Armstrong, and she won't comment on the piece of paper.'

'She doesn't know him,' Randolph said. 'Does she, Laura?'

Laura said nothing. Both men found the silence significant. 'She *does* know him?' Pharaoh asked.

She shook her head, refusing to meet their eyes. Suddenly she stood up and left the kitchen. Randolph stared at Pharaoh in bewilderment. 'Now what?' he pleaded, but Pharaoh couldn't help him.

Laura came back with glasses and a bottle of Scotch.

'Sun's not over the yard-arm,' Randolph said automatically.

'It is today.' She poured generous measures and took Randolph's glass to the tap. She went back to her chair, drank and set down her glass with a crack.

'Mabel doesn't know Armstrong,' she said. 'But I do.'

Randolph gaped. 'Why on earth—'

She held up her hand. 'Let me tell it. He's a friend of a friend to whom I owe a favour. He – Armstrong – got involved with some people – I don't know the details, and I'm not bothered. He needed a place to hole up for a while and I knew Hollins was empty so I sent him to you, Dad.'

'But why all the secrecy?' Randolph was lost. 'Why were you so—'

'The point is' – she was incisive but Pharaoh thought it was to hide embarrassment – 'I don't know what he's mixed up in and I thought it was better that you shouldn't. I mean, look at you! As soon as you know there's something going on, you want to know what it is!'

'But if it was criminal—'

'Who says it was? Dad, I owed a friend a favour. All that was wanted from me was a – a safe house if you like, and no questions asked. You haven't done anything illegal. Anyway, he's gone now.'

'Well,' Randolph looked round the table, then at Pharaoh, as if looking for words, 'all I can say is, it's as well he has done a flit. Sounds fishy to me.' He looked apologetic as if Pharaoh had been burdened with family matters. Pharaoh took it as a cue.

'So he did give Roy money?' he prompted.

Laura's eyes were cold. 'Of course. He had to get Roy off his back.'

'If you can blackmail a chap—' Randolph began, but stopped as Laura turned on him. They all knew they had a delicate subject here – and Pharaoh stayed at the deep end.

'He's not a writer,' he said flatly.

'No—' Laura cut it off but too late.

'So where did the manuscript come from? Don't tell me. Mabel wrote it.'

Her eyes narrowed. Randolph was agog, Pharaoh alert but patient. She was as hostile as she had been at their first meeting, and tense as a spring. Under his steady regard she relaxed visibly, taking deep breaths.

'Mabel wrote the book,' she admitted. 'But they never met. I took the typescript to him in batches.'

'Why?' Randolph breathed.

'As cover, Dad! A man can't come and live in the dale without everyone speculating about him and his background and his motives but who's bothered about a chap who's writing a book? Lakeland's full of them.'

'But Roy sniffed him out,' Pharaoh persisted. 'And tried a spot of blackmail – and succeeded.'

'He couldn't do anything else; he had to get rid of Roy.'

'That's an unfortunate choice of words,' Randolph pointed out.

'Armstrong left the night Roy was killed,' Pharaoh said meaningly.

She licked her lips. 'He couldn't stay,' she protested. 'He thought they were ganging up on him: Claire and Roy. First she approached him and implied Becky was at Hollins or had been there. He'd never even *met* Becky! He knew Claire was up to no good when she said he'd invited Becky to visit him – and then along comes Roy. Armstrong was paranoid about discovery; he even wondered if the kids had been sent by someone. He had suspicions about you, Pharaoh, come to that.'

Pharaoh said carefully, 'If he thought Roy was a threat it makes him a suspect.'

Laura's eyes wandered. She fidgeted with a teaspoon. 'He had nothing to do with Becky's death.'

Randolph's expression sharpened. 'You're on to something.' He leaned across the table. 'Did Roy kill Becky?'

'No.' Her lips thinned. 'It was Claire.'

The ticking of a clock was loud in the kitchen. Trudy's claws scraped as she chased hens in her sleep.

'Why?' Pharaoh asked.

'They'd been playing a game,' she reminded them. 'A drama with Dad cast as the murderer, and suddenly they come across a real crime and it wasn't a game any longer. Probably Becky said she'd tell Isaac and Claire would be dead against that – because she knew, or guessed Mason was the poacher. Marlene will get the venison from him. They quarrelled and Becky compromised and typed the note and dropped it in the Volvo.'

Randolph was frowning. 'If they'd quarrelled how did Claire persuade Becky to go to the top of Falcon Crag on – when did Becky fall?'

'She was pushed,' Laura corrected, 'on Tuesday morning. They'd met and made it up on Monday evening when Claire waylaid Becky after she'd shown Pharaoh the short-cut to the Boathouse.' She paused. 'Was she already thinking that she'd have to kill Becky because she knew Mason was the poacher?'

'No!' Randolph shouted. 'Even an adult wouldn't be as vicious— That's evil.'

Laura gave him a thin smile. 'Children are.'

'I don't think so.' Pharaoh was thoughtful. 'Not that children aren't vicious but that if Claire did kill Becky I don't think it was premeditated.' He stopped and considered while the others watched him, Randolph too astonished for words, Laura speculative. 'Simply because,' he went on, 'she had no motive – well, not enough motive.'

'For – killing – Becky?' Randolph still couldn't believe what he was hearing.

'For premeditation,' Pharaoh said absently. 'I think it's more likely there was another quarrel – at the cave – only an argument perhaps, and then a push. And there again, it could have been an accident: Becky stepped back, or wavered and lost her balance. Climbing accidents happen like that: one moment's lapse in concentration, and if they were arguing at the time . . .'

'Her bike was taken away,' Laura reminded him. 'And you said the cave had been cleaned. Claire smokes. There would have been cigarette ends and spent matches.'

'And people die by accident, and other people hide the bodies in a panic or out of guilt.'

'Claire knows guilt?' Laura laughed without amusement. 'And can you imagine that child panicking?'

'It could have happened like that,' Randolph put in. 'I'd prefer to believe it did. The inquest will be next week,' he told Pharaoh. 'Will you say anything?'

Pharaoh shook his head. 'It's all surmise – although it does fit. Why didn't Buckle tumble to the possibility of Claire being involved?' He answered his own question. 'Because he'd never suspect a child could kill another child. It happens though.'

'Buckle doesn't know her,' Randolph said.

'He knows she was in Mason's cottage – ah! That's when she saw the deer meat. She suspected, she went down in his cellar and she found it hanging there. And then set to work to shift the blame to Roy,' he mused.

'Roy,' Laura repeated. 'Now that must have been an accident. You keep harping on about the position of that hammer,' she told Pharaoh, 'but no one else sees any significance in it. How can you say someone else threw it down? Roy used it—'

178

'He would have left it there: on top, beside the peg.'

'Why? He wasn't a climber. He wouldn't know the correct procedures. He'd have taken it down with him thinking that he'd need it, maybe to help him get back.'

'Hammers are used for pitons,' Pharaoh said stubbornly. 'He had none with him when he fell. He didn't *need* the hammer. He left it on top and someone used it and threw it over the edge, no doubt meaning to imply that Roy *was* carrying it when he fell.'

'There are no Press in the dale,' Laura said. 'That means the police are saying it was an accident: he didn't hammer the piton home and it lifted out when his weight came on the rope. Perhaps the rope whipped the hammer off as the piton came out. Another thing: the police must have kept quiet about finding Becky's bike, otherwise we'd have been besieged by reporters.'

'What happened to Armstrong?' Randolph asked. 'Where is he now?'

She looked at him. 'I've no idea, and I don't want to know. My guess is that we won't hear from him again; our only use to him was to provide a safe house.'

Chapter Seventeen

'I'd do it again,' Mabel said. 'It was an amusing exercise and the money was useful. We're always short; you can't run a car on the old age pension and a weekly item in the local paper.'

She was skinning a rabbit on the chopping block, deftly handling a lethal-looking knife, surrounded by attentive cats.

'Thank God we don't have myxomatosis,' she said. 'Rabbits supply us with the bulk of our protein. Which we're going to need,' she added darkly.

'You could write books yourself,' Pharaoh pointed out. 'I mean, and submit them under your own name.'

'I'd thought about it but while Armstrong could use my work, supplying him was the easiest option. There wouldn't be a lot of difference in the money, and I was doing Laura a favour. I never met him, you know; I wasn't interested. Were you surprised when you found out?' She threw the skin to the cats and set about jointing the carcass.

'There was obviously something going on but I was surprised at the nature of it. There were pointers; there was that rogue page in the typescript of your nature notes, which you implied was from your private journal but what I saw was fiction – and similar in style to the scrap I saw at Hollins that was supposed to be Armstrong's work.' He hesitated, then added gently, 'You knew he was in hiding.'

She picked up the bowl containing the joints and went indoors. He followed and sat at the kitchen table while she washed her hands and dried them, taking a long time about it. At last she turned to him.

'I didn't ask questions. I had an arrangement, a contract: I was to supply one or two chapters at a time and I'd be paid a hundred pounds for each chapter. And I would keep quiet about it. Of course the work must be submitted under someone else's name but for that kind of money who cares? It was trash anyway. I don't care for people and the only way I can write about them is to transpose my feelings for animals, and that makes me sound effusive.' She looked surprised. 'But someone bought the stuff so it fulfilled a demand.'

He stared at her. 'You don't really think it was passed to a publisher?'

'Why not?' She was affronted. 'It wasn't that bad.'

'You thought the reason behind the enterprise was merely that Armstrong should publish a book under his own name?'

'I told you, I didn't ask questions.' She was flustered. 'That was – I considered that part of the agreement.'

'You guessed you were doing something illegal.'

'I wasn't.'

'A moot point. But it never occurred to you that you might be helping someone – oh, never mind.' He sighed. 'Forget it.'

'That's the ex-Serviceman speaking; you have to learn to think for yourself now, to adjust. We have a different code here, not' – she was suddenly fierce – 'not the same as Mason and his gang – Heavens, diametrically opposed! All this smart talk about countrymen being custodians: that concept goes right back to the tribal chiefs. *We* know how the money should be spent, where it will do most good.'

'Laura seems to have a foot in both camps.'

'She has to keep up appearances in her business but she's not ostentatious. Successful women drive Porsches. Not Laura. She spends her money on the estate.'

'I think she's laundering money.'

'What does that mean?'

'She paid you for the book in cash?'

'Yes. Ah, dirty money! She told me about that; the people who spend a lot on the kind of parties she caters for may be laundering money themselves. But look at what we do with it!' She gestured widely, embracing the dale. 'I wouldn't disapprove if this estate were being run on the proceeds from bank robberies.'

'Yes, you would.'

'Well, maybe.' She sat down. 'But not if the money came from tax evasion and so on. We know how best to use it.'

'What are you going to tell the police?'

She shrugged. 'I'll answer their questions but' – she smiled sweetly – 'old people get so confused by authority. I wrote romantic trash and sold it, that's all.'

'Buckle will want to know the purpose behind it.'

'He'll ask Laura.'

'But when he comes to you it'll be because she told him the writing was a cover for a man in hiding—'

'Oh, my dear boy! As if I'd know anything about that!'

'He'll check and discover—'

'Check what? With whom? Armstrong's disappeared and Laura can't tell the police any more than what he told her.'

'She says he's a friend of a friend.'

'Then they'll check with him.'

Pharaoh considered this, and put it aside. 'There's Hollins,' he said thoughtfully, and let it hang.

Mabel looked puzzled. 'Why should they go there? They'd have to apply for a search warrant.'

'With Claire's latest accusations against Armstrong and his disappearance the night one of the victims died, a warrant's a foregone conclusion.'

'I don't believe this,' Buckle said. 'Here's an obvious villain obviously holing up, with an elaborate cover involving a couple of local women, and neither of them asks questions because they say they owe favours! And Laura didn't tell her father, and he didn't ask for references from a long-stay tenant. They're all lying in their teeth.'

They were standing on the grass outside Hollins. They had collected the key of the padlock from Randolph and searched the place. Now they were waiting for a man and a dog.

'They didn't have to tell us,' Fleming pointed out. 'Armstrong's left the place clean. If Steel hadn't reported it we'd never have known anything.'

'There's nothing to know, damn it! All he's told us is he provided a safe house for a man who has to be a villain, and his daughter and an old woman provided the cover. No one's as public-spirited as that.'

'He had to tell us that part because of Claire's story. I mean, that's important and he knows it: Armstrong paying Roy thirty quid—'

'It's that thirty quid that proves he's a villain. What did he have to hide?'

'Being involved in Becky's death – if young Claire's speaking the truth.'

182

Buckle took a turn across the grass and came back. 'Were all the kids in it? All of 'em blackmailing him? They suspected something. Becky tried it first and he pushed her off the top of the cliff and hid her bike.'

'No one's talked about her bike being found,' Fleming said. 'Leastways it hasn't reached the media.'

'They're a clannish lot – until they want to do the dirty on someone. Here's Laura saying she saw a white Volks bus with a German registration turn into the quarry on Wednesday night; well, that could be true, the Germans had to be somewhere while they were waiting for dark. They certainly weren't at the party with Roy. That's another example of doing the dirty on your mates: that lad saying Roy was drunk at the party and boasting he had a job on that night.'

'If Roy was drunk,' Fleming said, 'his fall could have been an accident. We keep coming back to how his killer could have got past the Germans.'

'So what you're saying is that Armstrong leaving about the same time Roy was killed was a coincidence.' Buckle stared at his sergeant and chewed his lip. 'You wait here for the dog; I'm going to speak to Laura Steel again.'

'The police are searching Hollins,' Claire said, sitting down beside her mother and picking up the remote control. Marlene had closed the curtains, the better to appreciate the new 24-inch television set. A bearded man was talking about the burial of nuclear waste at Sellafield. The sound stopped.

'What happened?' Marlene asked, panicking. 'Something fused? *You* did it with that thing! Get the sound back; they're going to talk about Roy.'

'I know about Roy. I've just come down. They got uniforms and plainclothes at Hollins—'

'What's that got to do with Roy?' Marlene was leafing through pages of instructions.

'He murdered Roy,' Claire said. 'Probably Becky too.'

'Here's a diagram. Now, where's the sound?'

Between them they got the right mix and sat through an interview with a farmer whose sheep were still affected by fall-out from Chernobyl. The camera returned to Mike Neville whose tone lowered a notch as he spoke.

'It appears that the teenager whose body was found yesterday at the foot of a Lakeland crag was bird-nesting when he fell three hundred feet to his death. The police say that taking the eggs of many birds is illegal and can result in heavy fines. A spokesperson for the mountain rescue team that recovered the body pointed out that rock climbing is a highly specialized activity and should be practised only under the supervision of experts.'

'Tonight,' Wendy Gibson said, 'we have in the studio an author who—'

'Switch it off,' Marlene said. 'They didn't say anything about murder.'

'Course not. They want Armstrong to think he got away with it. There's a sniffer dog at Hollins: a yellow Lab. They're looking for drugs.'

'Your imagination'll be the death of you, Claire Fisher. So what if Armstrong smoked a joint now and again? Everyone does. I don't,' Marlene added quickly. 'It can lead to hard drugs.' She sighed as Claire reached for the cigarettes. 'I wish you wouldn't; I'll swear your voice is getting hoarser.'

Claire ignored her and struck a match. 'That's a hell of a hassle for a few joints,' she observed. 'There's them two detectives as were here, but the boss went away in the car and left the other one to wait for the guy with the dog.'

'How do you know?'

'I was watching from the other side of the tarn, wasn't I. In the bracken.' She flicked a glance at her mother and looked back at the blank television screen. Her feet didn't touch the floor and she drummed her heels on the sofa like an infant.

Marlene said, 'What makes you think Armstrong killed Becky and Roy?'

'He hid Becky's bike and he paid Roy money and murdered him before he could ask for more, and then he split and no one knows where he's gone.' Claire regarded her mother thoughtfully. 'You never had nowt to do with him, did you?'

'No!' Marlene stared. 'Why d'you ask?'

'You never went up there?'

'To Hollins? Never. I mean, not since he's been there.'

'Nor you weren't in his car ever?'

'What is this? I never met the feller!'

'Just as long as I know.'

*

184

Summoned by phone Buckle came racing back to Hollins from an abortive search for Laura. Inside the cottage the yellow Labrador was working diligently up the stairs followed by an equally absorbed handler. Fleming was in the kitchen doorway and stood aside as Buckle approached. The sergeant had a powerful light which he shone on a gap in the floor where a board had been lifted. The floorboards sat on joists above a bed of dusty earth and mouse droppings which appeared to be undisturbed.

'The dog went mad here,' Fleming said, playing the light this way and that. 'My guess is that something's been spilt. Ask me, as far as the dog's concerned the place reeks of it. And look at this.' He shone the light on the window where putty showed fresh and clean round the new pane. Someone had taken down the old net curtain and left it on the draining board. A piece of string was threaded through the upper hem. Fleming shone the light in the corners of the window frame.

'The string would have been stretched between these nails,' he said. 'And see here.'

Peering, Buckle could make out a few dark fibres clinging to the head of a galvanized nail.

'Another curtain,' Fleming said. 'When the light was switched on in here, anyone outside could see through the net, but not if there was a blackout curtain in place. It would make a dark-room too.'

'LSD,' Buckle breathed, his eyes shining. 'Making up tabs. We've got ourselves an acid factory.'

'I reckon. And that there: under the floorboards, in the cracks between 'em, could be where they spilt some crystals. Doesn't show to the naked eye in all that dirt but if we can find just one crystal . . .'

'I'm not supposed to let people in the house when I'm alone,' Claire said primly. 'My mam's gone to town.'

'I know,' Pharaoh said. 'I passed her on the road. She waved. She didn't seem bothered that I was headed this way.'

'Why should she? She's got nothing to hide.'

'We have to talk.'

'Wouldn't it be better outside?'

'Let me be the judge of that.'

'You're the boss.'

She was so sharp she must cut herself sooner or later. He

185

followed her into the parlour where she levelled the remote control with both hands and switched off the television. She sat in the middle of the sofa, he took a chair.

'That's a magnificent set,' he said.

'It's rented.'

'Renting costs too.'

Her eyes wandered. 'You'd have to ask my mam about that. She knows about money.'

'Someone came by a hundred pounds recently.'

'They did? Oh, you mean the money from Miss Cooper's wallet.'

'Fingerprints,' Pharaoh mused. 'They're everywhere: all over her cottage . . .' He spoke slowly, giving himself an excuse to pause at that point.

'Of course,' she said. 'We were in there when we ate the trifle, when she left the door open.'

'When you climbed in through the skylight,' he continued in the same tone. 'All over the skylight,' he added. Her lips thinned but she said nothing. 'And on the larder window sill,' he went on, 'but you missed a spot on the wallet.' She sighed heavily and it wasn't a contrived sigh. 'When did you put it under Roy's mattress?' he pressed, and shook his head. 'It doesn't matter; obviously all the Hartleys were away from the farm. You know how I got on to you? Because every time you were about to be rumbled you shifted attention to Roy, and it was always you – or Becky – who blamed Roy, except for the poaching, when you quarrelled with Becky and didn't have time to tell her to put the blame on Roy. But she corrected that as soon as you told her to. So all the things that Roy got the blame for were things you did. You left your fingerprints behind.'

'I told you about the trifle.' Amazingly, while he'd been speaking she had regained her poise.

'But your prints,' he pointed out. 'You can't argue with those. Even the binoculars. And there will be prints on Laura's car.'

'Not so long afterwards.' And now she was grinning. 'Even if Becky had stole 'em.'

'Oh, no!' He was shocked. 'You're not blaming Becky?'

'Roy—'

'Roy's prints aren't on them—'

'No, they'd be covered by hers.'

'But yours are.' When would she accuse him of inventing all this? He was guessing but with every guess confirmed, his confidence grew.

She had hesitated for only a fraction of a second, then: 'I used 'em. I handled 'em. Everyone's prints would be on 'em.'

'And your prints are on her bike,' came Laura's voice.

They turned in astonishment. She stood in the doorway, ignoring Pharaoh, her eyes on Claire. How long had she been there, listening in the passage?

'It's the bike that gives you away,' she told Claire.

Pharaoh had the feeling that the child relaxed once Laura appeared on the scene, which was curious considering the nature of the accusation.

'When did you decide you had to kill her?' Laura asked.

'Becky?' Claire's face was blank.

'Why? You killed someone else?'

Claire blinked in bewilderment and Laura inhaled sharply. 'I asked when you decided she had to die?'

Pharaoh realized that he was holding his breath. Laura sat down at one end of the sofa and turned towards Claire, presenting him with her profile. Claire didn't move away from her. Her feet didn't touch the floor and this made her look very young and vulnerable.

'It's a silly question,' she said.

'Not at all,' Laura countered. 'Becky got cold feet and she was a threat. Hugh is your mam's fellow and if Becky spilled the beans Hugh and Marlene could go to prison and you'd be put in care. So you quarrelled—'

'Sunday morning—'

Laura smiled. 'And you made it up after Becky showed Pharaoh the short-cut to the Boathouse, the night before she was killed. You went up to the cave together next morning and you pushed her over the edge, and you cleaned the cave and dumped her bike in the old quarry because it was close to Hollins, and you could put the blame on Armstrong if it came unstuck with Roy. Roy might have had an alibi.'

'Didn't have to put the blame on Armstrong,' Claire said smugly. 'He pushed her.'

'And then there was Roy.'

'Oh, yes!' She was jubilant. 'I were up there in the storm and I knew how to make him fall. That weren't a push, that were to do with – with a hammer, like knocking out a nail. And it was me drove him back from Kelton?' She grinned.

'No,' Laura said. 'The people who were going to buy the eggs brought him back.' She stopped there.

Claire said nothing but she looked at the television set and her hand stole towards the remote control.

'You've got a new television,' Laura said tightly. 'That cost an arm and a leg.'

'It's rented.'

'Is that where Mabel's hundred quid went?'

'Renting is sixteen pound a week.'

Laura looked round the parlour, searching for evidence of other recent acquisitions. Claire watched her. 'They got a sniffer dog at Hollins,' she said.

Their eyes locked. Pharaoh too stared at Claire.

'So?' Laura was icy. 'And what have they found?'

'I came away. I saw the dog go in, that's all. 'Sides, they wouldn't tell me what they found: heroin, cocaine, whatever.' Without a change of tone she added, 'Armstrong knew Roy'd come back for more money.'

'What are you trying to say?' Laura was close to losing control and yet the child wasn't intimidated.

'Not trying to say anything; just there's millions of pounds in drugs. Roy didn't know what was happening or he'd have asked for more than thirty. I would have.' She waited for the inevitable rejoinder.

'Oh, yes, we know *you* would have.'

Pharaoh said quietly, 'You see a lot of what goes on, don't you, Claire?'

She was suddenly wary. It occurred to him that she was frightened of him where Laura only amused her, perhaps because he didn't make direct accusations. Laura betrayed herself, but the extent of Pharaoh's knowledge was debatable. 'You were out at night when the deer were taken,' he said. 'Were you out the night of the storm?'

She hesitated, then shook her head vehemently.

'So all you've got against Armstrong is that he gave Roy thirty pounds.'

You could deduce nothing from her silences. She might be refusing to speak because she didn't know the answer, or because she thought a response might incriminate her, or because she was considering how to play it. She said now, 'You'll know more about it after they've finished searching Hollins.'

'Christ!' Laura exploded, appealing to Pharaoh. 'We don't have to take this!'

He tried again, keeping his voice down, thinking that Laura and he were doing the bad cop good cop routine but that it wasn't following the rules because Claire seemed to be more at ease with the bad cop. 'Claire,' he said gently, compelling her attention, 'they can tell from your fingerprints if you were inside Hollins before today.'

'I wasn't—' she began, and checked. She went on carefully, 'I went in today to see if he'd had Becky there. It was the first time.'

'No one's going to believe that—'

'I tell you I never. How could I? He always locked up.'

'How do you know?'

She was trapped only for a moment. 'If I was passing I'd go and knock on the door, see if he was in. Then I'd try the door.'

'Why didn't you call when he was there? After all' – Pharaoh stated the obvious – 'if the car wasn't there, nor was he.'

Claire looked at Laura. 'Because I knew he wouldn't want anyone else there.'

Laura said, 'Because he was writing a book and didn't want to be bothered.'

'He didn't mind you.'

'She's going to work for MI5 if she grows up,' Laura told Pharaoh.

'We used to play games,' Claire said, also addressing Pharaoh, reminding him. 'It was even more fun at night because no one expects little girls to be out in the dark. *Mr* Armstrong' – Pharaoh's antennae bristled – 'he had a thick curtain over his kitchen window but he wasn't writing a book in there, no sound of typing like at Miss Cooper's.'

Laura was breathing hard. 'And you told Roy this.'

'And Becky.'

Laura said to Pharaoh, 'I think we'll go and talk to the police now.'

'Then they'd find Armstrong,' Claire said. 'And it wouldn't be right for him to go to gaol, would it? Just because of something I said.'

'I don't believe this is happening,' Laura hissed. 'You've said too much; you can't pull back now. You've accused Armstrong, but it was only to get yourself off the hook. You pushed Becky, didn't you? *Didn't you?*'

'Prove it.' Claire reached behind a cushion and came up with cigarettes and matches. They watched in a welter of emotions as she lit up, inhaled, and expelled smoke. Pharaoh thought that the worst kind of brothel must be something like this. 'We kept diaries, Becky and me,' she went on. 'I've got Becky's now, of course. I hid them, but someone knows where they are, and it's not my mam. Mr Buckle knows that little girls don't murder their best friends. And he knows that when silly gits like Roy Hartley threaten drug barons they're going to be wasted—' Laura gasped. 'But Becky and me,' Claire went on, 'we wrote it all down: what we saw, what happened up there on the cliffs; so no one's going to throw me over the edge, are they?' She appealed to Pharaoh.

'How do you suggest we get in touch with Armstrong?' Laura asked acidly. 'Because you're saying that if he keeps quiet about you pushing Becky, then you'll not say anything about him being responsible for Roy's death. Is that it?'

'Was I saying that?' Claire was amused. 'You read it how you like.'

'I can't think why you never even thought of asking him for references.' Incredulous before, now Buckle was suspicious.

'Why should I?' Randolph blustered. 'He couldn't do any harm. There was nothing worth stealing at Hollins and he paid his rent in advance. You don't expect your tenants to start using the premises to manufacture drugs.' His eyes came round to Pharaoh, who blinked. He hadn't been asked for references either, not by Randolph. Laura had mentioned them originally but not since.

It was later the same evening and they were in the drawing room at Burnbank. A preliminary examination had revealed LSD crystals in cracks in the floorboards at Hollins.

'You had no idea what was going on?' Buckle persisted.

'Of course not,' Randolph protested. 'I can't believe it now.'

'A pity you respected his privacy so much, sir.' He addressed Randolph but he was looking at Laura.

'When I took him the typescripts,' she said, 'I never saw anything suspicious. Of course I didn't go in the kitchen and I never stayed long, just dropped off the typing and left.'

'It never occurred to you that such an intricate cover had to be hiding something criminal?'

She closed her eyes wearily. They'd been over this and he couldn't shake her, could do nothing in the face of her insistence that she had neither known nor cared about Armstrong's motives for renting an isolated cottage. She admitted that a factor in her attitude was the money that Mabel earned and no, she hadn't been repaid; probably the notes would arrive in the mail some time. If they didn't she could stand the loss. And it was she who had dreamed up the idea of the book when Armstrong said he needed a reason for taking Hollins that would satisfy the locals, not least her father. Both she and Mabel had thought the book scam amusing – and lucrative.

'You cleaned the place,' Buckle said now, accusingly.

'Someone had to do it. But you can analyse the ash heap; I emptied the Hoover on it.'

'We've taken samples. We'll know more tomorrow.' He was morose.

'What are these crystals?' Randolph asked. 'Where do they come from?'

'They're imported, probably made in a laboratory in the States. They're diluted with vodka and spotted on cards. It's done with a pipette, a drop at a time: ten pounds a drop at its street value. One gram of crystals makes thousands of doses.'

'At ten pounds a time?' Randolph said. 'It's incredible.'

They were quiet, absorbing the implications. It was Randolph who broke the silence. 'You think Roy suspected? Even knew?'

Buckle spread his hands. 'The motive's there for blackmail – and murder. Millions at stake and even with a number of people involved each share worth a fortune if it's a long-running scheme, and Armstrong, being the chemist, would get more than most.' His glance travelled round the company and came to rest on Laura. 'But how can we trace him without a name? You can be sure Armstrong was an alias and he won't be using it now.'

'It's not important,' Randolph said. 'It's enough to know what he was up to.'

'The point is, sir,' Fleming put in, 'if we knew who he was we could trace relatives, like his wife or mother or girlfriend. He could visit any of them, might even be with them now.'

Pharaoh thought that a good chemist, a good bent chemist, would have been spirited out of the country already; it was too risky to allow him to stay in the UK. He caught Laura's eye and saw her lips tighten. Before they'd left Starfoot he'd approached her car. 'Claire's implying you know where Armstrong is,' he said.

'She can imply what she bloody well likes,' she said viciously. 'Tell her to prove it!' But now, in Burnbank's drawing room, she said nothing.

'We'll know more tomorrow,' Buckle repeated. He sat, moodily

191

considering the situation. 'If we catch him,' he mused, 'when we catch him, he'll confess. They always do, they're not used to lying under pressure, like your common villain. He'll talk and incriminate the rest of the gang.'

'I doubt if he knew them,' Pharaoh said.

Buckle raised his eyebrows. 'I'd forgotten you were there, Mr Pharaoh! You don't think he knew them?'

'He didn't have to. He only produced the tabs. The person who delivered the – what do you call them: constituents? – would have taken away the finished product. Armstrong would buy the vodka locally. Probably he knew only one person. That's the courier, isn't it?' His jaw dropped as a thought occurred to him. He caught Laura's eye and looked away.

Buckle was saying, 'And the courier could be this friend of yours, miss, who gave you a false name and address and who doesn't have a phone number – at least under that name.'

'I told you,' Laura said, 'I didn't know him well; he was more of an acquaintance. And it was just a matter of running into him in a pub where I'd met him before, and him saying his friend needed a cottage for the summer. And I told him to contact my father.'

'So it wasn't a case of you owing him a favour after all.'

'Yes it was; he put quite a bit of business in my way.'

'And the book scam?' Buckle sounded tired.

'Armstrong had told my father he was an author. I provided the props and incidentally saw to it that Mabel made something out of it – look, we've been over all this—'

'And we're all exhausted. Quite right. We'll call it a day for now . . .'

When the police had gone and Randolph was shutting up the hens, Laura said to Pharaoh, 'You had a brainwave there when you were working out Armstrong's contacts. What was it?'

'Not a brainwave, only a chance thought. Buckle could be right when he said Armstrong would incriminate everyone else if he was caught – so since it's such a profitable enterprise he mustn't be caught. It occurred to me that perhaps he never left; that he's buried somewhere or dropped down a shaft. But of course he isn't.'

'What makes you so sure?'

'He's far too valuable. It's two days since he left. What's the betting that he's already installed in another country, even another continent, waiting for his new courier?'

Chapter Eighteen

'You're leaving, Mr Pharaoh?'

It was eight o'clock in the morning. He'd heard the engine before the familiar car appeared and by the time it stopped and Buckle came walking across the gravel the adrenalin was surging but he said, almost lazily, 'Short tenancies start and finish on a Saturday.'

'So they do,' Buckle said. 'Now where did I get the impression you were staying for the summer? Can you spare us a few minutes?'

'Of course.' Such courtesy was suspect. 'I'm sorry I can't offer you coffee; everything's packed.'

'That's fine, we're not staying. Perhaps you'll follow us.' Pharaoh frowned and Buckle smiled slyly as if he'd scored a point. 'We're going to the top of Falcon Crag,' he added, turning to survey its walls that were outlined by the sun, the corners deep in shadow. Pharaoh stared at the site of the nest.

'Providing we don't disturb the birds,' he said.

'Ah, the peregrines. After only a week you've got your priorities straight.'

'They were straight before I came here,' Pharaoh said coldly but Buckle was walking back to his car.

He went in the Boathouse for one last look round, then he locked up and put the keys in his pocket. Fleming had turned the car and their silhouettes looked like cardboard cut-outs facing the crag but he knew they were watching him in the mirrors. He climbed in the Transit and the police car started up the drive.

On the escarpment Fleming turned into the parking place for Falcon Crag and reversed. Pharaoh ranged alongside, amused at this similarity between police and ex-Servicemen (and criminals?) who parked facing out, the better to make a quick getaway.

They crossed the road to the top of the crag, keeping to the

193

side where the cave was so that they wouldn't disturb the birds. They were feeding the first chick now; he'd been up since five, watching them in the intervals of packing. He'd miss the peregrines.

'Where are you going?' Buckle asked, stopping a few yards from the edge.

'To Scotland.'

'Armstrong went to Scotland.'

'Probably. He won't be there now.'

'How much did he tell you?'

'Nothing about his movements.'

'And yet you're following him to Scotland.'

'I reckon he made tracks to the nearest airport, like Prestwick. I'm going as far north as I can get.'

'Tired of people?' Buckle suggested.

'And crime,' Fleming said.

Pharaoh just stopped himself from saying he was tired of hassle. A buzzard mewed and he listened for the peregrines but heard only a curlew bubbling from the direction of the Roman road.

'Laura Steel was in Scotland,' Fleming said. 'On Wednesday: the day the balloon went up. She said she was in Carlisle.'

'I remember Randolph saying something about Carlisle.'

'She had to find another safe house because things were getting sticky here after Becky's death.'

'That's ridiculous,' Pharaoh said, but without much hope. 'You're implying she knew what was going on.'

'Exactly,' Buckle said.

Pharaoh met his eye steadily. 'So you think Armstrong's holed up again just across the border.' Buckle said nothing. 'Where do I come in?' Pharaoh asked.

'You could be the courier,' Fleming said.

Pharaoh nodded slowly. 'I see. You want me to bring the Transit to Kelton and you'll go over it – with a dog?'

'Right.' But Buckle made no move.

'And there's the Boathouse,' Fleming said. 'And your person.'

'My—' Pharaoh blinked, caught on and sighed. 'I thought you brought me up here to discuss murder, not drugs.'

'Now why would you think that?' Buckle asked.

Pharaoh was surprised. Why had he thought that? 'Probably because we've lived with the possibility of murder for days, and there was a time when every man was a suspect, but drugs are new; we haven't got used to them yet. It never occurred to me that I might be suspected of dealing in drugs.' He grinned. 'I don't show much evidence of money.'

'Nor did Armstrong, but you have a point,' Buckle conceded. 'Murder fits you better.'

'Which murder?' Pharaoh was curious. 'Becky or Roy, or both?'

'It would have to be Becky. Roy's was an accident.' Pharaoh was expressionless. 'He wasn't a climber,' Buckle went on. 'He didn't abseil, he didn't know how; he went down the rope hand over hand. We've been talking to the experts. It was his weight on the rope pulled the piton out of the crack. The Germans were here, they saw it happen. Nothing they could do so they got out sharpish, but they'd left Roy's bike in Botchergate. That puzzled us for a while: why hadn't they put it in the Volks? But we decided Roy meant to go back to the party and the Germans would have run him back to Kelton if he hadn't killed himself. It'll be brought in as accidental death at the inquest.'

'Weren't there any fingerprints on the hammer?' Pharaoh asked.

'They were smudged. He would have tucked it in his waist next to the skin.'

He was being taken into their confidence and this made him increasingly suspicious. 'So you've got me lined up for Becky,' he said, and waited. So did they. 'What do you want me to say?' he asked reasonably. 'I can't think of a motive. Can you? It wasn't a sexual attack.'

'Unless she was running away from you,' Fleming said.

Pharaoh snorted his derision. 'She'd never have come up here with me—' He stopped.

'She came across to the Boathouse,' Buckle murmured.

'And visited Armstrong,' Fleming said. Pharaoh looked hard at him but held his tongue. They had only Claire's word for that.

'Yes,' Buckle said, watching him. '*That* was why he asked Becky to visit him: because he knew the little girls had been snooping round his place and they'd seen something they shouldn't. She was one of those kids with no fear of men; those are the ones who get into trouble. She took him up on the invitation and bingo! He probably stunned her with a blow and threw the body over here.'

They all looked at the edge of rock above the cave.

'You said little girls,' Pharaoh pointed out. 'Why didn't he go after Claire too?'

'Claire's too wily.'

'Roy wasn't.'

'Read my lips, Pharaoh. The Germans were here; Armstrong couldn't have got past them. He left because Roy'd started blackmailing him, not because he'd killed the lad. Laura found another safe house across the border and came back and made him leave as soon as she heard Roy had demanded money, and that's where he is now, hidden away in the Southern Uplands.'

'Have you arrested Laura?'

A shadow swept the rock as the buzzard drifted out over the dale. There was still no sound from the falcons.

'We're just having a conversation,' Buckle said, as if a different question had been asked. 'You're helping us with our enquiries.' He grinned like a Rottweiler. 'It doesn't make you a suspect.'

'That wasn't my impression earlier on.'

'Just our little joke,' Fleming said.

'Buckle came here for her,' Randolph told Pharaoh. 'He must have gone straight to you afterwards. There's no answer from her flat and her partner isn't expecting her. What's happening?'

'Nothing that she didn't intend,' Pharaoh said drily. Laura had left Burnbank last night. 'She's going to lie low for a while,' he went on. 'Wait for all this to blow over.' He wasn't sure where he was with Randolph.

He glowered. 'She could phone me. And she said she was going back to work.'

'She wants to keep you out of it. When did she say she'd be back?'

'Not for a while, she said. Keep me out of what?'

'I think she may have had some idea of what was going on.' Pharaoh was feeling his way.

'For Heaven's sake! All she did was provide accommodation for a crook.'

'That's not how the police view it. And they want to know where she is.'

Randolph pursed his lips and tried to look innocent. 'Yes, well, all *I* know is she said she was going back to work.' His face changed, becoming concerned. 'There's nothing else, is there – like – they can't think she's involved—'

'They're convinced Roy died accidentally,' Pharaoh said firmly. 'But they do think Armstrong killed Becky.'

'Good, good.' Randolph nodded dismissively. 'We've got some sorting out to do here. Laura insists Marlene has to go and she's

196

quite right: Starfoot's no better than a brothel. Mason can go with them so they won't be without protection.'

Pharaoh was grimly amused at this order of dominance. Like the police, it would appear that Randolph had closed his mind to the truth.

Trudy was nuzzling his thigh, pleading for a biscuit. 'How will you get rid of Mason?' he asked. 'He owns his cottage.'

'We'll buy it from him; he won't need any persuading. In the circumstances. I wish I could persuade you to stay on; I need another man here.' He sounded lonely and depressed.

'There's Mabel. You share the same interests.' Pharaoh knew he needed company more than practical assistance.

'Mabel's rather extreme at times, a bit tiring. You've got a sense of proportion.'

'That's why I'm leaving.'

Randolph looked as if he'd been hit below the belt. He pushed the coffee pot across the table. 'I wish I didn't feel so heavy,' he muttered. 'She will come back, won't she?'

Pharaoh grieved for him. 'The dale comes first with her every time,' he said, and took the plunge. 'She only did it for the money.'

'That's what I keep telling myself.' Pharaoh had broken through at last. Randolph shook his head and sighed and said on a high contrived note, 'No more where that came from, but we have enough to modernize Hollins and Mason's cottage, and the rents from those and the others will keep us going for a time, even pay for a few improvements. I know a fellow with earth-moving equipment and he owes me a favour; I'll get him to scrape out some sites for ponds. We can manage.' His face fell. 'This place needs a new roof though.' His eyes roamed the kitchen and fastened on the window. 'But nothing's as important as the land; that always comes first. Go and say goodbye to Mabel and reassure her.' His eyes came back to Pharaoh and they were steady. 'Reassure her,' he repeated, making certain that there was no mistake. 'I understand your disapproval, but you never owned land. I'm sorry you think you have to go but there, you have your principles too.'

Mabel was picking stinging nettles in her drive, accompanied by the tortoiseshell queen. He told her that he was leaving but she'd know that already by way of the telephone.

'I'm not surprised,' she said. 'I knew that you'd never give up once you'd started to unravel the truth, and that was easy in the circumstances. We're not criminals; we give ourselves away, don't we?'

'You're too modest. The police are way out in their deductions. I've been up on Falcon Crag with them.'

'I know, I saw you on top. Let's have coffee and you can tell me all about it. I think we have enough of these.' She handed him her basket and peeled off her rubber gloves. 'Nettles are full of iron,' she told him. 'We live on them for a few weeks in spring. I must see what goodies we have to speed you on your way. Where are you going?'

'To Sutherland and Wester Ross.'

They strolled to the garden gate. The white cat came running and butted her legs. He opened the gate and they walked up the path. She left him on the bench and went indoors.

The crag was in shadow on this side. The black cat leapt on the seat and came softly along the slats to sniff his wrist. He spoke and it started to purr. The buzzard was back, soaring on thermals above the dale but keeping well clear of the crag.

'Do buzzards take chicks?' he asked when she came out with the coffee.

She glanced up. 'No, it's safe. When the peregrines attack they're defending their territory.'

'Why don't they attack now?'

'The female doesn't want to rock the boat, and he's waiting for the pigeons.'

'Oh, come on! How do you know that?'

'The binoculars are on the dresser; you'll find the male on a pinnacle about thirty feet below the summit of Grey Buttress.'

He did as he was told. She was right; the falcon was standing to attention where she'd said, immobile.

'He's not watching the buzzard,' he said.

'I told you: he's waiting for the pigeons. They're lying low because of the buzzard but they have to go and feed some time. They have young too.'

He sighed. 'I'm going to miss this.'

'Why don't you stay? Randolph needs help badly, particularly now.' Her voice dropped. 'She's going to be away a long time.'

'I'd stay to help Randolph but Laura can't come back while I'm here.'

'Did you quarrel with her?'

'No, we parted quite amicably, except that I didn't know she planned to leave last night, although I should have anticipated it. She's only a jump ahead of the police.'

'She can trust you.'

'That's what you say but she doesn't know that.' Mabel looked puzzled. 'Let me put a scenario to you,' he went on: 'an hypothesis. First you must accept that the police suspect Laura – I don't know how far, but definitely that she was involved in the drug factory. They say that on Wednesday she went to Scotland to find another safe house and that when she came back she learned that Roy had started blackmailing Armstrong. The police say Armstrong killed Becky, which was why he had to move, and that Laura was at least an accessory.'

'This isn't an hypothesis, dear boy; you're giving me the police theory.'

'Right, so here's the hypothesis. Laura was in the Borders on Wednesday looking for a safe house. She'd do that on principle, they'd never stay in one place for long; it was probably the reason she was here anyway: to look for alternative accommodation. The catering business is genuine but it's a front, isn't it?' He didn't wait for a response but went on: 'Becky's disappearance brought things to a head; if she'd been killed and it was a sexual attack every man would be suspect. When Laura came back – perhaps before, because she could have phoned Armstrong – she learned not only that Becky had been found dead but that both Claire and Roy had been to Hollins and Armstrong had panicked and paid Roy blackmail money. Armstrong had to leave right then, that night, during the storm. They cleaned out Hollins and he left.' Pharaoh stopped deliberately.

'Wednesday evening,' Mabel said, not looking at him, 'you were at Burnbank.'

'In this scenario Laura would have gone up to Hollins after I went home, perhaps after Randolph had gone to bed. I don't think Randolph knew the truth until last night, perhaps not all of it then. This morning he thought Laura had gone back to her job.'

'Where's your proof?'

'There isn't any. It's a story, although there could be witnesses, except that they'll never come forward: the German egg collectors. Let's say they were near the top of the crag and they were approached by someone claiming to be a ranger and asked their business. That would be Armstrong. The Germans would leave

199

in a hurry – which is why they weren't there when the piton was knocked out and the hammer was wiped and thrown down. When they did go back there'd be no sign of Roy or his equipment and they'd assume he'd climbed back to the top but they'd have no way of contacting him. Eventually they'd have to leave.'

'What need was there to kill Roy if Armstrong was leaving?' Mabel asked.

'There were two motives. One was that since Roy knew he was on to something he could direct the police to Hollins out of spite, and Laura knew they could find traces of drugs there. The hunt would be up for Armstrong and that could lead to herself and even to you and Randolph. The second was hardly a motive, it was an opportunity. Roy was in the act of stealing the eggs and there was the hammer and there was the peg – and the rope taut as Roy went over the edge – perhaps showing up in a flash of lightning. It was a murder waiting to happen.' Mabel turned to him, her face full of despair. 'The police are convinced it was an accident,' he told her.

'Are they?' She paused, then said carefully, 'So' – she let her breath go in a long sigh – 'we're in the clear – for Roy's murder?'

'If Buckle doesn't think it was an accident, or if he were ever to change his mind, he can't prove it was anything else. On the other hand, he says Armstrong killed Becky.'

'That's as well. We don't want Claire suspected. Of course it was Claire: either a slip or a push is immaterial, but it was more likely a push because she hid the bike.'

'And the ironical bit for Armstrong is that Claire never thought Becky was at Hollins, but having gone up there to hide Becky's bike she had to have an excuse in case the searchers saw her on top. She had to be searching too. Going to Hollins was a smokescreen.'

'But she was also laying a trail that pointed to Armstrong's involvement in Becky's death. Why didn't she hide the bike the previous morning, after Becky fell?'

'I think they both cycled up there but Claire couldn't afford to be seen returning alone. But she had to get home quickly to give herself an alibi of sorts so she ran down one of the easy gullies to Starfoot. She must have hidden both bikes temporarily and hoped they wouldn't be discovered. Next morning she went back the same way, dropped Becky's bike into the old quarry and then went to Hollins to lay her smokescreen.'

'That's a dangerous child.' Mabel lapsed into silence for a few moments, staring at the profile of the crag. 'Why did Buckle take you up there this morning?'

'I thought it was to convince me that Armstrong killed Becky.'

'What did they expect to gain by that?'

'Oh, my God, that wasn't it at all! It was to persuade me that the police thinking is that Roy's death was an accident, the idea behind that being to put Laura off her guard. They're not bothered about Becky; they're after Laura.'

'They'll never find her – nor him. They've left the country.'

Pharaoh slumped on the seat. 'I guessed it. They'll set up shop in the States.'

'Listen to me, Pharaoh.' She turned to him, her face alight with sincerity. 'No one forces people to take drugs. Think of all the estates that are run on tobacco profits – and on alcohol. How many people does tobacco kill in a year? As for Roy, like you said, that was an impulsive act; the opportunity presented itself and Laura took it. She's not like Claire, who's a cold killer: a budding psychopath, but with her background: drink, prostitution, the only man about the place a criminal, what can you expect? I wonder if she'll come back at some future date, I wonder about her diary. Laura said she had one. It's a potential for blackmail.'

'No.' He was certain on that point. 'I was there, listening to them; they showed their hands to each other. Claire went too far with her threat of the diaries – Becky's too, she said. And then that she'd told someone, but that it wasn't Marlene! Suppose they did exist: those kids lived in a fantasy world; the diaries could be a record of fantasies. I think Claire's bluffing but Laura can't *know*. It's a psychological stand-off; each is saying she knows the other killed, but neither can prove it: the ultimate deterrent.' He smiled thinly. 'They'll be looking over their shoulders for a while, at least, Claire will. But it's in Laura's interests for attention to focus on Armstrong. The last thing she wants is Claire suspected of causing Becky's death. If the child was questioned she'd hit out at Laura and precipitate matters, so Armstrong has to be the scapegoat. After all, Laura knows he's safe.'

The black cat walked across the grass to the shade of a juniper and collapsed like a dog.

'We're in for another dry summer, I'm afraid,' Mabel said absently, and then, 'She was only the courier, you know.'

He didn't believe her but he admired her spirit. 'I'm leaving,' he said. 'She could come back secretly, but not if I'm here. She'd always be afraid of me. I'm not about to change my principles, not my attitude to drugs anyway, and suppose I did, she'd never know, wouldn't believe it if she did know. She's got too much to lose. She won't come back while I'm here.'

'I see.' And he knew that she did now. 'But you'll call in some time when you're passing?'

'I promise.' He stood up. A breeze stirred the birches and as if it were a signal there came a distant clapping of wings.

The pigeons came low and fast from the north, like small planes dodging ground defences although the danger wasn't on the ground. Above the garden they started to wheel, heading for the conifers on the shore. Behind them came the peregrine: faster than a falling stone, a speck growing magically in size as it hurtled through the air.

The flock scattered and the falcon rose with its prey. Feathers spread like a soft burst of fireworks. The bird landed above the nest and his mate greeted him hungrily.

'The pigeon must die of shock,' Pharaoh said.

'Actually peregrines kill by a bite on the nape of the neck. It severs the spinal cord.' He looked at her. 'True,' she assured him. 'They're very efficient killers. Nature *is* efficient; she's had longer at it than us.'

The last blue feather floated down and was pounced on by the white cat with the bicoloured eyes, watched benignly by Mabel and the tortoiseshell queen.

'You know what's wrong with you,' Mabel said. 'You get too involved. You must learn to see things in perspective.'